BY EVELYN SKYE

FOR ADULTS

The Hundred Loves of Juliet

One Year Ago in Spain

Damsel

FOR YOUNG ADULTS

The Crown's Game
The Crown's Fate

Circle of Shadows
Cloak of Night

Three Kisses, One Midnight

FOR CHILDREN

Princess Private Eye
Princess Private Eye and the Missing Robo-Bird

One Year Ago in Spain

One Year Ago in Spain

EVELYN SKYE

DEL REY

NEW YORK

A Del Rey Trade Paperback Original

Copyright © 2024 by Evelyn Skye

Published in the United States by Del Rey,
an imprint of Random House, a division of
Penguin Random House LLC, New York.

Del Rey and the Circle colophon are registered trademarks of
Penguin Random House LLC.

ISBN 978-0-593-49927-6
Ebook ISBN 978-0-593-49928-3

Balcony image: Sally Fama Cochrane

Printed in the United States of America on acid-free paper

randomhousebooks.com

2 4 6 8 9 7 5 3 1

First Edition

Book design by Edwin A. Vazquez

To Anne Groell—
for seeing my stories . . . and me.

Para Leo Teti y su equipo en España—
quienes me ayudaron a entender la cultura española.

One Year Ago in Spain

CLAIRE

⁓

THEY KISSED LIKE THEY WERE TALKING ABOUT THE WEATHER. And not the tornados of the Midwest or the searing wildfires of California. Just a tepid peck on the lips, as exciting as a partially cloudy evening.

All around them, Manhattan heaved like an impatient dragon, its sidewalks shimmering like scales sweaty with humidity. Streetlamps blazed, and the horns of taxis wailed. Everything in the city was alive—feverish, irrepressible.

Everything except Claire and her date.

It was the third time she and Glenn had been out together, and now they stood outside the perfectly acceptable restaurant where they had both eaten perfectly acceptable chicken with a sautéed vegetable medley. The conversation had been perfectly acceptable, too—not bad but not great. Just . . . fine.

Glenn smiled at her. He was tall enough that she couldn't see the balding patch on the crown of his head, but she knew it was there. He had nice teeth—he was a dentist, so he'd better have—and he seemed to wear a uniform of standard-issue polo shirts in tame shades of blue, paired with tan chinos.

They were supposed to be heading to the opening of a new exhibit by a Spanish artist. Claire's best friend—one of the lawyers she worked with—was married to the gallery owner, and he was throwing a swanky party with cocktails and a live band tonight.

"Should I get us a ride?" Claire asked.

Glenn kept smiling in that mild way of his.

"Um . . ." She looked around them to see if she'd missed a cue about what was going on, but no dice.

He took her hand. "I was wondering," Glenn said, shouting a little to be heard over the street noise. "Would you like to be exclusive?"

Claire blinked at him. "Exclusive?"

"You know, not seeing anyone else?"

She frowned, but just a tiny one—the kind that only the person frowning really knows is happening while the rest of the world goes on blissfully unaware. "Oh, I know what exclusive means, but . . . why?"

Glenn let out a short laugh. "Because I thought it might be nice if we didn't kiss anyone else."

She didn't think he *was* kissing anyone else. And Claire certainly wasn't seeing other men. She was a corporate attorney at one of Manhattan's top international firms, on the cusp of partnership, which meant nearly all her waking hours were spent at the office. It had taken her and Glenn weeks to find a compatible evening in their schedules for this third date.

"Also," Glenn was saying, "because we'd be good together. We're both smart and we have our lives figured out—which, to be frank, even though we're both thirty-one, is no longer a given for our generation. We're both practical and clearheaded. It's the foundation for long-lasting success."

Claire sighed. She'd grown up on epic love stories and movies, like the *Outlander* books and *Titanic*. So Claire wanted fire and passion, a man who stayed with her not because it was sensible, but because he couldn't imagine a life without her. And Glenn's speech was nowhere near what she'd once dreamed of as a romantic declaration.

But she wasn't getting any younger, and he *was* the kind of man you wouldn't be embarrassed to bring home to the family—if Claire's parents were still alive or she had any siblings, which she didn't.

Yet if she and Glenn were this bland at the start, what kind of future would this relationship hold? Besides a high probability of predictable stability?

A taxi pulled up at the curb near them, vomiting out passengers onto the sidewalk. Immediately, two different couples—red-faced from the heat and humidity—lunged toward the open door, fighting to claim the car. Getting a ride on a Saturday night in Manhattan was no small feat.

Glenn stepped away but didn't do anything to help shield Claire from the melee. Not that she needed a man to save her, but she wouldn't have minded a little chivalry.

"So, what do you say?" Glenn asked once one of the couples had victoriously crammed themselves into the cab and left the other pair growling and punching at their phones, trying to find an available ride.

"Say to what?" Claire asked, her mind still on the minidrama over the taxi.

"Being exclusive. You and me, together."

"I think . . . Well, I like you, Glenn."

He grinned at her with his very straight teeth.

"But the thing is . . ." Claire took a deep breath. "Don't you think we deserve more? I mean that in the nicest way possible.

Maybe you're right and we would be a good team, but don't you deserve something more than just a well-functioning team member by your side? Don't you deserve someone where, when she's gone, you still think about her all the time? Someone you want to text whenever you have a break in your schedule? And after a long day, you want nothing more than to curl up next to her and hear all about *her* day? Because, if we're being honest, I doubt you feel that way about me. Right? And I . . . I respect you, Glenn, but I don't feel that spark with you, either."

Glenn crossed his arms across his polo shirt, which was now sweat-soaked at the pits. He closed his eyes briefly—had she gone too far? But he'd said he appreciated Claire's clearheadedness, right? Like the attorney she was, she'd laid out a well-thought-out argument for their respective happiness. It just didn't involve being together.

When he opened his eyes, he nodded calmly, as if he'd just considered a patient's description of a toothache. "What you described is, indeed, the fantasy. But that's all it is—a fantasy. And, Claire, come on, you care more about practicality than passion. Look at your life. You're a lawyer. And you chose to go out with *me,* a dentist. We are people of responsibility. A little boring, a little uninspired, perhaps, but steady. Fantasies are for dreamers, not for dentists and lawyers like us."

For the second time in just minutes, Claire found herself blinking at him. If Glenn had gotten angry or stomped off or something else dramatic, she could have taken it. But instead, he had returned her careful line of reasoning with a rational argument of his own—one that walloped her in the stomach far harder than if he'd told her to fuck off.

"Claire?"

She shook herself out of her thoughts.

"No," she said.

"I'm sorry. What?"

"No," Claire said, looking him in the eye. "You're really nice, Glenn. And maybe you're right, but I'm not ready to give up yet. I still want—"

"The impossible?"

She bit her lip, then nodded. "Yeah."

Glenn laughed without humor, but he was too placid a person to be angry. "All right, then. Best of luck to you, Claire. I hope you find the love of your life."

"You, too, Glenn."

He nodded once, then headed off toward the subway station.

Claire allowed herself one more long exhale. And then she turned in the other direction and began to walk toward the gallery where her friend Yolanda was waiting for her.

CLAIRE TRUDGED THROUGH GREENWICH VILLAGE, MOSTLY oblivious to the people and storefronts as what Glenn had said about her echoed in her head.

Boring.

Uninspired.

You care more about practicality than passion.

Was it true?

Claire's life *was* remarkably predictable. She woke every morning at 5:30 A.M., went for a run through Central Park, came home and showered, then made the same oatmeal with raisins, walnuts, and cinnamon for breakfast. She left her apartment at 7:25 to catch the train, which got her through the front doors of the law firm at 7:47—enough time to grab a coffee from the break room and read through any emails that had come in overnight before hopping on client calls starting at 8:30. The only thing Claire couldn't predict was when each workday would end, because sometimes there were calls with clients on the West Coast or even in Asia.

But my reliability is why my clients love me, Claire thought, trying to reassure herself.

And being reliable wasn't mutually exclusive with wanting to hold out for a bigger love. Right?

Then again, if she thought about the epic love stories she'd grown up with, they always involved a large dose of spontaneity and upheaval—time travel, sinking ships, and giving up everything and everyone you'd ever known.

It was a lot to ask.

Oh god, what if Glenn had been right about her?

Claire wove around some of the stinking trash bags that had been left out to fester on the sidewalks. Deep in her thoughts, she almost walked right past the Rose Gallery and its exhibition *Surreal Delight*.

But the dead streetlamp above her suddenly flickered on and illuminated the plate glass window, and Claire drew in a breath in surprise.

There was a long oil painting of the Manhattan skyline on a rainy day. At first glance, it was just another realistic steel and gray view of the city. But then Claire's eyes traveled to the bottom half of the painting, where a small girl in a yellow rain jacket crouched next to an enormous puddle that spanned the length of Manhattan. And in its watery, upside-down reflection was a whole different world—one where the skyscrapers were towering sunflowers, and the little girl was a euphoric bumble-bee.

The next painting was also realistic on its face: a Spanish chef laboring over flames and a large pan of paella. The kitchen staff around him sweated and bustled, and the rich, deep colors of the painting reminded Claire of classical European art.

But the exhibit was called *Surreal Delight,* and on closer inspection, she noticed that the saltshaker in the chef's hand was scattering not salt, but tiny hearts, the little red confetti tumbling down onto the saffron rice in a shower of culinary love.

"I want *that,*" she said out loud. Not the literal painting—although she wouldn't mind having it on her wall—but that *feeling,* that twinkle of joy in her otherwise orderly world.

Behind her, the gallery door opened.

"Claire!" Yolanda Davis—her best friend, colleague, and the wife of the gallery owner—popped her head out. She was, as usual, impeccably put together, her dark skin contrasting beautifully with a pale pink silk blouse, her natural hair blown out. "I thought I saw you through the window. Come inside! And where's your date?"

"Glenn went home early."

"That bad, huh?"

"No, not really," Claire said. "Just . . . not enough."

She followed Yolanda inside and sighed gratefully as the icy blast of air-conditioning hit her skin. The melodies of a saxophone and flamenco guitarist echoed through the high rafters, and a ritzy Fifth Avenue crowd milled around the gallery, drinking sangria and rebujitos while occasionally looking at the paintings on the walls.

"Claire Walker, haven't seen you in ages." Jason—Yolanda's

husband—came up and greeted Claire with a hug. "What do you think of the exhibit?"

"I've only had a chance to see what was in the window, but . . . it's extraordinary."

"Can I get you a drink?" Yolanda asked. "The sangria is great, but the bartender's also making tinto de verano, which is kind of like sangria, but fizzy."

"Yes, please. I could definitely use a drink."

Yolanda darted off to the bar. Jason started to tell Claire about the nearest painting but then broke off and, looking over her shoulder, said, "Oh, there's the artist. Do you want to meet him? I'll introduce you. He's from Madrid, but he's going to be here in the States for a couple years as a visiting professor at the New York Academy of Art. He's a classical realist—with a touch of the imaginative. Monstrously talented and passionate, which is so refreshing in this age of soulless AI art, you know?"

Jason waved at someone. Claire turned around. She was only five-four, so she couldn't see over the heads of the people in front of her. But it didn't matter, because the crowd parted, and there he was.

"Matías de León," Jason said, "I'd like you to meet a friend of mine, Claire Walker."

He was just like his paintings, viscerally real and rendered in warmth: Waves of black hair. Olive skin. Broad shoulders and muscled forearms that were proof of hours working with his hands.

But then, like the title of his exhibition, there was the glimmer of surreal delight—his eyes were like pools of honey in morning sunlight, rich and gold with promises of undivinable depths.

"*Un placer.* A pleasure," Matías said, his English gently accented with Spanish.

Claire's mouth opened, but no words came out.

Yolanda reappeared with drinks. But when she saw Claire speechless—and knowing how, as a lawyer, Claire was *never* without something to say—Yolanda winked at Jason and said, "Why doesn't Matías give Claire a personal tour of some of his paintings in the back of the gallery? You know, since she arrived late and missed the introductory speech?"

Without missing a beat, Jason said, "What a fantastic idea," and steered Claire and Matías away from the music and the bar and the majority of the guests. Jason and Yolanda then melted into the party without even a glance back.

Claire laughed nervously. Yolanda wasn't known for her subtlety, but what the heck was she thinking? There was no way a gorgeous Spanish artist was going to be into Claire. She dated balding dentists and the occasional accountant.

"I am so glad you could come tonight," Matías said as they made their way deeper into the Rose Gallery. Heads turned wherever he walked.

"You are? Why?" Claire didn't mean to blurt that last bit out, but her nerves had the reins right now.

"I was worried no one would attend my gallery opening," he said. "But Jason has done a wonderful job with it. Are you having a nice evening?"

"Not until now." Claire immediately felt her face flush the same red as her drink.

Matías grinned, and it was charmingly lopsided—nothing like Glenn's perfectly symmetrical smile.

What is going on? Claire never spoke before she thought; you learned that in the first year of law school.

They reached the back wall. There were only a couple of

other guests back here, so Claire and Matías had this part of the gallery pretty much to themselves. Matías was close enough to her that she could smell the pine and spice of his cologne, and her heart thrummed a little faster.

"Although Jason asked me to give a speech earlier tonight," Matías said, "I do not really like to talk about my work. I put everything I have to say into the art itself, you know? So, please." He waved toward the paintings that hung around them.

Claire's pulse sped up more, but for a different reason now. Publicly, she pretended to like paintings and sculptures and such because it was the kind of sophisticated thing that all the partners at the law firm seemed to enjoy. Being Yolanda's friend also meant she heard a fair bit about the art world.

Yet the truth was that Claire had never been the sort who was particularly moved by art—not like the people who had annual passes to MoMA who could stand in front of a canvas and talk for hours about its complexity. Paintings were just pictures to Claire. So she started psyching herself up to come up with some eloquent lies to tell Matías.

But then she was face-to-face with his work again, and it was like trying to walk during an earthquake while the ground was still shaking. Basic assumptions weren't straightforward anymore.

Each of his pieces was painted in a style reminiscent of classical European masters, done on wood panels rather than canvas, which seemed to give the colors a richer, almost glowing quality. Matías's style was very realistic, except that in each painting there was one incongruous, imaginative element.

There was a portrait of a man and a woman at home, him drab and slouched and slack-faced on the couch watching mind-

less TV, completely unaware that beside him, his wife was glee-
fully reading a book from which a cute, thimble-sized red alien
had emerged and was waving from the pages. Claire laughed out
loud, remembering her own amazement when, after moving to
New York and having some subway commuting time to kill,
she'd rediscovered the joy of reading.

Next, she stood for a long time in front of a painting of a
little boy in a field blowing on a dandelion, but rather than seed-
lings, there were tiny drones, dutifully flying off into the blue sky
with his wishes. A trill of happiness vibrated through Claire; this
was a vision counter to all the doom-and-gloom headlines about
how computers and robots were going to devour humanity. Instead, Matías had found a way to show a path forward where
technology was infused with hope.

But it was a painting in the quiet corner of the gallery that
knocked the breath out of Claire. In it, a gap-toothed, smiling
monk held out a partially peeled orange to the person gazing at
the painting. But it wasn't an orange peeking out from under the
peel—it was the planet Earth.

Peace, cupped in his hands and offered to every single person
who stopped to look.

"Oh my god, Matías," she whispered.

He'd stood quietly next to her as she walked through his
work, understanding that sometimes the best tour is one the
traveler leads herself on. Now he smiled, and those golden eyes
glimmered under the gallery spotlights.

If it were possible to know someone's soul without knowing
the person at all, this was how. Matías's art was his pureness, his
sanguine exuberance, his belief in the promise of the world.
And—just like when Claire first saw his painting of the Man-

hattan skyline reflected in a puddle as a forest of sunflowers—
she thought,

I want *that*.

I want *him*.

But ordinary people only get to mingle with the extraordinary for brief interludes before they have to return to the normal
world. Claire knew to savor these moments because she wouldn't
get to have them again once she walked out of the Rose Gallery's doors.

Unfortunately, the adoring crowds soon found Matías again.
A group of society matrons converged on him and swept him
away before Claire could even thank him for sharing his work.

She stood there alone then, with his art, wondering if someone like her could ever inspire a similar passion in someone as
vibrant and original as Matías.

But after a few seconds, Claire laughed at herself. She had
had her brief interlude with the extraordinary, and now it was
time to return to the norm.

HE CALLED HER AT HER OFFICE THE NEXT DAY AT 9 A.M.

"Hi, Claire? It's Matías. I asked Yolanda for your number. I
hope that was okay. I'd like to take you to dinner."

Claire gawked at her phone for a moment. Was he really asking her out?

Her voice squeaked when she answered. "Um, dinner sounds
good. What date were you thinking of?"

"Tonight, if you're available."

Tonight? Attorneys were never free on such short notice.
Claire's calendar was often booked a month in advance.

"Unfortunately, I'm busy all this week," she said.

"Oh, okay. I understand. If you are not interested, I am sorry for bothering you—"

"No, wait! I am! Interested, I mean. But I have to work late."

Matías laughed softly. "All right. Well, what if it is a *late* dinner tonight? You have to eat, don't you?"

"I do," Claire said. "But I honestly don't know how long I'll be working. I have a call at seven that will last at least two hours, and I'll have some follow-up work I have to take care of afterward. I might be here until eleven or so. I was planning to just grab a salad from the cafeteria before they close and eat at my desk after my call."

Matías made a disapproving *tsk* with his tongue. "Claire, that is no way to live. In Spain, meals are more than just nourishment. However, I understand that you're busy, so I'll tell you what—I will bring food to you at the office after your call tonight. Give me thirty minutes for a break, and I will prove to you that dinner can be efficient *and* pleasurable."

The way he said *pleasurable* sent a warm rumble straight through her core.

WINDSOR & BLACK LLP WAS SPREAD OVER TWENTY FLOORS IN a skyscraper in Midtown. Floor 1 was security; floor 2, a reception hall as elegant as a Four Seasons hotel; floor 3 was the copy center and gym; and floor 4 was the free employee cafeteria. Floors 5 through 7 were glass-walled conference rooms, and then the rest of the levels were attorneys' offices. Every lawyer at Windsor & Black LLP had their own office with a heavy oak door, and their secretaries and paralegals sat outside their re-spective attorneys' offices in pods in the center.

Just after nine, Matías arrived, and Claire brought him up-stairs. The usually bustling floors were empty now, other than a handful of attorneys still in offices here and there, their doors shut to avoid all distractions so they could finish their work and hopefully get home before midnight. Her own desk was so cov-ered in binders and stacks of paper that there was nowhere to eat, so she led him to the law library.

It was a beautiful space, all soaring ceilings and marble col-umns, that sadly no one used anymore because research was all done digitally now. When Claire had first started working at Windsor & Black, she'd sworn to herself that she would visit the library every day to remind herself that law and justice were re-vered, noble concepts, not just a glowing computer screen and endless conference calls. But that promise had fallen by the way-side, long ago consumed by demanding partners and even more demanding clients.

She let out a contented sigh, though, as they stepped into the library now.

"Intimidating," Matías said as his gaze brushed across the towering shelves of leather-bound tomes.

Claire smiled. "Nah. It's all a facade. Attorneys are just nerds who like big words, and lots of them."

"You sell yourself short," Matías said. "But there *is* one thing I have in common with lawyers—we keep late hours." He held up the cooler and canvas bag he'd brought. "Spaniards eat dinner at nine or ten at night, too."

Claire laughed and led him deeper into the library, to a table in the back corner.

Matías pulled out a tablecloth. It was brightly colored, like blue and yellow ceramic tiles, and he lifted it into the air like the parachute game children play, tablecloth hovering for a long moment, before letting it settle gently onto the otherwise ordinary table.

He unpacked real plates—not paper—and weighty silverware and cloth napkins, too.

"Three courses in thirty minutes," Matías declared, and Claire laughed.

"Where did you order from?"

He furrowed his brow. "What do you mean?"

"The food? Where did you get it?"

"Oh! Well, let's see. The Manchego, I purchased from Murray's Cheese. The olives and almonds, I bought from Despaña in SoHo. The fruit and vegetables are from the farmer's market near my apartment, and the vinegar and olive oil I bought the first day I was in New York, from Mercado Little Spain."

Claire stared at him with her mouth open. "Wait. You mean you made me dinner from scratch?"

Matías made a face. "Of course. Why wouldn't I?"

She didn't want him to figure out that many New Yorkers never cooked. They just ordered delivery through apps, with the food arriving slightly soggy but still pretty warm at their door.

To begin, he artfully arranged a shaved-apple salad with arugula, Manchego cheese, Marcona almonds, and a tart cider vinaigrette. Claire gasped at the crisp sweetness of fruit contrasted with peppery greens and the richness of nuts and cheese.

"This puts my cafeteria salad to shame," she said.

"I hope so."

But it wasn't just that it was leagues more delicious than regular salads. It was that he'd made it *for her*.

Next, Matías presented her with empanadillas de atún—half-moon pastries filled with tuna and green olives—then spooned a sauce made of tomato, onions, garlic, and bell peppers, cooked until deeply caramelized.

"Should I use a knife and fork?" Claire asked, not wanting to commit a cultural faux pas on their first date.

"You can," Matías said. "Or you can just pick it up like this—"

He bit into an empanadilla and *oh god*, his mouth. The pastry crumbled in a shower of buttery decadence, and Claire wanted to crawl across the table and lick the stray smudge of sofrito sauce at the corner of his lips. But she restrained herself because (a) she was Claire Walker, who didn't do things like that, and (b) they were in a library, for goodness' sake. Even if it was a deserted one after office hours.

But then Matías brought out a small glass jar filled with what looked like speckled caramel.

"This is bienmesabe canario," he said. "An almond dessert from the Canary Islands, where my great-grandparents were from. This is an old family recipe and my favorite from childhood."

He dipped a spoon into the jar.

Leaned toward her. "Try it . . ."

Claire parted her lips.

The silver tip of the spoon touched her tongue. Sweetness hit her taste buds, and she moaned.

Every woman has her limits.

She pushed aside the remnants of the picnic, climbed across the table, and kissed him, their mouths like molten sugar.

Claire had never slept with anyone before the sixth date, but Matías was not made for rules.

He laid her down on the plush carpet of the library and disassembled her carefully pressed suit, piece by piece. She yanked his shirt over his head and fumbled at his fly.

Despite the air-conditioning of the staid library, their bodies melted together like the heat that shimmers in the air in the middle of summer days.

When she came, she held in her scream, but the books shook on the shelves around her.

When it was his turn, he whispered her name.

The full, contented silence that followed said everything else they needed to know.

And that was how Claire Walker fell in love with Matías de León.

CLAIRE

~

ELEVEN MONTHS LATER

"I CAN'T WAIT TO SHOW YOU AROUND SPAIN," MATÍAS SAID AS he grabbed his empty suitcase to begin packing. He was about to set it on the bed when Claire yelped.

"Wait, don't put it there!"

She ran to his closet and returned with the luggage rack she'd bought him. "It's just . . . remember I read that article about all the germs on suitcase wheels?" She wrinkled her nose. "I'm sorry, but I—"

"You don't have to apologize, *churri*," Matías said, using his favorite endearment. He leaned in and kissed her, right where her nose was scrunched. Then he took the luggage rack from her, unfolded it, and set his suitcase on top.

Claire sighed. He was good to her, he really was. But in the eleven months of their whirlwind romance, some . . . *differences* had emerged. Matías was chaos, whereas Claire was order. For instance, he tried his best to put things where they belonged, but he wasn't always successful. That had been good enough in the early days of being together, when Claire had laughed whenever he set his keys on her kitchen island instead of the entry table by the door, or when he put the coffee mugs on the water glass shelf.

But it had been bothering her more lately. Maybe because

the hurricane of their relationship was slowing down to a normal breeze, and it was a lot easier to spot flaws when you weren't in the middle of a storm.

Right now, she had to avert her eyes as he tossed improperly folded T-shirts into his suitcase.

Don't be so rigid, she told herself.

Still, to avoid watching, Claire walked over to the dresser in the far corner of his room to retrieve some socks and boxer briefs. If she got to them before Matías did, she could roll them up nicely to prevent them from wrinkling.

As she reached for his socks, though, her hand hit something hard in the back of the drawer. What the—?

Claire angled herself so her body would block Matías's view, and she pulled the mystery thing out of the drawer.

It was a sock, but stuffed inside it was a velvet ring box.

Her stomach flipped, and she wasn't sure it was entirely in a good way.

He's planning to propose. On this trip to Spain. In front of all his family and friends . . .

Only, Claire already knew she couldn't go. The merger she was working on was utter madness, but she hadn't found the right time yet to break the news to Matías.

Also, she didn't know if she wanted to say yes to marrying him.

She and Matías were complete opposites—which, judging by Claire's friends' relationships, usually did not work out. And her model relationship—her parents—had been one based on shared personalities and occupations. Mom and Dad had both been postal workers, and because of that, they'd understood how to live in the ebbs and flows of each other's days. They had driven to work together each morning. She worked in the post office itself and he delivered mail, so they touched based during the day whenever he stopped in for a new batch of packages and mail. And at the end of the day, they'd sit next to each other on the sofa, their feet soaking in respective foot baths in front of the TV, where they inevitably murmured their commiseration every time a delivery person showed up onscreen and got chased by dogs.

Mom and Dad had died in a car accident right after Claire graduated from college, but she still thought of them every day. Missed them. Hoped that the life she was leading would've made them proud.

What would they have thought about her and Matías?

The velvet box seemed to grow heavier in Claire's hand.

Part of her didn't want to peek, because that would make it more real.

But the lawyer part of her that liked facts wanted to open the box to make sure she wasn't making this up. Because maybe it wasn't an engagement ring. Maybe it was a pair of earrings for later, like Christmas, even though it was only July now.

If you're going to do this, you'd better be quick, she told herself. Matías could decide to come over at any second.

She bit her lip and opened the velvet box.

Inside was a small, glittering sun—a ring with a round diamond, surrounded by tapered topazes like flames. Because of course Matías would promise nothing less than to give her the sun.

It was too much.

Claire stuffed the box back into the sock and shoved it into the recesses of the drawer where she'd found it.

How could Matías spring something like this on her? Didn't he know by now that she needed her life calendared? And who in this day and age surprised people with engagement rings anymore? All her lawyer friends had discussed getting married with their significant others long before the question was popped, and even then, it was a foregone conclusion because they'd already done the ring sizing and shopping together.

And besides, Matías ought to know that they wouldn't work out in the long run. This proposal was too soon, too rushed. If he waited another year, he would inevitably realize that she was too bland for him. Claire was all white blouses and pressed trousers, while Matías was riotous color and wild imagination. Over the past eleven months, she'd tried to enjoy every moment with him that she could because, deep down, she'd known it could never last.

How could she ever say yes to a proposal, when she knew she would only weigh him down for the rest of his life?

Still in a daze, Claire turned back toward Matías's suitcase with neither socks nor boxers.

In the few minutes that she was gone, he'd somehow managed to cover his bed with various sprawling, unruly cables, seemingly random scraps of paper, his passport, gum, and toiletries. That was the thing about Matías. If there was any available space, his exuberance spread out immediately to cover every surface.

Claire glanced over at the bookshelf next to his bed. Unlike the shelves at her apartment, which were lined with books neatly organized by genre, Matías's was full of his various hobbies—a ukulele and accompanying sheet music. A box full of blocks of wood and whittling knives. A chess board, a deck of cards for practicing magic tricks, and a sketchbook and set of charcoal pencils. Not to mention the weekly letters from his ninety-two-year-old *abuela*—his grandmother—from the past eleven months. The stacks of envelopes with her beautiful handwriting had tipped over and knocked over all the others like cascading paper dominoes.

"I'll be done soon, and then we'll head to your place so you can pack," he said, smiling as he looked up from his suitcase.

Her heart clenched. He'd been so excited about the trip that she'd put off telling him that she was bailing.

Except now, not going to Spain with him seemed even worse. Before, it had just been about work. But discovering the ring box changed this trip from a mere vacation to a Significant Life Event, and Claire's cancellation felt like it might actually be an ending.

I don't want to break up with him, though.

The last eleven months had been the most exhilarating of her life. Claire was like a stick well established in the mud, but Matías showed up and wrested her free. She still loved her routines and schedules, but often, when there was an opportune gap in her calendar, he would insert himself into it and whisk her away for an impromptu picnic in Central Park or a wine tasting at a pop-up cellar. On the nights she worked late, he would sometimes swing by when she was ready to go home, and instead of taking the car that the firm would have paid for, they would walk together through Midtown. If the streets happened to be empty, Matías would whirl her into the middle of them to dance for no reason.

And the sex . . . God, the sex. This was not the way tight-laced lawyers and accountants did it. Matías in bed was like his art—he paid extravagant detail to every inch of her body, and he moved with luxuriant, confident grace. Sometimes they made languorous love in the mornings, still groggy from sleep but waking, slowly, together. Other times, they would have to pause in the middle of dinner and fuck in the kitchen, overcome by the rich, sensuous flavors of the meal he'd prepared and unable to keep their hands and mouths off each other a second longer.

Claire loved Matías, and she wasn't ready to let him go yet. She just needed to slow things down, to buy herself more time to think. But she did need to tell him she couldn't go to Spain.

"Matías . . ."

Saying his name, though, made him grin. Claire was self-conscious about committing fully to a Spanish accent, but she also wanted to respect his heritage, so what always came out was a hybrid where the first part sounded Spanish and the second half, American. Which Matías had decided was adorable.

She softened at the reminder of how much he loved every single thing about her—even the imperfect bits.

"I know what you're thinking," she said, a reluctant smile curling the corner of her mouth. She picked up a pillow and threw it at him.

Matías laughed. "Say *guacamole* for me. With a proper Spanish accent."

"No." But now she was trying not to laugh, too, because this was his favorite way to tease her, and even though she'd practiced over and over, she still couldn't get *guacamole* right.

"*¿Por favor?*"

"I can't!"

"Yes, you can. Just go easy on the *g*."

Claire screwed up her face. Then she took a deep breath and did her best, which she knew was still embarrassingly wrong—"wa-ca-mo-lay."

Matías swooped her up in a hug and kissed her. "I love when you speak Spanish. And when we get to Madrid, you'll get to put your lessons to good use."

She winced. Claire had declared months ago that she was going to learn Spanish, but after an enthusiastic start, things at work had really heated up, and she hadn't made much progress on the language since.

Plus, she was about to bail on the trip completely.

Claire let herself be held for a moment longer. But then it was time to face the music.

"I have bad news," she said.

"Oh?" Matías frowned, but leaned against the window ledge, giving her his full attention. He did that every time—set down his phone or magazine or ukulele to listen to her when she started to talk. It was amazing, and at the same time, maddening how incredible he was, because Claire could never be as wonderful back. He set an impossible standard.

"I can't go with you to Spain."

"What?" His face crumpled. "Why?"

"This merger I'm in charge of . . . It's at a crucial juncture, and I need to be here to manage it. I'm so sorry. But if I nail this, they'll make me partner. Honestly, I still have to pinch myself that I'm running it all. It's a *billion*-dollar deal for Intelligentsia Tech, and I can't just leave in the middle of it. I'm really sorry, hon."

"But we planned this," Matías said.

"I know," Claire said. "And I thought the timing would work

out, but the firm needs me. I'm the linchpin of the whole acquisition."

"I was really looking forward to showing you where I grew up," he said. "And for you to meet my family."

"I've sort of met your family on video chats?" she said, trying to be conciliatory.

"It's not the same."

She knew how important his family was to him, and how much he'd wanted them to meet in person. Claire leaned against the window ledge, beside him.

"I feel terrible about this."

"What if you came with me, but we set aside some time for you to work remotely?"

She shook her head. "It's not the kind of job I can do well if I'm not in the same office as my team."

Matías was thirty-six and an accomplished artist, but right then, he looked like a boy who'd just lost his favorite toy.

"Hey . . . Look, I *do* want to meet your family. Let's promise to go to Spain together in the future, okay?" Claire said. "But this time, just go have fun. You haven't been back home since you came to New York almost a year ago."

He glanced in the direction of his dresser, and Claire was pretty sure he was thinking about the thwarted engagement.

"Maybe I'll stay here, too," he said.

Claire tensed for a second but plowed forward.

"No, don't do that, Matías. It's your summer break. You have no classes to teach till August, and you don't have another gallery show until the fall. You should go to Spain and do all the things I wouldn't want to do. Oh! What about that trip that Diego, Carlos, Facu, and Leo wanted to go on?"

Matías cocked his head as he thought about it. His childhood friends had proposed a week of jet skiing and skydiving and all manner of risky outdoorsy stuff that made Claire want to hide under a table just thinking about them. Matías had declined his friends' plans when Claire was coming to Spain, but now that she wasn't, he wouldn't have to be held back by her anymore.

"That *would* be a lot of fun," he said.

Claire rested her head on his chest. "I appreciate you understanding about my job. And when you get back and my merger is done, I promise I'll make some time for just us. Some sort of romantic getaway—even if it's only for one weekend."

She could almost see the thoughts churning behind his eyes, setting aside one proposal location for another yet to be determined. So be it. Maybe by then she will have figured out just what to do.

But one thing she did know. "I *am* going to miss you a lot," she said, looking up from where her head lay against his chest. She always felt safe here, nestled against Matías—a warm, temporary respite from whatever else may be going on around them.

He was quiet for a second. Then he said, "I think I have a solution for that."

Matías carried her to the edge of the bed and set her down. But instead of making love to her, which was what she thought he intended, Matías took Claire's left hand and spread it open. He brought it to his mouth and pressed a lingering kiss onto her palm. Then Matías curled her fingers closed around it.

"This kiss is for you to keep until I come home," he said, "so you can carry me with you while I'm gone. If you find yourself missing me too much, just press your lips against your palm and imagine your kiss meeting mine, and I'll be right here with you."

"You are such an over-the-top romantic," Claire said.

But even so, she looked down at her hand and kept her fist tightly closed, keeping the kiss he'd left her safe.

CLAIRE

⌐

IT TURNED OUT TO BE A GOOD TIME FOR MATÍAS TO BE GONE. Over the next few days, Claire spent seventeen hours a day at her office. As the senior corporate associate in charge of an enormously high-profile merger, she was the quarterback of every minuscule detail and thousands of pages of documents. She had multiple teams working with her—intellectual property lawyers negotiating technology licensing agreements, environmental attorneys dealing with EPA issues at a couple of the target company's sites, a real estate group investigating some expired leases, and more.

Just before 3 P.M., a pair of first-year associates filed into her office to listen in on her upcoming conference call.

Being a senior associate meant that Claire had a semi-corner office, which was a room larger than the normal offices and next door to one of the powerful partners. Sometimes Claire sat at her mahogany desk and just stared at the wall between her and the partner's office and daydreamed what it would be like when she, too, had a corner office of her own.

She just had to navigate this Intelligentsia Tech merger safely home.

"I like the painting behind your desk," Julia, one of the first-year associates, said.

Claire smiled and swiveled to look at it. It was a large still life of a fortune cookie, broken open to reveal the white ribbon of paper inside, connecting the halves like a bridge. Sitting on the paper were miniature versions of Matías and Claire, having a picnic of Chinese takeout as if they were in a park rather than inside a cookie.

"Thank you," Claire said. "It was a welcome home gift from my boyfriend a few months ago. I'd been traveling for work for ten days straight and finally flew back here on a red-eye. I was exhausted and all I wanted was a shower and to fall asleep in my own bed. But when I unlocked my apartment door at 6 A.M. and stepped inside, there was coffee brewing, and Matías greeted me with fresh churros and a mug of melted dark chocolate to dip them in. But the pièce de résistance was the easel in the center of the kitchen table, covered by a sheet of fabric.

"When I unveiled it, it was this painting. I don't know if you can read the fortune inside the cookie from where you're sitting, but it says, 'This is what happiness looks like.'"

Julia sighed. "That is the sweetest story I've ever heard."

Claire allowed herself a moment to ponder what a fortune cookie would say now about her future with Matías.

But then it was back to business. She prepped the first-years for the call and let them know what their assignments would be afterward.

They opened their laptops as Claire dialed in on speaker-phone. The general counsel of Intelligentsia Tech loathed video calls and would only do voice. Claire had to admit she was glad for at least one respite from the back-to-back Zoom meetings so she could sneak in a few bites of the salad she hadn't finished earlier.

That was another thing she missed about Matías's not being at home. Whenever he wasn't working late in his studio or teaching at the academy, he would make the most delicious dinners, and the leftovers were Claire's lunches. Without him around, though, she had to settle for cafeteria fare.

The conference call center connected her, and she introduced herself.

"This is Claire Walker, Windsor & Black."

"Hi, Claire. No one else has joined yet." Mitch Tahir didn't bother to say his own name, because he assumed he was important enough that people would just know him. He was the general counsel of Intelligentsia Tech, an old-school lawyer in his late fifties who'd run the legal departments of some of the biggest companies in Silicon Valley. Mitch was brusque and legendarily hard to please. If he asked you to bring him a talking fish, he expected a talking fish. In his wake were hundreds of lawyers who had wilted under his demands.

But not Claire.

"Good to talk to you again, Mitch. We're just a couple minutes early, so Yolanda and Kwame will be here shortly."

As if on cue, the conference call center connected the employment attorneys.

"Yolanda Davis, Windsor & Black."

"Kwame Jones, Windsor & Black."

"All right," Claire said. "Thanks, everyone, for being here. Let's get started."

Yolanda and Kwame launched into an update on where negotiations stood with the officers of Einstein Corp., the company that Intelligentsia was trying to acquire. Across the desk from Claire, the two first-year associates typed notes furiously on their laptops.

Claire had a yellow legal pad on her desk, just in case she needed it. But mostly she didn't. She lived and breathed this merger and knew every nook and cranny. She'd written all the main acquisition documents, and if she wasn't the author of all the side agreements, she had read them at least a dozen times.

"So," Yolanda said. "Jennifer Kahale-Brewster is demanding that Intelligentsia double the number of RSU grants in her employment agreement, or she won't sign."

Claire put the phone on mute to explain to the first-years. "RSU stands for restricted stock unit, which is incentive compensation given to executives." The associates dutifully scribbled down the definition.

Mitch blew up. "Double the RSUs? Who does she think she is that she can hold this deal hostage?"

"To be fair," Claire said, "Jennifer *is* their chief technology officer."

"I don't care if she's the fucking president of the United States," Mitch said. "Tell her that if she insists on being so damn unreasonable, then how will she feel when the merger falls apart and she gets *zero* Intelligentsia stock?"

The first-years had gone still, eyes wide. But Claire pursed her lips and tried not to laugh, because she knew Mitch well enough after working with him for the past eight months that she understood how to manage him. Mitch Tahir led with fire, and he only respected those who could fire back.

"You need her, Mitch," Claire said bluntly. "She can hold this deal hostage and you'll end up giving her exactly what she wants, because without her, you have nothing. There is no point in buying Einstein Corp. if you don't have Jennifer on board. So let's not waste your time—"

"Fine, fine," Mitch grumbled. "Give Jennifer what she wants. Next?"

Claire winked at the first-years, who were looking at her like she'd just defused a bomb with her bare teeth.

Kwame, the other employment lawyer, began explaining the pros and cons of lengthening the chief operations officer's contract.

The door to Claire's office opened. Her secretary, George, popped his grizzled head in and waved to catch Claire's attention.

She shook her head and pointed to the phone. Why was George interrupting her? It was obvious she was on a call, and he could easily look at her calendar and see that it was a very important one.

But George, who was usually great at anticipating Claire's needs and requests, took another step into her office and made his hand into the shape of a phone with pinkie and thumb extended, and put it up to his ear.

Annoyed, Claire mouthed, *Not. Now.*

George, however, started to look panicked. Then he strode over, grabbed the yellow legal pad from in front of Claire, and scrawled in Sharpie and underlined twice.

There was an accident.
Matías's sister is on your other line.

Claire's heart went into freefall.

She couldn't move.

But she could hear every pound of her pulse. Feel every twinge of nerves as their focus shifted from the adrenaline of a billion-dollar merger to the terror of something happening to Matías. She choked as she tried to remember how to breathe.

"Claire?" George whispered.

"Oh god!" she shouted as the weight of George's message truly hit her. She jumped up from her chair, loudly knocking over her mug of pens in the process.

The call went silent for a second.

Then Mitch said, "Is there a problem, Claire?"

"I—I have an emergency. Continue without me," she said, already halfway out of her office.

"This is unacceptable, Claire—" Mitch was saying, but she didn't hear the rest because she was hurling herself into the hallway after George.

"Matías's sister is on hold," he said. "You can take the call at my desk."

Claire careened around the edge of George's cubicle and snatched the phone, hands shaking as she pressed the blinking red button.

"Hello? Aracely? Th-this is Claire."

"Claire? *¡Ay, dios mío, algo terrible pasó! Matías y sus amigos estaban en la playa y hubo un accidente. La lancha—*"

"Wait, what?" Claire gripped the armrest of the chair with white knuckles, completely lost in a rapid-fire conversation she *had* to understand but couldn't. "Slow down, please. My Spanish is really bad and I don't—"

"There was an accident," Aracely said in English, with the same beautiful, soft accent as Matías; it made Claire want to cry. "The guys . . . their speedboat crashed. Two of them . . ." Aracely choked back a sob. "Two are dead. Three in the hospital."

"Matías?" Claire asked in barely a whisper.

"Matías . . . he's in a coma. You must come. Now."

CLAIRE

THE LAST-MINUTE TICKET TO MADRID MEANT THAT CLAIRE was crammed into a middle seat between a snorer who fell asleep the instant they took off and a teenager whose phone was clearly not on airplane mode, as it lit up every two seconds with new messages from his friends. However, it was a better seating situation than if she'd been next to the chatterbox one aisle back—clearly an oversharer who liked to interrogate those around her. Claire wouldn't have been able to take it. She felt as if her personal armor had been punctured a million times, and now her heart and the rest of her insides were leaking through it like a sieve.

"Hello, everyone. This is your captain, Amanda Cheasequah, speaking. We've reached our cruising altitude of forty-one thousand feet so I'm going to turn off that seatbelt sign. Unfortunately, it does look like there will be some turbulence as we get closer to Spain, but I'll keep you updated as we approach the storm. For now, sit back, relax, and enjoy our seven-hour, twenty-seven-minute flight."

Claire squeezed her eyes shut. *Turbulence as we get closer to Spain.* That was an understatement if she'd ever heard one. Her entire future was on life support. Matías was on oxygen and a feeding tube. She was going to meet her boyfriend's family but she didn't know if they knew he'd been about to propose, and how they felt about her abandoning her planned vacation with Matías at the last minute. And on top of that, she'd run out of the office in the middle of one of the biggest mergers her firm had ever handled, possibly cratering a career she'd toiled for and taken massive law school debt to build.

Seven hours and twenty-seven minutes. Claire had mapped Hospital Universitario La Paz from the Madrid airport, and thankfully, it was only sixteen minutes away when there wasn't traffic. Still, with deplaning time and passport control and customs, that was over nine or ten hours until she could see Matías.

Ten hours too long.

Please, Matías, don't leave me. Hold on. I'm coming.

Claire bit back a sob. The teenager next to her rolled his eyes. Claire normally would have said something, but she didn't have the energy right now for insignificant fights.

Oh god, all those insignificant little fights she'd had with Matías . . .

She should have been more forgiving. What did it matter if he left water glasses all over the apartment because he would forget that he already had a cup and just grabbed another one from the cabinet? Why had she tried so hard to make him follow her organizational rules—things that made sense to her but might as well be arbitrary to anyone else?

Plastic wrap and foil should be lined up in the drawer with their openings facing to the right.

If there is a white tea towel on the oven handle, then the other towel should be a blue terry one because they have different levels of absorbency.

Also, towels don't get washed with clothes because it encourages pilling.

Claire had never thought of herself as persnickety, but now that she started cataloging the myriad requirements of participating in her life, she wondered how Matías hadn't run out the door screaming on day one.

Because he was a saint. He picked up her dry cleaning. He carried her to bed when her feet were too achy from being crammed into heels all day. He painted her body with colors he made himself from ground blackberries, rose petals, bee pollen, and honey, then kissed every inch of her clean and made love to her like she was a masterpiece.

I don't deserve him, she thought.

He'd said he loved her because she was strong, and he'd been surrounded by strong women his entire life. But Claire wore armor because she'd lost her parents too young, and because she worked in a field still dominated by men who talked over everyone else since they were spoiled by an old guard who always listened to them.

Underneath the warrior's clothing, though, Claire hid the raw, tender parts of herself. And they were exposed now, vulnerable to every terrible what-if she could imagine.

"Please God," Claire whispered, tears streaming down her face. "Please let him live. I will do anything . . . just let Matías make it through."

CLAIRE

⌒

NINE YEARS AGO

"CONGRATULATIONS, PUMPKIN!" DAD PULLED CLAIRE CLOSE TO kiss her on the cheek, bumping her graduation cap off onto the grass.

Mom picked it up and beamed at it, then at Claire. "Oh, sweetheart, we're so proud of you! Not only are you the first person in any part of our family to go to college, let alone graduate, but you're also off to law school!" She re-pinned the cap onto Claire's head and adjusted the tassel so it was on the left side now that she'd officially been through the graduation ceremony.

Claire wrapped her arms around both her mom and dad and brought them into a group hug. It had always been just the three of them. Jim and Sarah hadn't been able to have kids of their own, so they'd taken Claire in as a foster child when she was two—her biological parents had died of drug overdoses—and as soon as it was possible, Jim and Sarah made it official and adopted Claire. They were all the family she'd ever remembered, and all the family she'd ever needed.

"I love you, Mom. I love you, Dad," Claire said.

"Not as much as we love you," Dad said, which was the same retort he gave every time she said that. And it made her smile every time.

"So," Mom said, "how about a celebration dinner at Applebee's?"

"That sounds perfect," Claire said. Most of the kids in her class would be out at fancy steakhouses or upscale Italian restaurants tonight. But Applebee's felt like home to Claire, who'd grown up in a house full of love but not much money. Applebee's with her parents was exactly where she wanted to be.

Over boneless wings and pub pretzels with cheese dip, Mom talked about the rest of the RV trip they'd planned. They'd driven up from the little town in Florida where Claire had grown up to New York to be at her graduation, but then they were veering west to go see the Grand Canyon and a few other notable stops—like Carhenge, a "Stonehenge" made of cars—along the way.

"Wish you could come with us, sweetheart," Dad said.

Mom swatted him affectionately. "Oh, stop it, Jim. Don't guilt the girl. She's got dreams bigger than Carhenge. Claire's going to be a Big Apple lawyer someday, aren't you, honey? Just like those shows on TV."

Claire grinned from behind fingers covered in honey-garlic sauce from the wings. "Yep, just like TV, except maybe with less romantic drama."

Mom laughed. "I hope so. Those TV lawyers are always sleeping with each other *and* all their clients. Pretty sure that's a conflict of interest."

Dad winced. "Sorry. Can't think about my sweet little girl grown up and, uh, having relations with anyone."

Claire leaned across the table and gave him a sticky, sauce-covered kiss on the cheek. "Don't worry, Daddy. No matter what, I'll always be your little girl."

———

TWO HOURS LATER, CLAIRE'S PHONE RANG. HER PARENTS HAD wanted to take her to a movie after dinner, but she'd planned to go to a graduation party with her friends, so her mom and dad had decided to hit the road to get some mileage in before the sun set.

She stepped out of the party, onto the lawn. "Hello?" She noticed that she'd missed four previous calls from the same unknown number.

"Claire Walker?"

"Yes?"

"This is Officer Grether from the Maryland State Police. I'm afraid I have bad news . . . There was a crash on I-95 involving an eighteen-wheeler and your parents' RV."

"What?" Claire bolted into the middle of the street, as if somehow she'd be able to see all the way down to the highway in Maryland from there and prove him wrong. "A-are they all right? I can drive down right away. No, shit, I've had a few drinks . . . Are Mom and Dad okay?"

"The big rig jackknifed on the highway and your parents' RV was crushed. I'm very sorry, Claire . . . Jim and Sarah Walker are dead."

CLAIRE

CLAIRE JOLTED AWAKE FROM THE HALF-FLASHBACK, HALF-dream, face wet with tears.

Mom ... Dad ...

She should have asked them to stay longer after her graduation. Then they wouldn't have been on the road when that trucker lost control. They would still be alive today.

If she'd gone with them to a movie like they wanted, their plans would have changed just enough. They'd invited her, just like Matías had asked her to come with him to Spain. And both times when she'd declined ....

Oh god. A violent sob racked Claire's body. The teenager next to her frowned and asked, "Are you okay?"

Claire shook her head. She'd been alone in the world when her biological parents died, and Jim and Sarah had swooped in like angels and made her part of a family. But then they'd died, too, and Claire had been left all alone again. She'd found some sense of belonging in law school and at her work, but it wasn't until she met Matías that she finally felt that she had found a safe haven again. And now she might lose him, too.

She sobbed again. The teenager rooted around his backpack and found a travel pack of tissues. "Here, ma'am."

"Thank you," she whispered as she accepted the proffered mercy.

"Hello from the flight deck," Captain Cheasequah said. "We're making our final approach into Madrid-Barajas Airport and will have you on the ground in about thirty minutes, so I'm going to go ahead and turn on that fasten-seatbelt sign. Please remain in your seats for the remainder of the flight, and thank you for flying the global skies with us."

Claire emerged from the plane puffy-eyed and red-nosed. She headed straight to a restroom and splashed her face with cold water.

I look like crap, she thought of her reflection in the mirror. Her hair had frizzed in all directions, her skin had simultaneously dehydrated and broken out during the flight, and there were purple-gray circles beneath her eyes. And then, because her brain was a scramble of dread and anxiety, she wondered, *Should I put on some makeup to meet Matías's family?* After all, she'd only talked to them a few times on Zoom, and this was her chance to make a first impression.

But then Claire glanced at her reflection again and actually laughed out loud, startling the poor woman at the sink next to her.

There was no fixing Claire's appearance. She looked like crap because how the hell *would* someone look if their almost-fiancé was in a coma, with two of his friends in similar critical condition and two dead?

She gathered her bags and trudged out of the restroom. The airport bustled with travelers eager to be on vacation, or striding purposefully to business meetings, or chattering in excitement to be reunited with friends and family. In another life, Claire might have been one of them. But today, all she heard was a cacophony of Spanish airport announcements she didn't understand, mixed with the noise of a version of humanity she couldn't comprehend—one that was looking forward to what came next.

Because of her stop in the restroom, her entire flight beat her to passport control, and the lines wound back and forth, doubling onto themselves at least ten times. With shoulders slumped, Claire took her place at the back of the queue. The massive hall was hot and humid since it was summer, and unlike wasteful Americans, Europeans didn't crank up their air-conditioning to high as soon as the thermometer reached seventy-two degrees. It must have been at least eighty-five in the room when all the sweating travelers were accounted for.

For once, though, Claire wasn't in a rush to get out of the airport. She would stay here in passport control for days if it could somehow slow down time and unmake reality. How could Matías, who was bursting at the seams with energy and life, possibly be lying in a hospital bed, unconscious? How could someone like that be put on mute, their creativity and joy paused like a TV show, abandoned while the rest of the world continued?

But eventually she made it to the front of the line. Her photo was taken, her fingerprints scanned, and when the immigration officer asked the purpose of her visit, she just whispered, fighting back tears, "I'm going to see my boyfriend and his family," and the officer nodded, stamped her passport, and waved her through.

She shuffled through customs and out into the Arrivals Hall. There, a sea of faces surged around her and Spanish hit her like a tidal wave. Gone were the flight attendant and pilot announcements in both Spanish and English. Now it was only the language Claire had just started to study—and after six months, she was only on chapter 4 of her textbook because her job kept her too busy.

Claire's heartbeat pulsed in her throat as she scanned the crowd for Matías's sister, Aracely. *Please let me remember what she looks like,* Claire thought, because she suddenly couldn't conjure an image of Aracely's face in her head. She never imagined this was how she'd meet them in person for the first time.

There were drivers holding up iPads with names of the passengers they were picking up. Friends with balloons and ¡Bienvenidos! posters. Eager, wide-eyed people, bouncing on their toes and shouting as they spotted those they were searching for.

And then Claire saw them. A woman in her early thirties and a man about a decade younger, their expressions as gray and eyes as bloodshot as Claire's. Aracely and Luis, Matías's siblings, stood like somber statues in the middle of the animated Arrivals Hall.

"Hola," Claire said when she reached them.

Aracely just reeled her into a tight, silent embrace. She was a soft, plump woman, and it was comforting, if only for a few seconds, to be in her arms.

"Thank you for picking me up," Claire said after they'd pulled apart. "How is he?"

"Matías is . . ." Luis hesitated. "He is the same."

Claire closed her eyes tightly for a moment. When she opened them, she found the courage to ask, "No improvement at all?"

Aracely bit her lip and shook her head. "You must prepare yourself to see him, because . . ." She started to cry and couldn't continue.

Luis hugged his sister. He was only twenty-three, the baby of the family and still a little lanky from youth, but he had the same hair as Matías—thick black and wavy—and even though his eyes were deep brown and not liquid gold like his brother's, they were the same shape, and the resemblance nearly made Claire dissolve into tears, too.

"Matías broke thirty-seven bones," Luis said in a low voice. "They were going one hundred and eighty kilometers per hour when they crashed and flipped over. Matías is in many bandages. There are a lot of machines . . . I-I'm sorry, I don't know what they are called in English."

"It's okay," Claire said, not wanting to know yet. *Thirty-seven bones. Coma. Speedboat accident with two of his friends dead.* It was already too much to take in.

"How are Leo and Facu doing?" she asked.

"Still in Valencia, but also in an intensive care unit," Aracely said, unburying her face from Luis's chest. "They're only a little better than Matías. We pray for them, too."

"Come," Luis said, putting his other arm around Claire protectively and steering her toward the airport exit. "Let us take you to Matías."

ARACELY

❧

As ARACELY DROVE, SHE STOLE GLANCES AT CLAIRE IN THE rearview mirror. Matías's girlfriend was quieter than Aracely had imagined, and smaller, too. He had described Claire as the quintessential take-charge American woman, someone who ran multinational billion-dollar deals by day and kept his life in order by night.

Good, Aracely had told him when he'd first begun dating Claire. *You need someone like that.*

It had always been Aracely who kept Matías on track when they were growing up, rather than the other way around, even though he was two years older. She had learned this very early, on her first day of primary school. Matías had proudly walked her to school, introduced her to her teacher, then left for his own class. But he'd left all his books and even pencils at home, so the day ended up a rotten one for him, and he'd gotten detention. Aracely had to stay late while he served out his punishment by cleaning the classroom.

Even that had taken longer than it should have because Matías kept getting exciting ideas for things to draw, and he would doodle on the whiteboard instead of making it pristine. Matías was artistic entropy personified, and he needed someone to contain him. Aracely ended up helping him put the room back in order, and by the time they arrived home, it was two hours later than it ought to have been. She resolved from that day onward to make sure Matías had all his homework and school supplies before they left each morning.

They were a good pair like that. Matías's looming presence on the playground meant Aracely was never bullied. And when she was older, it meant the boys in her grade were extra respectful of her because they knew that one stray, less-than-gentlemanly comment would result in being pounded by Matías after school.

Looking at Claire huddled in the backseat, Aracely felt a pang of kinship. They were both women who were quite sufficient on their own and yet had enjoyed the security of being under Matías's protective wing. They had also shared the role of letting Matías be the genius that he was, while helping to focus his energy.

And now they were rendered helpless. Nothing to do but wring their hands and pray.

Aracely looked away from the rearview mirror and reached over the gearshift for her other brother's hand.

"It will be okay," Luis said in English.

"How can you be sure?"

"You can't," Claire said from the backseat before she fell quiet again.

Matías

⌣

ELEVEN MONTHS AGO

MATÍAS PACED THE LENGTH OF THE ROSE GALLERY OVER AND over.

"Don't worry," Jason, the owner, said. "Your opening tonight will be a success. The RSVPs were excellent, and your work is incredible."

Jason seemed confident. Not just his words, but also the way he stood, with shoulders back and relaxed, and his smile effortless. Part of Matías's success as a painter stemmed from his ability to understand the minute details of the human form and what they meant—a small crease at the corner of the mouth, a slight flare of a nostril, a faint crescent bite mark on a knuckle. And what he read on Jason right now was tranquil confidence.

At least that's one of us, Matías thought as he surveyed the wide-open space of the gallery. In just half an hour, the doors would open, and strangers would pour in to pass judgment on his work to the soundtrack of champagne bubbles and a Spanish band. He had held gallery showings before, of course, but the unfamiliar crowd had always been punctuated here and there by smiles from family members. The de León clan in Madrid was big and gregarious and unfailingly supportive, so not only would his mom, dad, sister, and brother be at every opening night, but also his *abuela* and a dozen or more aunts, uncles, or cousins. Not to mention friends from art school.

But here in New York, Matías was . . . new. He was barely moved into his apartment—his only chair right now was an upturned paint bucket—and he had just this morning received the key to his faculty office at the New York Academy of Art. He knew no one, other than the professional contacts he'd been emailing before he arrived, the people in the university administration, and Jason here at the Rose Gallery. And no one knew Matías.

"Do you mind if I make a quick phone call?" he asked Jason.

"Of course not," Jason said with a congenial wave of his hand. "I've got a few last-minute things to check on anyway before we open the doors."

As Jason walked toward the front of the gallery where the band and caterers were setting up, Matías dialed his sister. It was the middle of the night, but Aracely would pick up. She knew how jittery he'd been leading up to this exhibition.

Aracely answered on the first ring. "*Lo harás bien,*" she said without preamble. You will do great.

"I'm sorry to call so late," Matías said. It was comforting, slipping into Spanish.

"I am hardly asleep yet," Aracely said. "I just finished dinner not too long ago."

Matías smiled at the reminder of home. American dinnertimes had been a bit of a shock to him. In Spain, he didn't sit down to eat until 10 P.M., and it was almost always with either his friends or family, so the meal wouldn't wrap up until half past eleven. In New York, a lot of restaurants *closed* at 10 P.M., and the ones that closed at eleven made it clear they didn't like customers walking in the door at what would have been a normal Spanish dinner hour.

"What does the gallery look like?" Aracely asked.

"I'll send you a photo." Matías snapped a pic of the closest wall, hung with two of his larger pieces. He sent that photo and another of the gallery's front window to Aracely.

"Oh, it's beautiful," she cooed. "Your New York skyline painting is so stunning. It will draw in passersby for sure."

"Do you think anyone will buy anything tonight?" Matías asked, pacing again.

"I do," Aracely said. "But it also doesn't matter. Tonight is only the opening; it's your entrance into the New York art world. People will get to know you, and even if they don't buy tonight, your work is so impactful it will linger in their minds long after the party is over, and they will tell their friends, and more people will come to the gallery during regular hours, and you are going to be a star, Matías. So don't worry. Tonight is not the end. Tonight is a beginning."

"Tonight is a beginning," he echoed.

"Yes," Aracely said as she yawned. "I love you, and you are amazing, okay? Now go wow those Americans, *hermanito*."

TWO HOURS LATER, MATÍAS'S DIMPLES HURT FROM SMILING SO much, but it was a good problem to have. The attendance was, as Jason had promised, excellent, even if most of the guests didn't quite understand Matías's work.

"It's so fun!" a woman in her fifties gushed to him while her ring of friends murmured in agreement.

"Your paintings remind me of *Highlights* magazine," another of the women said.

"I'm sorry," Matías said. "I am not familiar with *Highlights*?"

"Oh, right, of course!" she said. "You probably don't have that in Spain. It's a darling magazine for children. Every issue comes with a hidden pictures game, which looks like an ordinary illustration, but then there are always wacky, unexpected drawings in them. Like, it'll be a scene of two children playing a video game in front of a television, but when you look closer, you'll discover there's the outline of a spatula sketched into the girl's hair, or that the curl of electrical cords on the carpet is in the shape of an octopus. It was one of my favorite things about the magazine when I was a kid!"

"That sounds . . . enchanting," Matías said, his smile a little more forced now.

"Just like you are," yet another of the women said. "I bet everyone in this room would love to take you home after this party."

Matías laughed politely. "Well, unfortunately for them, the only things in this gallery going home with anyone are my paintings."

They giggled, but at least it started them chattering about how they'd rank the pieces.

Which was not a discussion Matías wanted to stay for, because no artist wanted to hear how his work was graded on a curve. He put everything he had into each painting, and they were all different. Patrons were welcome to have their opinions, of course; Matías just didn't need to hear them.

Thankfully, Jason was waving at him from near the front door.

"It was wonderful to chat with you all," Matías said to the circle of women, "but the owner is summoning me, so I'm afraid I must take my leave. I hope you enjoy the rest of your evening."

Matías wove his way through the crowd, which was thicker in this part of the gallery because it was near the bar and the band. The majority of the guests had already walked through the aisles looking at his paintings and were now just enjoying the free drinks.

A short distance in front of Matías, a young man shouted over the flamenco music to his companion, another blond man in his late twenties. "The gallery's choice of artist is a surprise. Classical realism is so outmoded."

"Maybe the owner is trying to be daring," the second man said.

"Or stupid," the first replied. "Nobody is going to buy this antiquated shit. Abstract art is so much more elevated."

The second man caught sight of Matías and froze. Then he said, as if still in conversation, "Oh, you're so funny when you're sarcastic, honey. Um, why don't we go get some more booze?" He whispered something hastily to his partner, then they fled to the bar.

Matías simply shrugged. He was more than familiar with the uphill battle of painting in a classical style, even if he did add an imaginative element to it. What they'd been saying wasn't wrong, exactly; global tastes did lean toward the contemporary. But as his mom, Soledad, always told him, "That's how you stand out, Mati. Because you're different from the rest."

His art wasn't for everyone. Matías just needed to find the kind of person who appreciated it, who understood what he was trying to say.

The musicians finished their song, and as the audience clapped, the crowd parted.

There, in front of him, stood Jason, along with a woman in a white blouse and beige pencil skirt. Her brown hair was neatly pulled back into a bun, just a few loose tendrils curling to frame her face like satin ribbon. She looked more like she belonged in the hallowed halls of a university library than in the middle of an extravagant gallery opening.

She stood out because she was different from the rest.

"Matías de León," Jason said, "I'd like you to meet a friend of mine, Claire Walker."

"*Un placer*. A pleasure," Matías said, bowing a little as he reached for her hand.

Claire's mouth parted, but no words came out.

Yolanda, Jason's wife, appeared out of the crowd with two drinks. But when she saw Claire standing there—and snuck a quick, assessing look at Matías, which he did not miss—she winked at Jason and said, "Why doesn't Matías give Claire a personal tour of some of his paintings in the back of the gallery? You know, since she arrived late and missed the introductory speech?"

"What a fantastic idea," Jason said. Smoothly, he steered Claire and Matías through the throng of guests and deposited them near the path that would take them deeper into the gallery. But before Jason left, he leaned into Matías and said, "Sorry about this. Just humor my wife. This is her best friend." And then he and Yolanda disappeared back into the crowd.

Claire laughed under her breath in a way she probably thought Matías couldn't hear. But even if he hadn't, he would've known she was nervous just by the way she subtly worried her lower lip—her teeth tugging, but barely, on the inside of that full, pink mouth—and the slight flush at the base of her throat, right where a simple pearl pendant rested. She was the opposite of the women from earlier, who'd wanted to take him home with them and devour him.

"I am so glad you could come tonight," Matías said as they made their way deeper into the Rose Gallery. He didn't, of course, know anything about her other than that she was Yolanda's friend, and what he could read from her body language, but he *did* know that he didn't want Claire to be nervous.

"You are? Why?" she blurted.

"I was worried no one would attend my gallery opening," Matías said honestly. He didn't like men who put out a facade of bravado; Matías preferred to lead with his heart, in both his art and his life. "But Jason has done a wonderful job with it. Are you having a nice evening?"

"Not until now."

Her boldness caught him off guard, and he grinned. *There* she was. He'd suspected from the first moment he saw her that Claire wasn't the meek type. She may have been more at home in a university library than at a gallery opening, but she didn't have the posture of a mousy bookworm. More like a young professor who knew she was a rising star. She was aware of her potential, but not egotistical about it—perhaps because she understood that talent alone was not enough to guarantee success.

Matías led them to the back wall of the gallery. There were only two other guests farther down on this aisle, so he and Claire had this part of the exhibition to themselves. She was a head shorter than him, and when a waft of the light citrus scent of her shampoo hit him, he gasped.

Seville orange.

Like the famed Spanish oranges of home.

His heart thrummed a little faster, and for a few seconds, he forgot how they had gotten here alone. But then he remembered that Yolanda was trying to set them up, and that Matías was supposed to explain his paintings to Claire.

Suddenly, though, Matías felt his hold on the English language loosen. Which was strange, since he'd spoken it fluently for nearly three decades.

He cleared his throat. "Um . . . although Jason asked me to give a speech earlier tonight, I do not really like to talk about my work. I put everything I have to say into the art itself, you know? So, please." He waved toward the paintings that hung around them.

Was that terribly awkward of him? He was supposed to be Claire's guide, and he had embarked on this endeavor not wanting her to be nervous, but now he'd just thrust her straight into his work without so much as an explanation of classical realism or even a background of his years of training.

But as he'd guessed before, Claire wasn't meek, just unaccustomed to the art world. As he watched her absorbing his work—taking her time with each one and giving it its due—he realized he'd been right to let her explore his paintings without the burden of his commentary.

And Matías could see the instant when Claire found the magic in each piece. She didn't laugh loudly or point at it like almost everyone else had tonight. Rather, she simply smiled quietly and held the detail inside her for a moment, as if turning it over in her mind and contemplating not just the image of it, but the *why* of its existence in the first place.

When they arrived at the painting of the monk offering the planet Earth inside an orange peel, though, Claire couldn't keep her reaction in.

"Oh my god, Matías," she whispered. And in those four words, he knew that she understood everything he was trying to say.

Matías smiled then, brighter than he had all evening, and his dimples didn't even hurt.

Tonight is a beginning.

CLAIRE

⌐

THE HOSPITAL WAS THICK WITH BEEPING AND THE SMELL OF antiseptic, with the padded footsteps of doctors in sterile shoe covers and the fog of patients' worry and families' fear. Claire's chest seized up as soon as she stepped inside.

When her parents had been hit by the big rig, they had died on impact. Claire hadn't even gotten to see them in the hospital, because they'd never had a chance. She used to wish that she'd had the opportunity to at least say goodbye, but now that she was here in that situation, she didn't know if it was better or worse—getting the bad news all in one blow or having it slowly trickle like water torture, not knowing how or when it would end.

Claire followed Aracely and Luis through the corridors, past signs in Spanish she couldn't read and rooms full of the heavy burden of waiting. There were halls and halls of patient rooms, and every so often, a nurse's station. It felt like they were walking in slow motion through Dante's rings of hell; the journey was interminable. In actuality, it was only three floors and four wards they had to cross before reaching Matías's.

As soon as she, Aracely, and Luis came through the double doors, the de Leóns descended on Claire. All of the extended family lived in Madrid, and every last one of them was here in the hospital. They gathered around Claire in a collective hug, talking all at once in a storm of Spanish.

"*Ay, pobrecita.*"

"*Claire, cielo . . .*"

"*He estado muy preocupado para Matías, pero ahora, estás aquí y espero que . . .*"

She was helpless, uncomprehending in the torrent of their emotion. Why hadn't she made it more of a priority to learn his family's language?

But Claire and Matías had been together for less than a year. She hadn't had enough time—to study Spanish. To meet his family properly. To sort through her own baggage enough to decide if she really wanted to marry him. If their connection was real, or just an illusion.

A woman who looked identical to Aracely but with more wrinkles put her hands on Claire's cheeks. It was Soledad, Matías's mother.

"*Mi corazón*"—dear heart; that was one phrase Claire knew from Matías—"You are strong. You can do this."

"M-may I see him?" Claire asked, her voice barely audible.

"He is resting," one of the many cousins said in English this time.

"The nurse said no visitors," another said.

The denial was too much. Claire's knees gave out. She almost hit the floor, but Luis caught her arms.

"I don't care about the nurse's rules," Soledad said. "Claire is no normal 'visitor.' *Va a ser la esposa de Matías.*"

Claire had enough Spanish to understand—She is going to be Matías's wife.

So he *had* told them his plans to propose, although they didn't seem aware that Claire knew. Otherwise, Soledad wouldn't have said that part in Spanish to keep it secret.

But now Claire didn't know if Matías would live long enough for her to become his wife, regardless of her own feelings on the matter.

She must have let out a whimper, because Aracely came over and pulled her in for another hug.

Soledad marched over to the nurse's station and spoke quietly to them, gesturing every so often at Claire.

A minute later, Claire was standing outside Matías's closed door.

Afraid to open it.

"*Ve*. Go," Soledad said gently. "Matías needs you."

Claire didn't know someone could have so many IVs and tubes and casts and bandages on him. After the accident, emergency surgery had been performed to stop internal bleeding, and now Matías was hooked up to nine different monitors—one to measure his breathing, another machine keeping track of his heart rate, a bank of panels administering half a dozen medications. There was a feeding tube and a catheter. What little of his skin that was visible was swollen and covered in bruises so deeply purple they were nearly black. They'd shaved part of his head to get access to his skull.

"Oh, Matías." Any armor Claire might have still had on now tumbled to the hospital room floor, and she collapsed by the side of his bed and wept. "Please don't die. Please hold on. I'm here . . . Can you hear me? I'm here."

She couldn't even hold his hand, because it was covered with tape and wires and an IV. There was no part of him she could touch—not his hair under the head brace or his battered cheek crisscrossed with scrapes or that muscled part of his neck that she liked to tuck herself into when she was scared or stressed.

What if he never woke up?

What if he did, but he was permanently broken? If he couldn't paint, if he couldn't play in his weekend volleyball league or go scuba diving with his friends? If he couldn't take part in all his hobbies—and the *life*—that he loved . . . how would he survive?

And what if he did recover, but he held it against Claire for not coming to Spain with him in the first place? She knew it was irrational, that he couldn't *really* blame her for the boat accident or the timing of the merger.

But she also couldn't help thinking it was always somehow her fault. Like with her parents . . . What if she had gone out for a movie with them that night? Then they would have been in the theater with her and not where the eighteen-wheeler truck jack-knifed . . .

If Claire had come to Spain with Matías, he would not have gone off on risky adventures with his friends. He would not have ended up on a boat at all, because waves made Claire seasick. And then Matías and Facu and Leo would be okay right now, and Diego and Carlos would still be alive, and, and, and . . .

The tears flowed faster now.

"I don't want to do this without you, Matías. Come back to me, okay? Please?"

The oxygen cannula hissed. The panel of monitors beeped. Nothing changed.

"I love you, Matías. Come back. I'll be waiting."

Matías

‿

Matías smiled in his kitchen as he smelled the ripe tomato in his hand. Meeting Claire last night had been an unexpected highlight of the gallery opening. The exhibition itself had been a mélange of emotions, as it was anytime Matías had a show—the stress of sharing his work with a new audience and the rush of mingling with art lovers, the high of a sale, the low of haughty comments about his style. But that brief time he'd spent with Claire had been pure joy.

She *got* him.

And now she'd agreed to dinner. Matías hadn't been on a first date for years—his last relationship had been quite long, and only recently ended—and he didn't know if there were differences in how things were done in the States versus in Spain, but there was one thing he knew: Food was a universal language.

So Matías had spent all morning and early afternoon visiting different purveyors around New York. He'd stopped into four different cheesemongers to sample their offerings before he circled back to Murray's for the Manchego that tasted closest to his favorite one at home—nutty and tangy, with just the right crumble. Then he'd browsed through Despaña for olives and Marcona almonds, and chatted his way through a local farmer's market, taking time to talk with each grower about where they were from and what they grew and why. It was the way he had been taught by his mom, Soledad, and his *abuelita*, Gloria. Meals were not just nourishment—they were love letters to the sun and the earth that grew the vegetables, to the farmers who nurtured the fruit and the artisans who pressed the olive oil, and most of all, to the people to whom you served the food. If you put love and care into your cooking, it would show with every bite.

It wasn't that far off from how Matías approached painting.

He glanced over at the open notebook on the counter: a collection of family recipes that his mom had compiled for him before he moved overseas. She'd been worried he would feel homesick, especially not being able to come over for family dinner every Saturday, so she and his abuelita had painstakingly handwritten over a hundred of the de León favorites. Aracely had gotten each recipe protectively laminated—because Matías's persona in the kitchen was best described as Chef Chaos—and then bound them into a single, neat book so he couldn't misplace any of them.

He was making empanadillas de atún con sofrito. He already had the half-moon pastries in the oven (some families fried theirs, but his had always baked them), and now he was working on the sauce of tomato, onions, garlic, and bell peppers. The onions were already browning on the stove in Spanish olive oil, filling his small apartment with their rich aroma while he chopped tomatoes.

What Matías knew from the art world was that first impressions meant a lot, so he was throwing everything he had into cooking for Claire.

He hoped this dinner would show her as much about him as his paintings had last night, and that she would like what those flavors revealed.

HER WORLD WAS SO DIFFERENT FROM HIS. INSIDE THIS TOWER of steel and glass was an entire industry Matías knew nothing about—high-powered corporate attorneys who helped drive the global economy. While he made pieces of art one by one, Claire and her colleagues helped build new companies and cement landmark deals for everything from cutting-edge windmill technology to fish hatcheries, luxury hotel mergers to Super Bowl beer distribution rights.

Increíble, Matías thought as Claire led him through the Windsor & Black offices. This woman in front of him had the power to shift the way the world worked, just with her words.

She took him to the law library, where she had said they would have more room to unpack the dinner spread he'd brought. Claire scanned her badge at the glass double doors. He held it open for her, and she paused for a second as she looked up at him and smiled.

"No one's opened a door for me in a long time," she said. "It's surprisingly nice."

"You need to be spoiled more," Matías said.

Claire laughed as she flipped on the library lights. "Not really. I mean, look at where I get to work."

"Oh wow." All around him were gleaming marble columns and shelves and shelves of polished oak filled with handsome leather-bound tomes. There was a circular desk—presumably for the librarians—and above it, painted in gold on the ceiling, was a quote from Jorge Luis Borges: "I have always imagined that Paradise will be a kind of a library."

Claire shook her head, although she was still smiling. "I'm not sure that quote applies to a *law* library . . . But I do like it."

"I like it, too," Matías said, but he wasn't looking at the quote; he was watching *Claire* look at it. Just like last night when she was studying his paintings, there was so *much* going on behind those eyes. Her intelligence was palpable, and he wanted to know every single one of her thoughts.

"Anyway," Claire said, "let's go deeper into the library. There are some tables back there where we can spread out and have a proper dinner. It would've been terrible if we'd tried to eat squeezed between all the stacks of paper in my office."

She turned to a corridor to the right, but before they left the library's foyer, Claire flipped off the lights.

"To save on the energy bill," she explained when she caught Matías glancing back over his shoulder at the dim room behind them.

He liked that she cared, even though the firm was the one paying for the lights.

When Claire had found the perfect table in the back corner of the library, Matías unpacked the bag and cooler he'd brought with him. A tablecloth his brother Luis had given him as a New York housewarming gift. A set of plates and silverware, which seemed to surprise Claire, probably because she was accustomed to eating off of paper or from disposable plastic containers. And of course the food—a tart apple salad with that delicious Manchego cheese, and the empanadillas and sofrito.

Claire ate with the same quiet expressiveness Matías was beginning to adore. She would take a bite, then close her eyes to let the flavors roll around in her mouth, and then she would swallow and a small smile would blossom across her face.

"This puts my cafeteria salad to shame," she said.

"I hope so." Matías grinned. She liked his cooking. She *could*—he was pretty sure—taste the passion he'd put into it. And he thought she might like him, too.

Claire asked him about painting and Spain, but he felt like they'd had plenty of his work last night at the gallery, so he asked about her life and her work instead. She gushed about the exhilaration of putting together multinational deals, of bringing together teams from different companies and countries. Her zeal for her work was something he understood, too—that thrill of losing yourself in something exciting.

But as they bit into the tuna pastries, Claire seemed to lose the thread of what she was saying. She went still for a moment, staring at his lips. The little hollow at the base of her throat turned a darker shade of pink.

Matías wiped away the bit of tomato sauce at the corner of his mouth.

She inhaled sharply, then shook herself out of her momentary trance. She creased her brow, as if having an argument with herself. The blush crept up her neck and bloomed onto her cheeks.

Yes, Matías thought. *She likes me.*

He had promised to take only thirty minutes of her evening since she still had work to do, but it would be hard to leave her.

When he unveiled dessert and fed the sweet almond confection to her on a spoon, she moaned. Then Claire bit her lip, contemplating for just a second, before she swiped aside the dishes in front of her, climbed over the table, and kissed him.

She tasted of sugar and heat, almonds and yearning.

Matías pulled her onto his lap and kissed her deeper, her lips parting, his tongue finding hers. And that would have been enough for him, just to hold her there, feeling her body against his, the pleasure of the meal he'd made her swirling through her veins.

But Claire's skirt rode up her thighs, and she pressed herself harder against him.

"Make me yours," she whispered.

Dios mío.

"Are you sure?" Matías asked, because even though he ached beneath her, Claire didn't strike him as the type to make love in a public place, even *if* it was an isolated corner of a locked library after hours.

"Some people are worth breaking rules for," Claire said.

He picked her up in a single, swift motion, and lay her down on the plush carpet between the shelves. Their clothes flew off, and for the next hour, they made love so fiery Matías was surprised the pages of the books didn't all light aflame.

Afterward, he cradled her against him, his body and mind the most relaxed since he'd arrived in New York.

She laughed nervously. "So, um, welcome to the Big Apple. I'm your tour guide, Claire."

Matías pulled her closer and kissed the top of her head. "I wouldn't want any other guide but you."

CLAIRE

⌡

CLAIRE'S HOTEL WAS FUNCTIONAL. IT WASN'T BEAUTIFUL OR remarkable, but it was clean and close to the hospital, which was all she really needed. The nurses had been kind enough to allow Claire a little bit of time with Matías, but it was only that— a *little* bit of time. Then they gently nudged her and the de León family out of the ward, with assurances that they could visit again tomorrow during regular hours.

Now, Claire was faced with a long stretch of evening and a night all by herself. Matías's family had invited her to come over to Aracely's apartment, but despite their good intentions, it was just too much. Aracely and Luis spoke English fluently, and Matías's parents, Soledad and Armando, also spoke quite well, but the other dozen or so of the extended family spoke mostly Spanish. Because of that, Claire was still figuratively alone, even in the warm ocean of their family's embraces and attention.

Just for some human connection, she turned on her laptop to let Yolanda and her other friends at the firm—as well as George, her assistant—know that she had arrived safely in Madrid.

While she waited for it to boot up, Claire lifted the corners of the bedsheets to check for evidence of bedbugs. She did this at every place she stayed—even at the five-star hotels that her clients booked her in during business travel. Then, satisfied that there were no bugs, she unpacked her suitcase. It had been hap-hazardly thrown together—ironic, given how meticulously she had wanted to fold Matías's clothes just a handful of days before.

It was only now that Claire realized she'd forgotten to pack any underwear.

She kicked at the now-empty suitcase, as if it were somehow *its* fault that it had failed to produce her underwear, then sank to the floor, head in her hands, and cried.

Her laptop chimed on the hotel desk.

"Not now," she said, and went on sobbing, even though it was probably her friends checking in on her and that had been the reason she turned on the computer in the first place.

Ding

Ding

Ding

"Later! Please!"

It went quiet for a minute and let her cry in peace.

Ding

Ding

Ding ding ding ding ding

Was it getting louder?

DING

"Ugh! Fine, I'm coming, I'm coming!"

Claire swiped her sleeve over her eyes and snorted in the snot that had clogged up her nose.

Incredibly unattractive, she thought.

And then, *But who even cares?*

The laptop chimed four more times.

She crawled over to retrieve it from the desk. The carpet left a disconcerting, grimy tackiness on her skin, like rug cleaner that hadn't been quite washed out, mixed with several decades of the dirt off other people's shoes.

On the laptop screen, the Windsor & Black internal chat channel was all lit up. There weren't just a few notes from her friends, but also hundreds—no, probably thousands—of messages she'd missed since she'd fled the office in the middle of the call with Mitch from Intelligentsia. Mergers didn't stop just because one cog was missing, but in this case, Claire was an incredibly important cog. The one in the center of it all. And that meant everyone had questions, because she hadn't had time to share any information before she'd had to drop everything and fly to Madrid.

But then, work could be good. It might keep her mind distracted.

She decided to go downstairs. Claire wanted to set parameters for herself, to keep from breaking down again, and being in public would help. She hated crying in public; the flight over had been mortifying, and so had collapsing at the hospital when she'd first been denied access to Matías. Claire was used to keeping her vulnerability under lock and key, and the recent overexposure had left her feeling too raw.

So she closed her laptop and headed back to the lobby. Next to reception, the hotel's café had plenty of open seats because it was only open for breakfast and lunch, and it was just after 9 P.M. now. Claire set herself up at a table that had a view of the street through the floor-to-ceiling plate glass windows, still flooded with the light of the slowly setting sun. She opened her laptop and dove into responding to merger questions. There were a number of "so sorry to hear" and "wishes for a speedy recovery" notes from colleagues who were acquaintances, not friends.

George had been the one to book her plane ticket while Claire raced to her apartment to pack, so she supposed word had gotten around the firm by now about what happened. Still, she resolutely ignored those messages of sympathy in favor of the purely practical.

> What is the status of open items in Disclosure Schedule 5(b)(ii)?

She quickly typed a reply.

> The Freshfields team in London is following up on the assignment clause in the Cunningham contract and will have an update to us by Monday close of business GMT.

> Claire, do you remember where we landed on sublicensing Einstein's "Project Titanium" database to Sine Wave Enterprises?

> Two-year sublicense, but *non*-exclusive. $150K per month.

> Not sure if we can get the Czech apostilles in time for closing this deal in two weeks.

> Reach out to Anežka Černý in the Prague office. She's a paralegal and has contacts in the notary community who can fast track this for us.

As expected, it helped to sit in the cockpit and feel like she was in control of something. Here in the middle of this merger, Claire was Puppet Master of the Universe. She understood every detail. She knew all the players and the timing and how to avert disaster when things went wrong. She had worked on enough deals in her career that she could preempt problems before they arose, and when something unexpected happened, she had the experience to come up with a solution. Unlike with—

Unbidden, her thoughts went to Matías, lying still and broken in the hospital.

Tears started leaking out of her eyes even though they weren't *allowed* to. She was in public, goddammit!

Fuck. Fuck fuck fuck *fuck*!

She couldn't do this by herself. The last time this happened— when her parents had died—Claire had at least still been living near her college campus, and not everyone had scattered yet after graduation. There were friends' shoulders to cry on; people who would bring her chocolate cake from the twenty-four-hour grocery store in the middle of the night.

But now Claire was in an unfamiliar country, where she knew no one except future family members she'd only met a few times via video calls. And she couldn't even go to a bakery to buy *herself* chocolate cake since she'd never learned the Spanish word for cake. It didn't occur to her that she could just point at a cake in the display case, because . . . because . . .

"I *need* you, Matías," she whispered even as she angled her body away from reception because one of the women there was already looking her way, concerned.

For almost a year, whenever Claire was stressed or when something went wrong, Matías was the one who grounded her and made her feel safe. With him, she could feel like the world would be okay, that whatever she was freaking out about could and would resolve itself. He always believed fiercely that everything would turn out for the best, even if that "best" wasn't at all what you had imagined it to be.

But the crisis right now was Matías himself, and he couldn't be there to help Claire through it.

Her computer dinged again, but she was too far down the well of grief for work to save her now. She slammed the laptop lid shut and curled her fingers into fists, as if she could hang on to hope and Matías by the strength of her grip alone.

Her fingernails dug into her flesh.

Her left hand tingled, and suddenly she remembered.

Matías, his lips warm against her skin.

This kiss is for you to keep until I come home, so you can carry me with you while I'm gone. But if you find yourself missing me too much, just press your lips against your palm and imagine your kiss meeting mine, and I'll be right here with you.

Through her tears, Claire unfurled her fingers and stared at her palm. She wanted to smash her lips against it, but at the same time, what if that used it up? Panicked, she curled her hand closed, as if that would preserve the kiss, and her brain began to fire off irrational hypotheticals. *If Matías dies, will this kiss always be with me and I can still have him forever? Or is this the very last I will have of him? And if I use it up, then what will be left?*

But in the end, she couldn't hold out. Claire's whole body shook from needing him—needing *some* connection, however small—and she opened her hand. Before she could change her mind, she pressed her lips against where his had been.

Matías.

The whole world trembled.

She felt his mouth against hers, the kiss he'd left her so tender and soft—a velvet caress. The memory of his touch dissolved her tension, and her muscles relaxed into the safety of Matías, of knowing that she had a partner by her side, someone to protect her not because she needed him to, but because they were stronger together.

Time froze, or maybe it went backward, because everything felt safe and secure and normal again. The kiss united her with Matías, and for that long moment, all was perfect.

She didn't want to open her eyes. Didn't want to pull her hand away from her lips and face the harsher reality.

But Claire didn't have a choice because too soon the feel of Matías began to fade. Her palm grew cold, her mouth dry and alone.

With a sudden hollowness in her chest, she reluctantly lifted her eyelids.

The summer sunset glared off the mirrored windows of a nearby skyscraper, nearly blinding Claire. She yelped and turned away.

Then the flash was gone, and in the spot that had been too bright to look at just a second ago stood . . . Matías.

Claire's breath caught.

"No, you're seeing things," she told herself sternly.

But it was him. She'd know him anywhere. Those broad shoulders in the blue canvas jacket with the splatter of green paint across the right sleeve. The waves of black hair, always tousled because he ran his hands through them whenever he caught sight of something that inspired him—which, with Matías's capacity for curiosity, was often.

But mostly, it was the gleam of those golden eyes, richer and more beautiful than any Spanish sunset could ever be.

It was impossible. Just a couple of hours ago, he'd been bandaged and bruised and hooked up to all those machines.

But here he was. It was really him, and he was healthy and whole and alive, and he must be looking for her!

Claire let out a small cry and ran out of the hotel into the driveway.

"Matías! What are you doing here? The hospital . . . you're supposed to be—"

He cocked his head and the corner of his mouth quirked up, as if she was another thing in the world that he found fascinating and might use in a future painting.

"I'm sorry," he said, and Claire thought she might faint at hearing the dulcet tone of his voice again. "But have we met?"

Every cell in Claire's body went rigid. There was no recognition in his eyes. None whatsoever. Was she hallucinating, casting some stranger as her boyfriend? But no, it was him, in every detail, from carriage to voice.

"I-I'm Claire."

"Claire. *Un placer*—a pleasure. I'm Matías." He gave her one of his charmingly crooked smiles. "Now, what were you saying about a hospital?"

The setting sun glared off the mirrored skyscraper again, and the beam went right through Matías.

He was still there, but—for that split second—he was transparent.

Oh god, Claire thought. A ghost.

Which must mean . . .

Matías was dead.

"No . . ." she breathed. "You can't . . . I . . ."

And for the second time today, Claire's legs gave out beneath her.

But this time, there was no one to catch her.

Matías

Eleven Months Ago

For his second date with Claire, Matías wanted to slow things down. He, himself, was not afraid of falling too fast—he believed in the momentum of fate and would not stop his heart from diving after her—but he had a strong feeling that their dinner in the library had gone several times the speed she was normally comfortable with.

So he had let Claire choose where they would go for their second date, and since she had appointed herself his tour guide—albeit, half in jest—they were now at Coney Island because she had declared it a New York initiation rite.

"You can't be a New Yorker until you've spent at least one summer day sweating in the lines at Coney Island, stuffing yourself with hot dogs, and spending way too much money at carnival booths under the misguided belief that *you* will be the one to beat the odds," she said.

He arched a brow. "Is that really a New York initiation rite?"

Claire grinned. "Probably not, but my freshman dormmates made me do it when I arrived here from Florida, so now I'm going to do it to you."

They started at Eldorado Auto Skooter, where music blasted while full-grown adults slammed into each other with bumper cars. Claire drove like she was trying to win the award for safest motorist, so Matías decided to chase her, bumping her into other cars while she laughed and screamed the whole time, trying to run away from him.

Next, she took him to two hot dog stands for a taste test—Nathan's Famous and Feltman's.

Matías had to work not to contort his face as he ate them. "This is . . . food?"

Claire cracked up. "It is *definitely* food. It's also payback for the bumper cars."

"Oh, in that case . . ." He crammed the remainder of the second hot dog into his mouth and washed it down with a swig of lemonade. "Well, I feel thoroughly American now."

She winked and grabbed his arm. "Okay, now that you've passed that part of the initiation rite, I have a reward for you."

"Please tell me it's not a roller coaster. I don't think I could handle it so soon after hot dogs."

"God, no. You'll never find me on a roller coaster."

Matías smiled. He was beginning to figure her out—driving her bumper car carefully around the perimeter of the rink. Small, measured bites of hot dog. No roller coasters.

"Okay, then, where are we going?" he asked.

"The Art Walls," Claire said. "It's like an outdoor museum of street art that changes every year."

They were huge panels, spread out like an open-air art gallery with the roller coaster undulating behind it. Matías sighed happily as he took them in—various styles from Lichtenstein-like comics to graffiti to an abstract representation of life lived through a phone screen. It was thrilling, too, to see the crowds milling around each piece, the teenagers taking selfies and the families posing for summer vacation photos. He could understand now why Coney Island was a quintessential experience Claire wanted him to have. This was New York, living and breathing—alive.

"I love this," Matías said. "Thank you."

She beamed. "You're welcome. But there's one more wall you have to see."

Claire tugged at his arm. She didn't see the abandoned teddy bear on the ground, though, and she tripped.

But Matías caught her.

She looked up at him, their gazes locked.

And that's how Matías knew he had fallen for good, because he didn't need to see any more of the Art Walls. He could just look down at Claire, and it was more than enough.

CLAIRE

"Señora . . . Señora, can you hear me?"

Claire blinked slowly, vision blurry at the edges from the sun in her eyes. Why was it so bright? It was like someone was holding up a mirror to a flashlight and pointing it straight at her—

Oh.

The skyscraper and the sunset. And the beam that cut straight through Matías.

Claire moaned and squeezed her eyes shut again.

"My colleague is calling for an ambulance," the woman from reception said. She was kneeling next to Claire, holding her hand. The hand that had, until a few moments ago, contained Matías's kiss but was now nothing more than an ordinary hand. "You hit your head when you fainted. Are you . . . How do you feel?"

I feel everything and nothing, all at once, Claire wanted to say. Matías was dead. All her fears since she'd received the phone call in her office—amplified by what she'd been through losing her parents—had come to a head now in the worst possible culmination. At the same time, she'd already wrung out all her emotions during the flight and the hospital visit and the time alone at the hotel. Somehow, there was nothing left inside her.

So Claire lay in the hotel driveway, numb. She opened her

eyes and looked at the concern wrinkling the receptionist's forehead but didn't have the energy to respond to the woman's query.
Instead, she turned her head toward Matías's ghost.

But he was gone.

"Wait . . . Come back!" The sharp knife of grief sliced through
Claire's numbness, and the force of it made her sit up.

"Señora, you must lie down!"

It was too late; Claire was already upright.

The receptionist said something in Spanish to another hotel
employee nearby. He ran inside, then came back carrying one of
the ottomans from the lobby lounge.

"If you will not lie down," the receptionist said, "then let us
help make you stable."

The man set the ottoman behind Claire so she could lean
against it while sitting in the driveway. "Please," he said, making
a *stay put* gesture with both hands. "Do not move. The ambulance is almost here."

Claire just stared at the space where Matías had been.

The paramedics arrived shortly, and they brought Claire inside the ambulance to examine her. As she sat on the narrow cot,
they asked in English when she last ate, how much water or
other liquid she'd drunk today, and whether she felt nauseous.
She answered flatly—I don't know, I don't know, and I have felt
nauseated ever since Aracely's phone call about the accident.

There was already a bump forming in the back of her head
where she'd hit the concrete, and they checked her eyes for signs
of concussion. The medics asked if the light was bothering her.

"No, there was a ghost in the light, and I want him to come
back."

The paramedics didn't know what to make of her answer.

"Señora," one of them said. "I think you have a concussion. We would like to admit you to the hospital overnight for observation."

"Hospital Universitario La Paz?" That's where Matías was.

"No, we are associated with La Moraleja University Hospital—"

"Then no. *No, gracias,*" Claire said before the medic could finish. If it wasn't Matías's hospital, there was no way Claire would let the medics take her. Because if they checked her in as a patient, she would be stuck there. And she needed to get back to the *other* hospital where Matías was . . .

Where Matías was dead.

The knife of grief stabbed her again, and Claire almost doubled over. But at the last instant, she held herself still and swallowed the pain. She had to keep herself together. It was imperative that she convince these paramedics that she was okay, that they release her from this ambulance.

"I feel fine," she said with what she hoped was a winning smile, or at least a persuasive one. "I just need water and aspirin and some food; I'm sure I'm dehydrated from the flight, that's all."

The medics consulted each other in Spanish, stealing glances at her every other sentence. Claire kept smiling at them.

Finally, they came to a conclusion. The one who'd been talking to her grabbed a clipboard and a form, then filled out some information.

Dammit, Claire thought. *They're going to admit me to the hospital anyway.*

"Okay, señora," the medic said, coming over with the clipboard. "This document confirms that we recommended further medical care but that you declined. If that is correct and you still do not want to come to the hospital, then I need you to sign here."

Claire stared at the form in all Spanish for a second. But then she realized the medic was giving her an out. "*Gracias*, I really appreciate it, you won't be sorry, I promise I'll drink lots of water and have a big dinner," she rambled as she signed the document.

The medic tore off a carbon copy for her, then gave her two boxes of juice and some packages of crackers before helping her down from the ambulance.

"I am going to watch you walk inside, okay?" the paramedic said. "To make sure you are steady."

She nodded. "*Muchas gracias.*"

Claire made a show of puncturing one of the juice boxes with a straw and drinking it while she went back inside. The kind receptionist hurried over, bringing Claire's laptop and briefcase from where she'd left them in the hotel café.

"They told me I just need to eat, drink, and rest," Claire said, even though that was a lie. But the receptionist didn't need to know that Claire likely had a concussion and that they'd wanted to admit her to a hospital.

"We were worried," the receptionist said.

Claire glanced over her shoulder to see if the ambulance had left yet. But the paramedics were still standing in the driveway, watching her. She couldn't just ask the receptionist to call a taxi for her to Matías's hospital; Claire would have to actually get in the elevator to convince the medics she was going upstairs to rest.

"I've got my juice and crackers," she said, holding them out for the receptionist to see. "All good here."

The receptionist hit the elevator call button.

Claire sipped on her juice.

The elevator didn't move from the third floor.

Claire finished the juice.

The elevator decided to go up instead of down.

The receptionist smiled awkwardly at her.

Claire smiled awkwardly back. "Um, you don't have to wait here with me if you—"

"No, no! I am happy to carry your bag and computer and escort you to your room to make sure you are okay."

Great.

Claire opened a package of crackers and nibbled one. Her stomach was not in the mood for anything to be put in it, but she was under the spotlight for now with the receptionist and the medics all watching her.

Finally, the elevator came to the lobby, and a rush of tourists spilled out, ready to hit Madrid in search of restaurants and bars.

The receptionist accompanied Claire all the way up to her room, looking as if she were afraid Claire might faint again at any second.

"Okay, thank you," Claire said as she unlocked her door and took the computer and briefcase from the receptionist.

"If you need anything—"

"Thank you!" Claire said, practically closing the door in the receptionist's face.

Safely back in her room, Claire leaned her back against the door and slid to the ground. Everything that had happened hit her at once.

She'd seen Matías's ghost.

She had had a conversation with it.

He was dead, and she was losing her mind.

Claire inhaled a jagged breath as the weight of loss began to crush her again, grinding her into the grimy hotel carpet, compressing her lungs so it became harder and harder to get air. Her heart panicked, pounding erratically like a drummer who's lost all control of the beat, and the only thing she could see was the image of Matías in bed, hooked up to all those machines.

Except now, the machines were quiet. No beeping monitors. No IVs administering medicine.

No need, because Matías was dead.

Claire moaned and tried to bury herself deeper into the carpet.

He couldn't be gone. It seemed impossible. How could a spark as bright as Matías be snuffed out, as if he were nothing more than a stray ember to be stomped on?

I can't . . .

She grappled for her phone in the briefcase. She just wanted to hear his voice one more time—or maybe ten more times or thirty. Claire would dial his number so she could listen to him on his voicemail, so she could pretend for just a little bit that Matías was still alive, that he'd get the message and call her back at any minute.

Claire opened the phone app and was about to key in his number when something occurred to her.

No one had called her. If Matías had died, Aracely would've called either Claire's cellphone or the hotel, right? Unless Matías's ghost showed up the moment he passed away, and there hadn't been enough time yet for the hospital to inform the family?

Claire checked the recent calls list.

She hadn't missed anything.

Her hands trembled. *Okay, okay . . . no missed calls is a good sign.*

I think?

Maybe she *was* just hallucinating. After all, she really *hadn't* had much to eat or drink since she'd left New York.

But she needed to be sure. Claire dialed Aracely's number.

"*¿Hola?*" Aracely answered before the second ring even began.

"Hi, this is Claire. I . . ."

But suddenly, she couldn't get the words out. She couldn't bring herself to ask, *Is Matías still alive?*

"*Hola*, Claire. Are you all right? I mean, under the circumstances?"

In the background, Claire could hear the noise of Matías's family. It wasn't lively, because of course everyone was worried sick. But it didn't sound hysterical, and neither did Aracely.

"Um," Claire said. "I was just wondering if there were any . . . d-developments? I'm sorry to bother you. It's just that I can't call the hospital myself because my Spanish is awful, and—"

"You should call me anytime you need to, Claire," Aracely said gently. "And no, there is no news about Matías other than what we knew when we left the hospital."

Claire walked up to her window and looked down to the hotel's driveway. The ambulance was gone now, and of course there was no trace of Matías's ghost.

"And we're sure the hospital would call if anything changed for Matías, right?" Claire said.

"Yes, they promised, and they will," Aracely said.

"Okay," Claire said. "So he's . . . we can assume he's still the same?"

"Are you sure you don't want to come over here?" Aracely asked. "Maybe it would be good for you not to be alone. Luis can pick you up."

"No, no, I . . . I probably need to sleep. You know, jet lag," Claire said. "But thank you."

"All right, then. But call me anytime, I mean it."

"Thanks, Aracely."

Claire collapsed on the bed, crushing one of the packages of crackers. Matías wasn't dead. He was in a coma and that was a terrible thing, but he was still alive, still alive.

It wasn't great, though, that Claire was in bad enough shape that she had imagined his ghost.

She forced herself to eat the broken crackers and drink the other juice box. Then Claire took two sleeping pills and fell into a restless sleep, dreaming of mergers and ambulance lights and Matías, waking from his coma and not remembering who Claire was.

LUIS

When Luis couldn't sleep, he drove. It was not only a significant part of his job—he was a test engineer for Stellantis, which designed Fiats and Alfa Romeos, among others—but it was also a comfort. When he was a baby—a fussy one—his dad had figured out that Luis would sleep if he was in his car seat with the engine running. As he got older, he fell in love with kart racing. He never became good enough to be a professional race car driver, but when he got to university, Luis discovered engineering and how he could make working on cars and driving them part of his career.

Now, in the middle of the night, he hit the freeway toward Valencia, settling into a speed fast enough that he could hear the wind resistance but not so fast as to be reckless, not after Matías's boat accident. It would be a seven-hour round trip from Madrid to Valencia and back, but there was an art to driving long distances that Luis had mastered from all those hours spent on racetracks over the years. He turned on his playlist of classical music, slowed his breathing to a meditative state, and did not allow himself to envision the end of the journey, only the road immediately beneath his tires.

But it was harder than usual to clear his mind, because of Matías. Older than Luis by thirteen years, he had been a different sort of brother. For as long as Luis had memories, Matías had basically already been an adult. It was Matías who had suggested that their parents allow Luis to try kart racing. Unlike the rest of the family, Luis and Matías shared the same fearlessness—and if not for his older brother's constant reassurances to their parents, Luis would not have the career he had today.

He clenched the steering wheel in a decidedly nonmeditative way.

Even though Matías could be absentminded about some things, he never forgot birthdays or their parents' anniversary. He picked up the phone anytime Luis or Aracely called, regardless of the hour in New York. Even his art was a gift, a smile in a world that too often frowned.

He is too good to die, Luis thought.

"You promised you would be there the first time I led a design team for Maserati," Luis said out loud as the road to Valencia curved and then stretched out before him. "I haven't done that yet, and since you always keep your promises, I guess that means you can't die."

He imagined Matías laughing at the joke.

It made Luis feel a little better. Not entirely, but enough for him to keep going.

And that was the most he could ask of this night.

CLAIRE

⌒

"BUENOS DÍAS," CLAIRE SAID AS SHE GOT INTO LUIS'S CAR IN THE morning. The bags under his eyes were even grayer than the day before, and there was a huge silver travel mug of coffee in the cup holder. "Did you sleep at all last night?"

Luis shook his head. "I drove out to the beach house Matías and his friends had rented near Valencia so I could pick up his things."

"Is it far?"

"Some would say so," Luis said. "But I did some thinking, so . . ." He didn't finish the sentence, but he didn't need to. Claire understood. A lot of times, having something to do was better than just lying in the dark with your fears.

"If the boating accident happened way out there," Claire said, "why is Matías in the hospital in Madrid?"

"Because a high school classmate of my parents is a top doctor here," Luis said. "She helped us get Matías airlifted to her hospital."

"Lucky Matías," Claire said, realizing as soon as the words came out that he wasn't lucky at all. He was in a coma. He still might die.

"What about Leo and Facu?"

"They're in the hospital in Valencia. Their dog and cat keep crying without them and won't eat."

Claire's eyes welled up.

She couldn't bring herself to ask about Carlos and Diego, the two who had already died. How were their wives handling the loss? And what about their children? Their daddies would never come home.

Luis grabbed a box of tissues from the dashboard and silently passed it to her.

They drove the rest of the way to the hospital without speaking, both lost in their own thoughts. When they'd parked in the garage, Claire opened the car door immediately, barely resisting the urge to sprint to the hospital building and throw herself over Matías's unconscious body.

But Luis opened the trunk first, and Claire gasped at the familiar sight of Matías's well-traveled suitcase, the edges frayed, the colorful baggage tag he'd designed while in art school, smudged with the dirt of age and international travel.

"I found something this morning that I think you should have," Luis said. He unzipped the front pouch of the suitcase and pulled out what looked like a small diary with a plain black leather cover, but the sides of the pages were painted in brightly hued paisley.

"What is it?" Claire asked.

"I didn't mean to pry," Luis said, "but it was sitting out on the living room table in the house they rented, so I had to look inside to figure out if it belonged to Matías or one of the other guys. Once I saw your name, I didn't read any more."

Claire opened the journal.

A first entry was dated two weeks ago.

July 7th

Dear Claire,

I am going to ask you to marry me soon, so I am beginning a project. This diary will be a collection of love letters to you, doodles, and random thoughts about us.

Marriage is a big step, and I know our relationship has probably gone at a faster pace than you would have chosen if you were in charge. But I hope that our upcoming trip to Spain—when you meet my family and see where I grew up—will help you fill in whatever gaps you need resolved to say yes when I propose.

With that hope in mind, I am going to start writing in this diary now, and then I will give it to you as a gift on our wedding day.

It will not be full yet, but over the course of our life together, I am going to fill this journal and so many others because there will never be enough pages for you.

~M

"Oh, Matías," Claire said softly. "You really are such a romantic."

SHE NEARLY WEPT WITH RELIEF AT SEEING MATÍAS IN THE hospital bed; he was not dead or a ghost. For once, the hiss of the machines wasn't sinister, but rather a reassurance. The oxygen cannula meant he was still breathing. The monitor measuring his pulse meant his heart was still beating. Even the feeding tube and the catheter signaled that his body was, generally, still working.

But because he had so many family members, the nurses had to limit the number of people who could be in Matías's small room to three at a time. His parents, Armando and Soledad, had organized a rotational system to cycle visitors in and out. Claire, though, could stay in Matías's room during all of visiting hours if she liked, because having his girlfriend near him would surely be a force for healing.

"This is your chair, *corazón,*" Soledad said, leading Claire to the far side of Matías's bed. "Everybody understands it is reserved for you, and no one will sit in it."

"Gracias," Claire said. "I appreciate you negotiating with the nurses for me to be here. But if I'm not here, someone else can sit—"

"Nonsense," Soledad said. "This is *your* chair, and Matías will know that, even though he is unconscious. Nobody else will use this space. It is yours."

Claire nodded. "Okay. Thank you."

The wise don't fight when a mother is doing something to protect her child.

Armando and Soledad's rotational system, however, meant that Claire never had Matías alone, save for the two minutes between visitation shifts when one set of relatives went out and the next hadn't yet come in. So most of the morning, Claire sat in the chair just watching Matías's chest rise and fall slowly, while across from her, various family members took turns talking or reading to him in Spanish and looking at her with pity. She wished she could communicate with them beyond sad pantomimes.

If you wake up, Claire thought to Matías, *I promise I'll work harder at Spanish.*

But then it occurred to her that "work harder" was a half-ass commitment. Matías had begun a notebook with plans to fill volumes of them during their lifetime. Claire could do better than "work hard" at Spanish.

Even if you don't wake up, I will *become fluent in Spanish, in your memory.*

But god, I hope you wake up.

Later, Armando came in with a tiny, gray-haired lady pushing a walker. Her face was entirely composed of wrinkles, and when she gave Claire a small smile, her eyes disappeared completely within the deep folds of skin.

"Soy Abuela Gloria," she said, pointing to herself.

Grandmother. Abuela was in one of the first Spanish vocabulary lists Claire had studied months ago. But she would have known the word anyway because Matías had a stack of letters from his beloved abuela, who wrote to him by hand every single week.

"Novia," Claire said, indicating herself as Matías's girlfriend. They hadn't met on video calls before, because Abuela Gloria didn't know how to use Zoom. She might not even own a computer. "Me llamo Claire."

Abuela Gloria nodded and said in her small, sweet voice, "Ya lo sé. Matías me ha escrito mucho sobre ti."

Armando helped his mother, who was ninety-two, into a chair and set her walker next to her, within reach. "She said she already knows who you are because Matías wrote a lot about you in his letters."

Claire bit her lip. She hoped he'd said good things . . . and not mentioned her strict silverware organization system, or how she insisted that coasters be used on every surface even if it was a counter that could easily be wiped off, or how she "reset the living room" every night before bed by straightening the magazines, putting the remote controls inside the coffee table drawer, and refluffing the pillows so it looked like a furniture showroom.

But Abuela Gloria was no longer thinking of Claire. She was fully focused on her grandson, lying on the bed in front of her. "Aah, cielo mío . . ."

Armando sat next to her, took his mom's hand, and said something low in Spanish.

She paused to consider it, then nodded.

"My mother used to sing to my kids all the time," Armando said to Claire. "And since the doctor said that Matías might be able to hear us, I thought . . ." He choked up and couldn't finish.

But his mom squeezed his hand, then took a deep breath and began to sing.

Her voice was rich and round, surprising from such a small, elderly woman who spoke barely louder than a whisper. Claire didn't catch any of the words except *Rosa de Madrid*, but she could feel the melody—light and almost playful, like a song sung by an old Hollywood starlet.

When she finished, Armando wiped a tear from his eye, and Claire clapped quietly.

More subdued clapping came from the doorframe, which was now filled with a doctor and Soledad, and Aracely and Luis behind them. Claire hadn't noticed the rest of the family come in, because she'd been so focused on watching Matías for any signs of waking during his abuela's song (though his eyelashes did not so much as flutter).

The doctor and everyone else filed in. Apparently, the visitation limit didn't apply when the doctor was present.

"Hello, you must be Matías's girlfriend," the doctor said in English with the calming smile of a professional who was used to talking to loved ones in difficult situations. "I am Liliana Rodriguez, the physician overseeing Matías's care."

"Thank you for all you've done for him," Claire said, her voice shaking.

"We are trying our best. The truth is that Matías is in very bad shape."

"He looks worse than yesterday," Aracely said quietly.

"The team in Valencia managed to stop the internal bleeding in that first series of surgeries," the doctor said. "But a lot of damage had already been done. Matías's body is trying to heal itself, but I cannot guarantee that it will be able to, or that he will wake."

Silence.

Soledad began to cry. Luis wrapped his arms around his mother.

Finally, Armando was the one brave enough to speak. "What about my son's brain activity? In the hall, you said there was a spike?"

"Yes," Dr. Rodriguez said. "Last night, around 9:25 P.M., there was a sudden increase in Matías's vital signs. Brain activity, heart rate, and respiration rate all increased for a short period of time."

Claire sat taller in her seat. That was around the time the sun was beginning to set.

And when she had seen Matías's ghost yesterday.

"How long did the spike in activity last?" she asked.

"About a minute," the doctor said. "Then everything returned to baseline."

A minute. That's how long Claire's conversation with Matías had been. Could the spike in his vitals somehow be related?

But then she shook her head. It was just a coincidence that her hallucination aligned with a momentary blip in Matías's heart rate. *Come on, Claire. You're too rational—you're a lawyer, for heaven's sake—to be trying to draw tenuous connections like this.*

Dr. Rodriguez checked all the monitors attached to Matías and reviewed the notes on his chart again. She stayed and answered his parents' questions, although they switched to Spanish because they didn't know most medical terms in English. Claire didn't blame them, of course. She was grateful that they'd spoken in English until now.

While they were talking, Claire looked again at Matías's partially shaved head, his bruised and scraped face. The stubble from before was getting bristly now; in a few days, it would be a scraggly beard. His beautiful eyes remained closed.

This both was and wasn't her Matías.

Claire fumbled for the journal Luis had found in the rental house. She needed to touch Matías's most recent thoughts, the last things he'd wanted her to know before this terrible turn of events. She opened the book to the mere handful of other entries.

July 10th

Dear Claire,

I can't help but think of you today, because this is the day Romeo & Juliet met, at least according to that novel you love.

Remember how—on our second date—you interrogated me about the types of books I read? It still makes me laugh, how horrified you were when you found out that I sometimes read three different novels at a time, and that I dog-ear the pages or splay the books out on a table instead of using bookmarks.

Anyway, here is a doodle of Juliet's balcony, to commemorate July 10th.

~M

July 14th

Dear Claire,

You aren't coming with me to Madrid.

I will not lie. I am disappointed. I wanted you to meet my family in person, especially my mom and dad, and my sweet abuelita, and my bossy sister, and my brilliant little brother. I wanted to introduce you to my best friends, who all grew up with me in the same neighborhood. And of course, I wanted to propose.

But maybe this is just the universe telling me it wasn't supposed to work out this way, that there is something better in store.

So I will be patient. Because I think we are worth waiting for.

~M

July 17th

Dear Claire,

Today is my first full day in Madrid—most of yesterday was spent on the plane, so it does not count—and I miss you already.

I have been swarmed by my family, though, which has been a welcome distraction from missing you, and my mom and abuelita have stuffed me with enough food that I could probably survive hibernation through the summer.

There's no time for hibernation, though, because tomorrow, I head out to the coast with my friends for La Aventura Loca. That's what Carlos has dubbed our guys' trip, ha-ha.

I wish you were here, churri!

~M

July 20th

Dear Claire,

Tomorrow, Carlos, Diego, Leo, Facu, and I are going to take a speedboat out onto the ocean. You would hate it, I think. Too fast, too reckless—especially the way that Diego drives—but it will be a lot of fun.

Yesterday, we went night diving. Everything was dark, Claire, darker than you can ever picture. When you are sixty feet deep in the ocean, it is astounding that there are no city lights, no stars, nothing to illuminate your way.

All we had were small, weak flashlights that allowed us to see the lobsters and the octopuses and the other nocturnal sea creatures that scurry out of rocks and swim among the coral. I wish you could have seen it! There is a whole other world beneath the surface, Claire. We exist above, in full light. But it's like they live in an opposite dimension—underwater in pitch blackness. They cannot comprehend our existence, and it's difficult to understand theirs.

We don't even have adequate words to describe how octopuses move. They are like mercury, liquid yet solid, changeable from one instant to the next.

I have never seen anything more beautiful in my life, except for you.

~M

Matías

~

In his early days in New York, Matías often felt that the city was an entirely different world from anything he'd known before, even though he'd come from just across the ocean. Madrid was a bustling metropolis, too, but New York's personality couldn't have been more opposite. There was the attitude toward food, of course. Matías was still figuring out New Yorkers' habit of eating straight from takeout containers while in front of their computers. But there was also the rush—Madrileños took their time with everything, from reading a book under a tree in the middle of the afternoon to catching up with a friend to barhopping. New Yorkers, on the other hand, always seemed to have an endpoint, a goal.

He *liked* the people of New York a lot; he was just adjusting to their differences. Like when Matías met the chair of the fine arts department of the academy for coffee, the first thing she said after she sat down was, "I'm so glad we could get together. Never fear—I won't take much of your time, because I've got a thing I have to leave for in half an hour. But I just wanted to have a chance to welcome you in person before the academic year begins." Matías had been momentarily confused because he hadn't been concerned at all about her taking up his time. Wasn't that the point of meeting up?

Yet none of this bothered him. To anyone else, the brusqueness of this city and the people's insistence on not making eye contact or saying hello when walking past each other might have been off-putting, but to Matías—with his insatiable curiosity—it was fascinating.

"It's like I'm inside a nature documentary," he said to Claire on their next date, a mid-Saturday stroll through Central Park.

"So we're the animals and you're David Attenborough?" she said with a smirk.

Matías laughed. "In the most innocuous, inoffensive way."

She took him on a long loop around the park. Claire walked fast—another New York characteristic, he'd noticed—but on her, it was charming. She was so determined in everything she did, whether it was the hours she worked at the office or the desire to show him all the best of her adopted city. He knew she'd researched and made itineraries for both the Coney Island date and this one, and Matías smiled as he watched her take charge, flattered by how much she cared about his having a good time.

First, Claire took him to Gapstow Bridge for a beautiful view of the pond, where he couldn't resist taking some pictures of her (much to her blushing embarrassment). Then they walked to a carousel, which Matías insisted on riding, even though Claire initially protested, saying it was an attraction for kids.

They went to Strawberry Fields—which Matías learned was named after the Beatles song, not the other way around—and then to Bethesda Terrace Arcade, with its gorgeous columns and arches and the yellow-and-blue patterned tiles on the ceiling that sort of reminded him of home.

There was another beautiful bridge, and then the Shakespeare Garden.

A Disney-like castle, with a viewing pavilion at the top of a winding staircase.

An Egyptian obelisk called Cleopatra's Needle.

After several hours of exploring, Matías's stomach growled. There was a concession cart not too far away, so he asked Claire, "Would you like some ice cream?"

"I'm always up for ice cream."

He smiled as they ordered because Claire immediately asked for vanilla, and even though this was only their third date, Matías had already known that was what she would want. He, on the other hand, took a while chatting with the vendor and exploring all the available flavor options in the freezer case before settling on a chocolate-dipped pistachio toffee ice cream bar.

When he took out his wallet to pay, though, Matías frowned.

"Is everything okay?" Claire asked.

"Yes . . . it's just that your bills all look the same. They're uniformly a faded green—not a color I would have chosen—and also the exact same size. Euros have different colors and sizes for each denomination."

"Don't worry, I'll help you," Claire said.

"You will?"

"Of course."

Matías could have done it on his own. It's not as if it was difficult; he just would have been slower than with Euros. But he loved that Claire wanted to help, that she offered it immediately. She gave pieces of herself freely, and that was rarer than most people might think.

When she'd paid, they found a spot of grass under a tree with great, arcing branches and settled in to eat their ice cream.

Matías devoured his in five bites, then watched, amused, at how slowly and carefully Claire licked her cone.

She looked at him out of the corner of her eye. "Why are you staring at me like I'm another animal in the wild?"

Matías shook his head and tried not to smile.

"I see your dimples. What're you laughing at me about?"

"Nothing. You're cute, that's all."

She arched a brow.

He gave up and let the smile crack across his face. "You rotate your ice cream when you're eating. It's completely symmetrical now."

She looked down at her cone and scrunched up her nose. "Huh. I had no idea I did that. I just didn't want it to drip on me."

"Looks like you're succeeding. But would it make you mad if I did *this*?" Matías darted in and stole a quick bite.

"Hey!" She swatted him away.

Now there was a distinctly unsymmetrical chunk of her ice cream missing. Claire squirmed a little on the grass.

"You hate it, don't you?" Matías couldn't stop grinning. "The fact that it's uneven."

She faked a pout. "It's kind of ugly now."

"I can help with that. I'll just take another big bite . . ." He pretended to come in again.

"No!" Claire stuffed the ice cream into her mouth to save it from him, vanilla everywhere as she laughed and tried to eat at the same time.

She was a mess.

She was beautiful.

And he wanted her, perfect imperfections and all.

CLAIRE

~

AFTER FIVE HOURS IN THE HOSPITAL, CLAIRE NEEDED A BREAK. The family was going back to Aracely's for lunch—Spaniards ate late, around two o'clock—and they invited Claire to come along, but she begged off, wanting fresh air and some quiet for a bit before she returned to Matías's bedside.

Outside the hospital, life in Madrid continued without notice that Claire's life had been put on pause. The sun beamed cheerfully on the poplar and juniper trees. Office workers took casual lunches with colleagues in sidewalk cafés. Grandmothers pushed strollers under the shaded arcades of the buildings, and everywhere birds chirped garrulously as if it were their midafternoon gossip break.

Claire knew she ought to eat—she'd promised the paramedics yesterday that she would—but she had no appetite. Who *could* eat in such circumstances? But with the heat the way it was in July in Spain, she at least had to hydrate or risk another ambulance visit, and the medics probably wouldn't let her out of a hospital stay the second time around.

There was a drink kiosk in the nearby park—Madrid was full of wide-open green spaces in the middle of all the hustle and bustle of the city—and Claire got in line to buy a Coke. The man working the kiosk had a kind smile, and his skin was lined and browned from hours each day in the sun. He greeted several of the other people in line by name. At least, that's what Claire could gather with her limited Spanish.

When it was her turn, he smiled and said something rapidly that she didn't catch.

Flustered, she resorted to pointing and a broken attempt that wasn't even a complete sentence. "Um. *Uno* Coke?" At the last second, she remembered to add, "*por favor.*"

"*Una Coca-Cola para la señorita,*" the man said. "*Será un euro veinticinco.*"

Claire fumbled in her purse and grabbed a few coins. But on top of not knowing what the Coke cost because she couldn't understand numbers in Spanish that fast, she was also unfamiliar with the denominations of euro coins, and she just stood there like an idiot with a handful of money, uncomprehending. Here, they made coins not only for cents, but for one and two euros. Why would you mix things like dollars and change? What god of discord was in charge of that decision?

"*¿Eres estadounidense? ¿Quieres hielo?*" the man asked.

She looked at him blankly, her heartbeat speeding up in her throat. If only Matías were here to translate for her, to take care of this thing that should be so easy but somehow, at this moment, seemed too hard.

"Um . . ."

"He's curious if you're American," a man said behind her. "And if you want ice with your Coke, since that's something Americans are known for."

Claire couldn't move. Because she knew that voice. It had whispered to her many nights while kissing the length of her skin. Greeted her in the mornings with strong coffee and toast.

Echoed through museums when showing her his favorite paintings.

Matías.

When she didn't answer either him *or* the man holding her Coke, Matías said, "If you'd like ice, you can say, *Con hielo, por favor.*"

"Con hielo, por favor," Claire repeated robotically.

The man nodded and filled a paper cup with ice.

Claire was still unable—unwilling—to turn around to look at the ghost or whatever it was of Matías's voice, lest he disappear like he had yesterday. So instead, she asked the man at the kiosk, "Er, how much was the Coke again?" while helplessly holding out the coins in her hand.

"I can help, if you don't mind?" Matías stepped forward into her line of sight, and Claire let out a small cry. He was so beautiful. So alive. Nothing like the comatose man she'd just left in the hospital.

This Matías had his full head of hair, none of it shaved off so the brain monitor diodes could measure activity. His bones were intact, his skin was tanned and free of bruises, and his eyes . . . oh god, those golden eyes . . .

"Oh!" he said, seeing her face. "It's you again. From the hotel. You seem to be feeling better."

Claire wasn't sure that was true. She was hallucinating again. *Did* she have a concussion? And did concussions make you imagine things?

But yesterday she had seen the vision of Matías *before* she'd fainted and hit her head.

"Let me help you with those coins," he said, "and then maybe we could go for a walk through the park?"

Claire nodded, still shocked by his presence—and his coherence, because do imaginary people make this much sense?—and she wordlessly held out the coins to him.

Being respectful of a stranger, Matías didn't touch her, but only pointed out which ones she needed to pay for her soda. She transferred the money to the man at the kiosk, whose eyebrows were now knitted quizzically at her. Could he see Matías? If not, her behavior must've seemed incredibly bizarre.

Claire and Matías walked toward one of the long, tree-lined paths in the park. She wasn't sure what to do. She was definitely hallucinating, and she didn't know if it was safe to indulge it. Would conversing with this imaginary version of Matías do her mind harm? Would it be better to block it out and go straight back to the hospital, where she could ground herself in the reality of Matías's true state?

And yet, she didn't want to give up this moment. She *couldn't*. Because here, right now, Matías was strolling slowly beside her. The familiar pine and spice of his cologne wafted over to her— just a hint, but enough for her to sigh. The sunlight might shine straight through him, but this was *her* Matías. The one she wanted to remember if the real Matías didn't wake up.

But maybe there was something she could do about that! His vitals had spiked at the hospital last night at the same time she spoke with the ghostly version of him at the hotel, right?

So maybe if Claire could keep Spirit Matías with her for a while, it would also help the real version in the coma?

It was worth a try.

"Thank you for helping me back there," she said.

He smiled his crooked smile, and Claire had to swallow the little whimper of wanting that almost escaped from her.

"It was my pleasure," Matías said. "I know it can be intimidating to speak a new language."

"Very."

"I still remember when I was a boy, learning English. We'd studied it for several years in school, so our teachers decided it was time for us to use our skills outside the classroom. They planned an excursion to a British candy shop owned by a former Londoner, where we could buy whatever we wanted, but only if we spoke in English.

"My friends and I were thrilled at the possibility of a sugar-fueled afternoon, but my stomach tied up in knots the moment we set foot in the store. Learning a language from textbooks and in planned dialogues in a classroom is one thing, but speaking it out loud with an actual British person—an adult, no less—was another entirely."

"Did you manage?" Claire asked, genuinely curious. She'd never heard this story from Matías before. Part of her knew it wasn't a real memory—her traumatized mind was making up this whole conversation—but nevertheless, part of her wanted to believe that this was truly something that had happened to the man she loved.

Matías laughed. "I made a mess of the English language that afternoon. So did all my classmates. But the shopkeeper was patient, and he rewarded us for our efforts, if not our accuracy. The day was, ultimately, a success, because not only did we get candy, but I was never as tongue-tied again in the future. I'd gotten through an embarrassing situation, so I knew I'd survive if it ever happened another time. Ironically, the disastrous field trip ended up being what built my confidence in English."

Claire smiled privately as she sipped her soda and thought of

Matías as a little boy. It wasn't a difficult leap to make, because he still had a similar kind of boyish wonder as an adult, evidenced by the kind of paintings he created and his ten thousand hobbies.

"I just started learning Spanish," she said, "but you're right that studying from a book and listening to prerecorded comprehension exercises is completely different from talking to a live human." She winced at that last part, not wanting to insult Matías. Then she winced again upon remembering that she couldn't insult him, because he wasn't real.

"What brings you to Madrid? It's Claire, right?"

Hearing her name on his lips liquified her heart. She wanted to throw herself at him, feel his arms around her, bury her face into the crook of his neck.

But he didn't know her. And even if he did—and even if he weren't made-up and transparent—Claire was pretty sure that no one else could see Matías. The kiosk man had definitely seemed puzzled by her, and since then, Claire had caught other people in the park looking at her oddly. Because she probably looked like she was talking to herself, and she didn't have earphones in to credibly be on a phone call.

So throwing herself at what might as well be a ghost would be a bad idea on many levels. Not to mention she'd probably end up in the dirt with scraped knees and the burden of disappointment.

"I'm in Madrid to visit—" Claire stopped herself before saying she was here because her boyfriend was in a coma. For stupid, inexplicable reasons, she didn't want Imaginary Matías to know she was in a relationship, because then Imaginary Matías might not want to spend more time with her.

Ridiculous. Illogical. What are you thinking, Claire?

But that was the point. She *wasn't* thinking, and she didn't want to. At least for a little longer. Her brain had conjured this fantasy to give her a respite from the worry of her real life, and she was going to take the out. Just during her lunch break.

"I'm visiting a client," Claire said, which *could* be true. Intelligentsia Tech did have offices all over the world, including in Madrid.

"Where are you based, normally?" Matías asked.

"New York."

Matías's eyes glimmered under the midday light. "Really? I'm moving to New York in two weeks. I'm a painter, and the New York Academy of Art has offered me a position in their fine arts department as a visiting professor for a couple years."

The Coke sloshed over Claire's hand as she stopped suddenly in the middle of the park path.

"You're moving to New York in *two weeks*?"

That professorship was why Matías had moved to New York just under *one year ago*.

"Yes," he said. "I was actually on my way to my studio to pack up my paintings when I ran into you. Before the school year begins, I'll be showing an exhibit of my work at a place called the Rose Gallery. Have you heard of it?"

"I have . . ." Claire whispered. The Rose Gallery was where she and Matías had met. Eleven months ago. The gallery that Jason owned.

"What's today's date?" Claire asked him.

"What?"

"Today's date," Claire said.

"July 23," Matías said promptly.

Claire inhaled sharply. Today was indeed July 23. "What year?"

Matías frowned. "I don't understand."

"Today is July 23 of what year?"

He let out a small laugh. "Oh, I see, you're teasing me. That's funny. Everyone knows what year it is."

Claire didn't laugh, though. Matías was evading the question, and she couldn't think of a reason her brain would make the hallucinatory version of him do that if she had in fact made him up.

So could it be that he *wasn't* a figment of her imagination?

That this was somehow Matías from one year ago today? But how?

They came upon a fountain sculpture of a family of toads, where one toad child carried an umbrella to shield the other little ones from the sprinkles of water.

"This was my favorite fountain as a kid," Matías said. "I loved the unexpected detail that a toad would hold an umbrella, and the subtle humor that they were afraid of getting wet."

"I can see why you'd like it." She didn't mention that she could also see how this fountain might have been an inspiration for the whimsical art he became known for.

"I think I also identify with it because I'm one of three kids," Matías said. "The one with the umbrella reminds me of my sister, Aracely, who is always looking out for me and our little brother, even now that we're all adults. She paid the rent on my studio when I was first getting started, even though she was still in college. And she actually offered to pack me a snack and dinner for my upcoming flight to New York." He laughed fondly. "What about your family? Do you have siblings?"

Claire furrowed her brow. Again, this was something her

brain wouldn't choose to rehash if it were in charge. But if this *was* a version of Matías from a year ago—from before he met Claire—he wouldn't know that she had no family, that both her biological parents and her adoptive ones had died tragically.

What in the world was happening here?

"I'm an only child," Claire said, answering his question without going too deep.

"I cannot imagine life without my brother and sister," Matías said. "But anyway, Claire-who's-in-Madrid-visiting-a-client, what type of work do you do?"

"I'm an attorney. I specialize in international mergers and acquisitions."

Matías whistled. "Impressive. But I would've thought someone as smart as you could figure out how to count coins for a Coke."

Claire laughed. "You're cruel."

"You're bad at math."

"I just got here a day ago! Give a girl a break and at least a week to figure out which coins are which, will you?"

"Fair enough. Anyway, it will be my turn soon in the United States to be confused by your money."

"Don't worry, I'll help you," Claire said without thinking.

"You will?" Matías looked at her in surprise.

Oh shit. She'd momentarily forgotten that this wasn't *her* Matías. That she was talking to an illusion. Or a Ghost of July Past? Whatever he was, he didn't know they would end up together, that this was more than a passing walk through the park with a stranger.

"Um, sure," Claire said, trying to figure out how to cover. "It's nice to have a familiar face in a new city."

"That's very sweet of you," Matías said. "So . . . could I have your number so we can connect once I'm there?"

"Yeah, okay . . ."

"I mean, if you don't want to, I understand—"

"No, no. It's fine."

It was just that, to Claire, Matías should have known her number by heart.

But she pulled herself together and recited it.

He keyed the digits into what must've been his phone, but Claire couldn't see it, even though he obviously could.

The reflection off the fountain's surface shined through Matías, rendering him momentarily transparent. Claire felt his flicker viscerally, the brief second he vanished hollowing her out, only to be relieved and refilled when he reappeared.

"Okay, I'm going to text you a message so you have my number, too," Matías said. He typed something and hit send.

But then he made a face at his phone. He jabbed at it again.

"Strange. It says the message can't be delivered."

A chill shivered up Claire's spine. Was she suffering a mental breakdown? Was her usually logical, lawyerly mind trying to make sense of her walking and talking with an apparition, and then concluding that a Matías of the past wouldn't be able to send a message to Claire in his future?

Matías was still looking at his phone.

"Oh no, I lost track of time!" he said. "I need to get to my studio—the boxes for shipping my paintings will be delivered soon. But it was very nice chatting with you, Claire. I'll call you when I land in New York in a couple weeks, if you're back by then? Or if you're interested, come find me. My exhibit will be at—"

"The Rose Gallery," Claire said.

Matías ran his hand through his hair and gave her a long, admiring look. "You have a sharp mind. Except when it comes to counting coins."

Claire laughed despite herself.

"I look forward to seeing you again, Claire."

And with that, he waved and jogged off in the opposite direction, back toward the part of the park where the drink kiosk had been.

Claire watched him. Her Matías.

Until a patch of sunlight hit him full-on, and he vanished into thin air.

CLAIRE

⟿

CLAIRE HURTLED INTO HER HOTEL ROOM, THE DOOR SLAM-
ming behind her. She grabbed her laptop from her briefcase,
flung herself onto the bed, and dove into research about what
had happened at the park.

What was that version of Matías she'd just spent half an
hour with? And the one who'd been here in the hotel driveway
the day before?

Besides what Claire already expected—concussion-induced
hallucinations or something else caused by the trauma of
Matías's accident and stress—internet queries were fruitless:

What you are seeing is a demon in human skin.

Are you doing shrooms?

Haunted houses often utilize projectors to create the image
of a spirit.

After their loved one's death, some report seeing or feeling
the presence of a ghost.

Then there were the pseudopsychological diagnoses of ques-
tionable veracity:

Hallucinations may be early indications of schizophrenia.

Imaginary friends will sometimes persist into adulthood.

A vision of a ghost of a person who is still alive may actually
be an astral projection, a condition in which the soul
separates from the body for indeterminate periods of time.

Wait. Claire paused on the last answer.
An astral projection? She asked for more information.

Astral projections are rare but can occur when a subject is
suffering from dire physical or medical conditions. The soul
may detach in such instances. For example, there have been
accounts of people watching their own surgeries from the
same operating room, as if they were a third party.

Is it possible to talk to astral projections?

There is little evidence of interaction between astral
projections and living people. In fact, astral projections are
not a verifiable phenomenon.

"You just said that astral projections have actually happened,"
Claire said, glaring at her computer. "But now you're saying the
reports aren't verifiable?"

She typed more questions into the program, fingers pounding hard on the keys.

The chatbot seemed to adjust to what she wanted to hear.
When she pushed on with curiosity, it served positive answers

about astral projections. When she expressed skepticism for some of its answers, it gave her responses undermining the existence of astral projections and the people who claim to have experienced them.

In a burst of frustration, Claire hammered out one final query: Who has the most knowledge and experience with astral projections?

It came up with a list of psychics. Lots of supposed psychics.

And one academic—Margot Hong, professor of parapsychological phenomena, Stanford University.

Despite having seen an apparition, Claire was too rational to believe in psychics. But a professor . . .

Five minutes later, Claire had found the professor's contact info and emailed a brief explanation of seeing Matías's spirit, along with a request for an urgent appointment in the early evening Spain time, which was morning in Palo Alto, California, where Professor Hong worked.

"GOOD MORNING," THE PROFESSOR SAID, SMILING INTO THE camera. Margot Hong had the kind of face that age didn't stamp—she could be twenty-five or forty-five—although based on the number of papers she'd published, she must be on the upper end of that spectrum. "Or should I say *buenas tardes*, since you're in Madrid?"

Claire tried to smile back, even though she could feel her nerves practically vibrating through her skin. "It's nice to meet you, Professor Hong. Thank you for taking my call on such short notice."

"It's not a problem. Although I must confess I am also doing this out of professional curiosity."

"Thank you. I . . . I don't usually believe in stuff like this. I mean, I'm a lawyer. I am all about fact-based inquiry and rational beliefs."

Professor Hong nodded. "Don't worry. I'm a scientist. I am quite inflexible on facts as well, although I do challenge the notion of what we consider rational and what we don't. Anyway, you emailed me a little bit about your situation, but do you mind telling me everything that's happened from the beginning?"

Claire fiddled with the hotel-branded pen on the desk. She'd reviewed what she was going to say over and over while waiting for this appointment, but now it flew out of her head and she was forced to improvise. How much to reveal? What was enough, and what was extraneous?

Stop thinking like a lawyer in negotiations, she told herself. This wasn't like work, where sometimes she had to strategically keep information back. If Claire was going to talk about the vision of Matías, she might as well go all in.

"My boyfriend, Matías, was in a terrible boating accident. Two of his friends died, and he and two other friends are in comas."

Professor Hong exhaled. "I'm so sorry to hear that."

Claire nodded. "It's been awful. Matías is on life support and not doing well. But the thing is . . . I've seen him. Not in the hospital. Like, I've seen a transparent ghost version of him."

"Hmm. Tell me more. Where? When?"

"The first time was here at the hotel. I was working downstairs, and there was a flash of light when the sun reflected off a window, and then he was just there in the driveway. I ran out and he saw me, and we talked, but then the light went through him and I freaked out and fainted.

"The second time was this afternoon. I had just left his bedside at the hospital. I went to the park to get some air, and he was there, just behind me in line at a drink kiosk. We ended up walking and talking for a while. But I don't think anyone else can see him."

"What happened when you parted ways?" Professor Hong asked. She was leaning in toward the screen now.

"He went back in the direction we'd come," Claire said. "And then some light hit him, and he disappeared. Not like I lost track of him. He was just gone."

"Hmm," Professor Hong said again. "Give me a moment, please."

She went offscreen, then came back with a lit incense stick in a small glass bottle. Professor Hong then closed her eyes and inhaled deeply, drawing the smoke straight in.

Claire frowned. This was what she might have expected from an internet psychic, but not a respected academic. What the hell?

But Professor Hong sat like that for nearly five minutes without moving. Claire fidgeted with the hotel pen. Then she checked several times to make sure the internet connection was still good and the screen hadn't frozen. Everything was working, though; the incense continued to sway and stream into the professor in a steady, if languorous, flow.

Am I supposed to be doing something, too? Claire thought. Closing her eyes and thinking about . . . what? Maybe she was supposed to focus on Matías?

Just as Claire was about to try that, Professor Hong's eyes fluttered open.

"Did you, uh, have any visions?" Claire asked.

The professor smiled. "Oh, that wasn't a trance or anything supernatural." She raised the bottle with the smoking stick. "Just eucalyptus aromatherapy. I have a photographic memory, but sometimes I need a smell to help me focus as I flip through the mental files of all the research I've done."

Claire didn't know what to say. She felt stupid for thinking the professor had gone into some kind of New Age hypnotic state. And she'd never met anyone with a truly photographic memory. The fact that Professor Hong had enough research on the subject to riffle through made Claire feel a *lot* better that maybe this thing with the vision of Matías was real and she hadn't lost her marbles.

"I believe Matías is looking for you," Professor Hong said.

Claire frowned. "But I'm right here. I went to the hospital straight from the airport yesterday and then again this morning as soon as I was awake."

"Yes, but he's looking for you in a different way. What you saw was what we call an astral projection. But I think you are already familiar with the concept because that's why you reached out to me, isn't it?"

"Right."

"Matías is lost," Professor Hong said. "His soul needs something to focus on, to hold on to—similar to how I use the stream of eucalyptus scent—and I believe that something is you."

Claire shook her head. "But from my conversation with him yesterday and today, that version of Matías is from a year ago. He doesn't even know me yet."

Professor Hong closed her eyes again, but she wasn't gone in her mental file cabinet as long this time. She reopened them a minute later and said, "Here's what the evidence suggests. Matías's physical body is in Madrid right now, so that is why his soul is there, too. But his soul is also lost, stuck in his own subconscious. To make sense of being in Madrid, his soul has retreated into the memories from the last time Matías was in the city—one year ago.

"But," Professor Hong said, "a *place* is not enough to tie a soul to reality. You are his soul's connection with this world, and you must make him stay. Based on the academic research, as well as on your *actual* relationship, I believe you must make sure Matías falls in love with you."

Claire furrowed her brows. "He already does love me, though."

The professor shook her head. "In his *waking* life, Matías loves you. But now that he's unconscious, his soul is confused. This version of Matías doesn't know about the accident, and he doesn't realize he's separated from his body. And he doesn't know *you*, because you were not part of his life one year ago."

Claire winced, even though it was true.

"Right now," Professor Hong said, "you are a stranger to him, just another part of this 'world' his soul has constructed to make sense of his surroundings. But you are also his anchor in the *real* world, and the only way for him to return here. If you can get this version of Matías to fall in love with you, then he will be tugged back toward his body, toward reality, so he can truly be with you."

"This is a lot."

"I know."

"I'm not sure if I believe it."

"I know that, too. But there's a reason you emailed *me,* a scientist of parapsychological phenomena, rather than a psychic or medium, right? Clearly, you have already accepted that you saw some sort of vision of Matías. So you emailed me because if I could back up what you saw with proof that such phenomena have been documented before, then that would give you enough rational basis to move forward. Am I correct?"

"Yes . . ." Claire said, letting the logic sink in.

"Well, I have enough research to substantiate my theory. And to tell you that you are not imagining things."

Claire massaged her temples, thinking. After a few moments, she shook her head and asked, "How do I make a soul fall in love with me?"

"The same way you two fell in love the first time."

Professor Hong said it nonchalantly, as if it were easy. But Claire and Matías's first meeting had been serendipitous. They'd had an extraordinary beginning and got caught up in the momentum of their circumstances.

If Claire had to re-create their relationship again from scratch, would they even work?

Boring and uninspired. That's what Glenn had said of Claire. She was methodical and reliable, which made her a good attorney, but not the most exciting woman to date. Matías loved her, but sometimes she didn't understand why. Her daily schedule was mapped out by tenths of an hour (billable increments for the firm), whereas Matías marched to whatever rhythm that day asked of him, ready for an adventure or a tangent of curiosity at any time. They were opposites, and . . .

I don't know if I'm enough.

"I must warn you," Professor Hong said, "that astral projections are very fragile. Souls are wispy, sometimes skittish things. You must be careful not to touch him because you will go right through him."

"Okay."

"And Claire, you absolutely *cannot* tell Matías what is going on with his body and the hospital, not until he's ready. Do you understand?"

She shook her head. "Why not?"

"His soul is very tenuously tethered to reality, and the revelation that the soul is not *actually* Matías might be too much."

"Okay . . . But how will I know when he's ready?"

"I don't know," Professor Hong said. "Perhaps when he's fallen so thoroughly in love with you that he would walk through fire—or other planes of existence—to be with you. But remember: You are the only thing tethering his soul to life. If that connection breaks . . ."

Claire choked back a sob. "Matías will die?"

"I hate to say it, but yes," Professor Hong said. "You will lose Matías forever."

Matías

~

Nine Months Ago

A GIANT RED MONSTER STUCK HIS FACE IN FRONT OF MATÍAS.

"Agh!" He staggered backward, where he bumped into a life-size Donald Duck.

Times Square was famous in movies, and Matías had looked forward to visiting it since he was a boy. He'd been prepared for the Broadway marquees, the buzzing energy of the tourists, the iconic bright lights and screens of the billboards . . . but not for being accosted by Elmo and Donald Duck.

Elmo came at him again with his furry red arms outstretched. "Hug? Only twenty dollars!"

"Er, no, thank you," Matías said.

Donald Duck advanced on him and quacked. "Selfie? Twenty-five dollars!"

"I don't think that's a worthwhile way to spend my money . . ."

"But Elmo loves you!"

"And Donald, too!"

"He's good, thanks, boys," Claire said, swooping in from behind Matías and deftly steering him out from between Elmo and Donald. She was so beautiful when she took charge; it felt like you could leave anything in her hands and know for certain that all would be well.

When they were safely away, Claire fake-chided Matías.

"You can't let them get too close or they'll take advantage of you."

"I never knew that Disney characters could grow up to be thugs," he said, and Claire laughed.

"Okay, now that I've rescued you from the clutches of Elmo's evil twin, let's go see what they have at the TDF booth."

The TDF booth, Claire had explained during their last date, was where they could buy theater tickets for 50 percent off. The catch was that you wouldn't know what shows were available until the day of the performance, since the tickets were whatever hadn't previously sold. But Matías had never had a problem with flexibility.

They walked up to a glass pavilion with a red overhang that was a lot bigger than he expected, with twelve ticket windows and people swarming all around it. He and Claire got in line, and she stood on her tiptoes, trying to see to the signs at the front that listed what shows they could buy tickets for. But she was too short, and besides, the signs were too far away to read.

A man joined his partner in line right in front of Matías and Claire. He'd just returned from the sign and started listing off what was available.

"Ooh, they're all so good," Claire said. "It's a hard choice. I don't know which you'd like most."

"What are they about?" Matías asked, and Claire and the other couple started rattling off synopses of the plots for him.

"*Lion King* is a classic," one of the men—Jordan—said. "If this is your first Broadway show, I highly recommend that as an entry point."

"Personally," his partner—Riley—said, "I like exploring the newer shows. *New York, New York* is supposed to be excellent."

"Or you might like *Sweeney Todd* or *Hadestown*," Claire said as the line moved forward. "Or *Life of Pi*! It's based on one of my favorite books ever. I think you might enjoy that one, too."

"Are you a Michael Jackson fan?" Jordan asked.

"Or what about the *Wizard of Oz*?" Riley asked. "Have you seen *Wicked*?"

"*Hamilton* is so, so good, too," Claire said. They were getting closer to the ticket window, and her fingers had started fluttering, something Matías had noticed she did when she was about to have to make a decision. Like on Coney Island, when it was almost their turn to order hot dogs and she hadn't decided yet which drink she'd wanted. Or in Central Park at the ice cream cart—even though she'd probably known she was going to order vanilla, her fingers still fluttered until she was right up at the register making the actual decision.

He smiled. He didn't think she was aware how her fingertips betrayed her, but it was helpful for Matías to know when Claire was feeling unsettled, because sometimes he could help.

"Maybe we should look up the reviews," she was saying, beginning to reach for her phone.

"Hey." Matías smiled, brought his hands to her shoulders, and turned her toward him, then slid his hands slowly down her arms until her fingers were clasped gently in his. The anxious fluttering stopped.

"It doesn't matter what we see," Matías said.

"B-but I want to make sure you love it. And if we look at reviews—"

"They are all new to me, so don't worry, churri. It will be great."

"*Churri?*" Claire looked up at him with wide eyes. "What does that mean?"

Matías felt his cheeks flush. *Churri* was a term of endearment meant for serious girlfriends . . . He hadn't meant to say it out loud, but things just felt so right with Claire. They were complements in a lot of ways—where she was nervous, he was calm; where he was forgetful, she had mental checklists for everything. They both went out of their way to make sure the other was having a good time on their dates. And most of all, she made him laugh. Claire was, he thought, the kind of woman he could build a life with.

"Churri is like sweetheart or . . . beloved." Matías's cheeks got even hotter.

A soft smile crept across her face. "Yeah?"

"Yeah," Matías said.

She stood up on her tiptoes again, but this time not to look at a Broadway sign. Just at him.

He could fall forever into the depths of her eyes.

"I don't care what show we see," he said. "Nothing else matters, as long as I'm with you."

CLAIRE

⌢

HALF AN HOUR AFTER THE VIDEO APPOINTMENT WITH PRO-
fessor Hong had left Claire in shock, her phone rang.

"Claire, what happened to you?" Aracely said on the phone.
"Why didn't you come back to the hospital after lunch? There
was another spike in Matías's vitals, for much longer than the
one last night!"

"Oh, really?" Claire smiled to herself. Maybe her theory was
right, that the more time she spent with Matías's soul, the stronger the real Matías became. That would make sense based on
what the professor had said, since Claire was his soul's connection to life.

"Are you okay?" Aracely asked. "Visiting hours are almost
over."

Guiltily, Claire looked at the clock on the hotel nightstand.
It was 7 P.M. She'd been gone from the hospital for five hours.

She lied. "I, uh, took a nap. I didn't realize I'd sleep for that
long."

"Well, I'm sending Luis to pick you up in a little while,"
Aracely said. "You're coming over to my parents' house for dinner. Mamá doesn't want you alone right now, okay? You need
people around you, and good food."

Claire smiled sadly. Her first date with Matías had begun with him trying to prove to her how important good food was.

She didn't know if she could handle his big family. Hers had been so small, just her and Jim and Sarah, and then they'd died and her family had been only herself.

Her fingers fluttered, and Claire frowned down at them. When had she started doing that?

"Dinner will do you good," Aracely said. "I'm not giving you a choice. Luis will be at your hotel just after eight."

"Okay." Claire sighed, her fingers stilling. "I'll be downstairs to meet him."

When Claire and Luis arrived at the de León's apartment in Parque de las Avenidas, Claire was surprised to find only Soledad, Armando, Aracely, and Abuela Gloria there.

"We thought maybe you'd prefer a quieter evening," Aracely said as she embraced Claire at the front door.

"Thank you," Claire said, holding her tightly despite the heat of the summer evening. She hadn't realized how much she needed the hug, but after an afternoon spent with the disembodied soul of her boyfriend and then a helpful—but still unsettling—call with Professor Hong, it was a relief to be with people who operated within the bounds of "normalcy."

Soledad, Armando, and Abuela Gloria hugged her, too, as she made her way into their apartment. Their home exuded warmth—dark wooden floors, fat armchairs and a patterned rug in the living room, and photos of Matías, Aracely, and Luis as kids. Claire swallowed a lump in her throat as she imagined Matías as a boy.

Of course, Matías's brightly colored paintings also graced the walls.

There, above the television, hung a painting of doting mother and father tigers with their cubs, resting on dry grasslands. Among the cubs, though, was a baby zebra, but instead of black-and-white stripes, it was black and orange. Different, yet just like the rest of its family.

Out of habit, Claire turned to see if Matías was there beside her, watching for that moment when she found the delightful, incongruous detail in his work.

But he wasn't there—neither the flesh-and-blood Matías nor his soul. Claire blinked back tears. She hadn't realized how much she'd hoped he would appear here in his home until he didn't.

"I asked Matías for a portrait of our family," Soledad said. "That is what he gave me." She laughed softly.

Claire nodded because she understood completely. Matías might look like any other human, just like everyone else, but his quintessence was something different. An orange-and-black zebra living among tigers.

"Mamá likes Matías to paint our family's emotional mile-stones," Aracely said as she pointed at another painting on the opposite wall, a portrait of baby Luis having his first bath. It must have been done when Matías was younger, because he would have been barely a teenager when Luis was born. The style was still identifiably Matías's, though—realistic with a small hint of the sublime—although Claire could see how he hadn't quite understood subtlety yet at that age. The water in the painting shimmered iridescent.

Luis stepped in front of the portrait. "Er, we don't need to look at that one too carefully."

Aracely snorted. "Luis doesn't like us looking at his baby penis."

"*Es muy pequeño*," Soledad said. "And so cute."

Even Abuela Gloria laughed.

Luis turned crimson.

Claire choked back a laugh because her basic Spanish was enough to understand. She spared Luis, though, and moved to the other side of the armchairs, to a watercolor of white houses on top of green cliffs, overlooking a deep blue ocean. "This one is different from the others I've seen."

"That is *my* painting," Armando said. "Of the Canary Islands, where my grandparents are from. Where my mother grew up."

Abuela Gloria beamed at the landscape.

"Armando, you're an artist, too?" Claire asked.

"An amateur."

"But it's where Matías got his talent," Aracely said, casting a quick but proud look at her papá.

Claire's heart throbbed, suddenly missing her parents. Even though she'd always dreamed of getting out of her small Florida town, she'd also admired her mom and dad's steadiness. For all of elementary school, Claire had dressed up on Halloween as a postal worker, collecting candy in a shoulder bag like her dad carried mail in. She enjoyed the reliability of her mom's macaroni-and-beef casserole and a Hallmark movie every Friday. She loved knowing exactly where home was—with them.

Could she have something like that again? If Matías woke up and recovered, could she say yes to his proposal and find family again with the de Leóns?

"Aracely," she said. "You mentioned that Matías's vitals improved again this afternoon?"

"Yes, for about half an hour." Aracely smiled softly. "I think that's a good sign, don't you?"

"I do," Claire said, blinking back tears. Just like the minute from last night corresponded with her minute with Matías's soul in the hotel driveway, the half hour today correlated with the time she'd spent with him at the park. Claire's being with him seemed to make Matías stronger. She would have to figure out how to meet with him again.

But now was not the moment to think about that, because Soledad ushered everyone into the kitchen, where yellow stools surrounded a tile counter, and a well-worn wooden table was crammed into the corner. Garlic filled a small red bowl to the brim; a larger blue one was piled with tomatoes so ripe they scented the entire room.

"Please sit," Soledad said, gesturing at the stools.

"How hungry are you?" Aracely asked. "Spanish dinner is usually very light—a salad, some ham and cheese and bread, and fruit—because lunch is our biggest meal. But I don't know if you got to eat much for lunch, because of your nap."

Claire bit her lip, because of course she hadn't actually napped. But even though she hadn't had an appetite since she left New York, suddenly being in a cozy kitchen with kind faces and the smell of tomatoes and garlic filling the kitchen made her stomach growl.

"Okay," Aracely said, taking that as an answer. "Mamá, Abuelita, we need to feed this woman."

Soledad nodded solemnly.

While Luis tossed a salad and Aracely cut fruit, Soledad and Abuela Gloria got some leftovers from the refrigerator and warmed a bowl of broth for Claire, followed by a huge plate of stewed meat, vegetables, potatoes, and chickpeas. Armando sliced crusty bread.

"This is cocido madrileño," Soledad said. "Spanish comfort food." She took food seriously, and Claire understood now where Matías inherited his reverence for it.

Claire took a bite of the meat, rich and hot and bursting with the flavors of bay leaves, cumin, tomatoes, garlic, olive oil, and vinegar. "Oh my god."

Soledad gave her a small smile—the kind shared among people who were suffering but still managing to find brief moments of peace. "A good meal cannot solve everything, but it can make things a little easier, if it is made with love."

Soledad

Hours later, Soledad lay next to Armando in bed, both staring at the ceiling.

"I can still remember how it felt to hold Matías as a baby," Soledad said, bringing her hands up to her shoulder as if cradling him. "He was so tiny, but so warm."

"He always put out more heat than I thought possible," Armando said.

"Our tiny furnace," Soledad said, sighing. She closed her eyes briefly and brought her head down, as if she could nuzzle against the memory of her infant son. He smelled sweet, like milk and fresh laundry and that indelible, pure something of newborns.

Thirty-six years later, he was still her baby. It didn't matter that Matías had been taller than Armando for two decades, or that Matías was well known in the international art world. Or that he was a visiting professor at a prestigious art school on the other side of the ocean. Soledad would always be his mother, and that meant he was her little Mati, no matter how grown he'd become.

If only she could fall asleep, nestling against the peaceful thoughts of the past.

But sleep only came in nips and snatches since Matías's accident, and Soledad reluctantly opened her eyes. She rolled over to face Armando.

"You have been quiet. What are you thinking, *cariño*?"

Armando shook his head. "Claire. The poor woman has no family. Matías said her parents died many years ago. She has no one."

"She has us," Soledad said.

"She hardly knows us. And Claire lives in New York. What happens to her if Matías dies?"

"Don't talk about that," Soledad snapped.

"It is a possibility, *amor*."

"No. It is *not*." Soledad flung off the covers and launched herself out of bed.

"Where are you going?"

"To pray. To beg God to take some of the years off my life to give to Matías."

"Soledad, por favor."

"I would sacrifice my entire life for my children!"

"But you don't need to do that."

There was a pause.

And then, barely audible, she asked, "How do you know?"

Armando didn't have an answer.

Soledad tried to swallow the fear in her throat, but it stuck.

He climbed out of bed.

"Wait for me, Soledad. I am coming to pray, too."

CLAIRE

TIME HAD BEEN PASSING LIKE CLAIRE WAS WADING UPSTREAM through molasses, but the next morning, she finally began to feel a bit stronger, buoyed by the love of the de Leóns. While the rest of his family read to him from books—or sang, if it was Abuela Gloria—Claire started playing Spanish audio lessons on her phone when she was with Matías, trying out new phrases and acting out the practice dialogues in his room in hopes that he would hear her trying to talk to him in the language he loved most.

Also, Claire had a plan about how to find Matías's soul again.

She arrived at Hospital Universitario La Paz as soon as visiting hours began and took her place in the chair beside Matías's bed. But today she had brought her computer. Between Spanish audio lessons, she was going to spend the morning researching ideas for things she could do with Matías's soul in Madrid—basically, dates—while also keeping the physical part of him company.

Then, at 2 P.M. when everyone else took a break for lunch, Claire would go back to the drink kiosk in the park where she'd seen him yesterday. The most logical place to find something you'd misplaced was to retrace your steps. She hoped it went for souls, too, even though she hadn't exactly "misplaced" him.

"Buenos días, Claire," Soledad said as she and Armando entered the hospital room.

"Buenos días," she said. "¿Cómo estáis?"

Armando made a low noise in his throat and shrugged. Claire knew what he meant. When someone you love is in a coma, just getting through the night is a victory.

"You are not working, are you?" Soledad asked, forehead furrowed as she glanced at Claire's laptop.

The thing is, Claire *had* been checking in with work once a day since she arrived in Madrid. It was impossible not to, because they needed her. But she wasn't working at this very minute. And yet, how could she explain that she was brainstorming dates to go on with Soledad's unconscious son?

"I'm writing down ideas for things to do in Spain with Matías when he wakes," she said.

Soledad touched the cross she wore. "That is good. Optimism is a form of prayer. Matías will feel it."

Armando squeezed Soledad's hand.

Claire began searching the internet for ideas—things she could do with someone who didn't have a solid body. She wasn't sure what would happen if Matías were faced with having to hold or lift something. He'd been able to key her phone number into his phone yesterday, but what if he had to touch something in *this* world, something that didn't already belong to him, like a fork or a glass of wine? Professor Hong had mentioned that Claire couldn't touch Matías because she'd go right through him. So maybe a fork wouldn't register and he'd gloss over it, like when she asked him what year it was and he got confused for a second, then brushed it off?

Or maybe it would jar his soul into realizing he wasn't really

Matías, and that might cause his tenuous connection to this world to break. And then the Matías who was lying in the hospital bed in front of her would be lost for good.

The third possibility was that Professor Hong was completely wrong about everything, but that wasn't a chance Claire was willing to take.

Okay, so meals are out, she thought. But even though food was a big part of the Spanish culture, there were plenty of things to do in Madrid that didn't involve eating.

- Prado Museum (although being in crowds might be bad; Claire imagined a tour group inside the museum walking straight through Matías, and how shocking that would be for him, so she crossed off museums from her list)
- Hot air balloon rides (she would just have to deal with the operator thinking she was off her rocker for talking to herself, because the operator wouldn't be able to see Matías)
- Visiting Plaza Mayor
- Wander through Sabatini Gardens, the botanical gardens next to the Royal Palace
- Take in a flamenco performance
- Explore Retiro Park
- Evening stroll along Gran Vía
- Check out Puerta del Sol, the Times Square of Madrid

The last one made Claire smile. She remembered Matías's horror when she took him to Times Square for the first time and Elmo and Donald Duck cornered him.

Matías's relatives cycled in and out of his room all morning and into the early afternoon while Claire browsed Madrid itineraries and sightseeing guides online. Though at other times, she just watched Matías breathe, the oxygen cannula's hiss as her constant companion.

Claire let out a sad sigh as she realized she'd become used to the hospital—the smell of bleach wipes and antibacterial floor cleaner no longer bit at her nose, and the open doors and nurses' constant glances inside didn't felt like breaches of privacy anymore. But she didn't want Matías's being in a coma to become the status quo, so Claire felt guilty, yet enormously relieved, when her phone's alarm vibrated at a quarter to two.

Time to leave one Matías and hopefully find another.

"UNA COCA-COLA, POR FAVOR," CLAIRE SAID TO THE MAN AT the drink kiosk. "Y . . ."

Ice? What was ice in Spanish?

"¿Con hielo?" the man asked.

"*¡Hielo!* Sí, por favor," Claire said as she opened her wallet.

But then she paused. It wouldn't be hard to pick the right coins out today—she remembered what she needed—but still Claire hesitated, hoping that Matías would appear to help her out. Her fingers hovered over her wallet, waiting . . .

No voice, no amused laugh that she was confused again by the euros; nothing.

She turned to see if he was in line behind her, but unlike yesterday, she was the only customer.

With a sigh, Claire plucked the correct coins from her wallet, paid the man at the kiosk, and took her Coke.

What was she supposed to do now? She'd been counting on the repetition of yesterday's meeting to trigger Matías's return. But if that didn't work, should she still hang around? At home, he was perpetually late—so much so that she'd started telling him appointments and events were thirty minutes (at least) earlier than they really were. It wasn't that Matías didn't respect other people's time; it's that he was often so lost in the ideas in his head or—if he was in his studio—so immersed in painting that time ceased to exist for him.

Maybe it was the same for his soul. After all, they were really parts of the same person.

The logic was shaky, and if it were a legal contract, Claire would've poked a dozen holes in it. But since she had no other ideas for how to get Matías's soul to meet her, she parked herself on the nearest bench and crossed her fingers that he would arrive.

Two hours later, she'd drunk all the Coke and really had to pee. The de Leóns would be back at the hospital from lunch and wondering where she was. And the man at the drink kiosk had started to look at her with pity. Was it that obvious that she'd been stood up by her date?

Not that Matías could stand her up if he hadn't known they'd had a date.

Claire rose from the park bench, the slats probably imprinted onto the backs of her legs from sitting in the same place for so long.

"See you tomorrow?" the man at the kiosk asked in tentative English.

"I don't know," Claire said. "Maybe."

THE REST OF THE AFTERNOON PASSED IN A BLUR OF BEEPS AND rotating family members in Matías's hospital room. Claire tried to analyze what she'd gotten wrong about her lunch break, but who knew what laws governed souls, or if there were any rules at all?

But even if she managed to find his soul, could she make the impossible happen twice? Somehow, Matías had fallen for Claire back in New York, even though he was a Tasmanian devil of paint and curiosity and she was a lawyer who planned out the calendar of her outfits a month in advance. How could she replicate their relationship here, when the odds of someone like him ever loving her in the first place had been so slim?

In the early evening, Claire took her leave from the hospital because she really needed to buy underwear. She had found an emergency pair in the side pocket of her purse—a backup in case of early periods—but washing her panties in the sink with hand soap and alternating between only two pairs was hardly ideal, so it was time to take care of that problem.

The store the hotel receptionist had recommended was far more upscale than Claire was used to. Being the practical sort and also having grown up without much money, she usually bought cotton underwear in bulk packs. So she stood in the entryway of Oysho for a few hesitant seconds, flanked by mannequins in lacy bras and panties that certainly required more care than just tossing them into the laundry with everything else.

Plus, I have no one to wear such pretty things for, she thought, her chest tightening.

No, don't think like that. Matías *would* wake up.

Claire forced herself into the store. Most places in the U.S. put their most expensive, aspirational clothes up front, and their cheap utilitarian stuff in the back, and fortunately, the Spaniards had the same idea here. Their "plain" underwear was still more stylish than the twelve-pack kind she bought at home, but Europeans seemed to have better fashion sense than Americans in general, so it wasn't a huge surprise.

The sign over the underwear display made the decision for her. Her translation app showed that if you bought nine pairs, you'd get one free. Claire counted out a set of ten and took them to the register.

As she waited her turn in line, she looked over the pretty underwear in her hands. Even the simplest designs had a line of tiny buttons on the front, or a small bow, or just a touch of lace trim.

Was she buying too many pairs, though? Because what if buying so many jinxed Matías's recovery, because it indicated to the universe that Claire was ready for the long haul? Like, it meant she didn't believe he would get better quickly and wake up tomorrow. Ten pairs was one and a half weeks of no repeats . . .

She clutched the underwear tighter, wishing again that Matías were here. He always had a way of simplifying things when she started overthinking decisions.

"¿Señora?"

Claire looked up. One of the cashiers was now free and waving to her. As Claire reached the counter, though, she glanced out the window.

There was Matías, walking by the fountain in the square.

Claire gasped.

"Please hurry!" she said to the cashier.

The girl shot Claire a nasty look.

"I cannot help you unless you give me what you are buying."

"What? Oh!" Claire was still clutching the underwear in her hands. "Here."

The cashier muttered something.

"I'm sorry," Claire said. "Un hombre . . . outside. I want to talk to him."

"Ohh," the girl said, a pierced eyebrow lifting appreciatively now. But she frowned at the tame underwear Claire had bought—maybe thinking that a few sexier ones would've increased Claire's chances with a man. Regardless, she rang up Claire's credit card, wrapped the purchases in pretty tissue, and slid them into a nice handle bag. "Good luck!"

"Gracias," Claire said, practically running out the front door. "Matías!"

He spun around, and when the sunlight hit him, she could have sworn he was slightly less diaphanous than he was yesterday. But maybe she was just imagining things, because he was definitely still transparent until he stepped forward, out of the sunbeam.

"Claire! Wow, what are the chances?"

She didn't know. She had no idea why he had shown up here, right now, when her more thought-out plan at the drink kiosk hadn't worked. But she wasn't going to let this opportunity pass.

"Go out with me!" Claire blurted.

Matías seemed confused for a second, but quickly recovered. "I'd love to. I probably need a week to settle in once I get to New York, but then it would be wonderful to see you."

"No."

"No?"

"I mean, go out with me tonight," Claire said.

"Oh, I'm sorry. I can't. I'm busy for the next two weeks, preparing to leave."

Déjà vu, but the mirror image of it, because the first time Matías asked Claire out—when he'd called her at the firm about having dinner with him the same day—she'd told him she was too busy.

Yet he'd persisted, and she'd given in.

"I refuse to accept no for an answer," Claire said, crossing her arms and trying her best not to look like she was bluffing.

But she didn't actually know what ultimatum she'd use if he declined again.

He cocked his head and studied her. "Are all American women this stubborn?"

She balked. "I am *not* stubborn!"

Matías laughed. "I believe that proves my point."

Claire made a face at him.

"However," he said, "I happen to be an expert in stubborn women, because my mother and sister are both incredibly strong-willed."

"Oh? And what does an expert say, then, about this situation?"

"An expert says if you're smart, you do what the stubborn woman asks." Matías winked. "Let's go out, then. I know exactly where to take you."

Museo Sorolla was only a twenty-minute stroll away. At first, Claire had balked at going inside, worrying about crowds walking straight through Matías, but it turned out that tourists were all museumed out by the time early evening came around because they'd spent their energy at the bigger names, like the Prado and Reina Sofía.

"Joaquín Sorolla is one of my favorite painters, because he was a master at playing with light in landscapes," Matías said as they approached the museum. "Oh, I didn't even think to ask before I brought you here—do you like art?"

"I do since I met you," Claire said.

He laughed. "One fainting outside a hotel and a walk around the park, and I've already made such a strong impression!"

Claire blushed. She had spoken the truth, but it was for the other Matías. It's just that his soul was so exactly like him, that she'd momentarily forgotten this Matías wasn't quite the same.

She paid for their tickets while he was distracted by a display about Joaquín Sorolla. But it turned out that she hadn't needed to buy two tickets, because the docent at the door took only one of them from her. He definitely did not see Matías, and thus Claire finally had confirmation that she was the only one who could.

Luckily, Matías was too enraptured by art in the entryway to notice that the docent had taken only one ticket.

"This used to be Sorolla's home," Matías said as they stepped into a room with vivid red-orange walls. Framed paintings hung in every open space—small ones of gardens and fountains, medium-sized ones of arched building facades and reflecting pools, and large portraits of girls in white dresses at the seaside, the salty wind blowing at their hats and parasols. There was an intricate metal-and-glass chandelier hanging from the beamed ceiling, and sculptures and vases and other curios lined every shelf.

No wonder this was one of Matías's favorite artists. Claire

could feel the hum of life here even though the painter was long gone.

"See how you can feel the sun in every one of his pieces?" Matías asked. His eyes gleamed and he breathed in deeply— signatures Claire recognized from whenever he was in awe of another artist. Her heart ached, missing Matías, even though he was also right here beside her.

"Tell me more about Sorolla and his paintings," Claire said, because all she wanted right now was to listen to Matías talk forever.

"Be careful what you wish for," he said. "I might bore you if you give me free rein."

"Never," she said.

Matías laughed. "Okay, you asked for it. Look at this one." He pointed at a portrait of a woman clad in all black, with an enormous black hat on her head. "The room behind the subject is dim; the curtains are drab and muted, and they disappear completely into a blur of murky olive color on the left. And yet, look at how Sorolla highlights the woman's face with light. You can almost feel the sun coming through a small, narrow window just to shine on her, and because of that, you can feel her solemnity more potently than if she were cast in shadow, too."

As he was waxing rhapsodic about Sorolla's use of light in the portrait, soft golden evening sun filtered through a small window in the room and landed on *Matías's* face. He went transparent, though definitely less so than before, so the sunlight was able to bring out the gold in his eyes and make the contrast of his black hair even more stark against his skin. A shadow of stubble lined his jaw, and Claire closed her eyes for a moment, remembering the roughness against her own cheek, how it felt to press her mouth against his. How sometimes, in the beginning of their relationship, they would kiss so ferociously and for so long that hours later, she would come away with sandpaper burns on her mouth, her lips red and swollen even the next day. At the office, George would ask her if she'd had an allergic reaction to something; Yolanda would just snicker knowingly, being married to a fiery member of the art world herself.

In recent months, Claire had stopped letting Matías kiss her like that. She'd tired of going to work looking like a teenager after a backseat make-out session. She would be up for partner soon, and she had to look the part.

Now, though, as Claire looked at him with the sun caressing his face, she wondered: *Why?*

Why should the joy of her personal life mean she couldn't excel in her professional life, too? Why had she started pushing Matías away, nitpicking at the idiosyncrasies that made him him?

Claire wanted to kiss him. She wanted to cross the small patch of museum floor between them, stand on her tiptoes, and taste the sun on his skin. She wanted to kiss his neck, scrape her mouth against the stubble, feel his arms wrap around her and his hands slip under the edge of her shirt.

But she couldn't touch him. Professor Hong had made that clear.

So Claire stood rooted to her spot.

Matías was still looking at the painting. Then he turned and smiled at her. "What do you think?"

I think you're extraordinary, she thought. *And I don't know why I didn't see how lucky I was before.*

———

They stayed until the museum was about to close. Claire never liked to be the kind of person who stayed in museums or restaurants until the very last minute. She imagined it was probably uncomfortable for the docents or waiters to have to go to each guest and politely tell them it was time to leave. So she always made sure she left early enough to save them from having to do that with her.

"What should we do next?" Claire asked as she and Matías stepped back out into the city. "It's only eight o'clock. The night is still young."

"Actually, I should go home," Matías said. "I had a really good time with you, but I have so much I need to do before I head to New York."

"That's two whole weeks away, though," Claire said. She didn't know when or how she'd see Matías again, and she didn't want to let tonight go. It was also still difficult to understand the fact that for him, going to New York was in the future, while for her, that was already well in the past.

And how much time did she really have? What if Claire wasn't able to make this Matías fall in love with her before two weeks was up, when his memories of Madrid were supposed to end and shift to New York?

Claire shuddered. She didn't want to think about that.

For now, she just had to be with him as much as possible, to keep his soul connected to her, his anchor. Their past interactions had seemed to help with the version of Matías in the hospital, and she hoped that his vital signs were perking up again tonight.

"You have two whole weeks before your flight. That's so much time," she said, although she was trying to convince herself, too.

"Well, you have to remember that I'm moving out of the country for two years," Matías said. "It is not as simple as taking a business trip or short vacation. There are many things I must take care of."

"Yes, but—"

"Claire." A touch of annoyance tinged his voice. "Maybe we can see each other once I am in New York?"

"I don't want to wait," Claire said.

Ugh. She sounded pathetic. Desperate. But too much was at stake to care about that.

"I really must go now," Matías said. "I have your number. I will look you up when I get to the United States."

But Claire had heard "I'll call you" or "We'll go out soon" from other men too many times in the past. They never asked for another date. It was the way they ghosted her, which was sadly ironic here.

It's possible Matías *did* mean to reach out to her when he got to New York. But it was just as possible that Claire had pushed too hard, and now he was retreating.

He waved and crossed the street. A bus drove by, briefly blocking Claire's view.

And when the bus passed, Matías was gone.

Matías

Four months into their relationship and on their sixth visit to the Met—New York's most famous museum—Claire confessed.

"Before I met you, I'd never actually come here before."

"What?" Matías said so loudly that it echoed through the gallery. A few patrons glared at him, and he raised his hands in apology.

He lowered his voice and shook his head at Claire, amused. "How long have you lived in New York?"

"I just . . . wasn't really into art before I met you."

"But you're friends with Yolanda and Jason."

"Yes, but that's because I like them as people, not because I was particularly into what Jason did for a living. I mean, he's married to Yolanda, but I think the only time she talks to him about work is when he asks her to help him fall asleep by telling him the latest developments in employment law."

Matías laughed. "Okay, that's fair. But have you been pretending about art around me? Please tell me I haven't been subjecting you to suffering for the last four months."

Claire got up on her tiptoes and kissed him. "No, art is so much more interesting with you. You explain each artist and painting like a story, rather than just a dry recitation of history. I like hearing about what was going on in the painter's life when she was working on a piece, like that she chose to use lemon ochre instead of Italian yellow earth because her husband had gotten in an argument with the owner of the paint company that made the Italian yellow. Or like how that one guy was deathly afraid of water, so he made his entire career about painting boats and the sea to confront his fear. And the way you talk about the paintings themselves—you bring art to life, and that makes me love it."

Matías's entire body warmed at the thought of introducing her to so much joy.

"So what should we see next?" she asked. "What about sculpture? We've never been to that exhibit."

Matías stiffened.

Claire's brows knit together. "You don't like sculpture?"

"I do . . ."

"But you're afraid you don't know enough on the subject and you'll be mortified when I find out?" she said, teasing.

Matías tried to school his face into something resembling neutral. "I used to date a sculptor."

Claire tripped on her own feet. "Oh. Um, you did?"

He shrugged. "Yes, but it's in the past. Anyway, I had my eye on the exhibit on costumes. What do you think?"

Claire's fingers fluttered, and Matías was pretty sure she was debating whether to ask more about his ex or not. He hoped she decided on *not*. At the end of each of his dates with Claire when he asked *When can I see you again?* she always seemed surprised that Matías was still interested. So he didn't want to talk about his previous relationship right now, because he knew Claire well enough to know that she would immediately compare herself to his ex, and he wouldn't be able to convince her that he was so much better off with down-to-earth Claire than another free-spirited artist like himself.

Maybe what Claire needed was to see herself more clearly—that she wasn't only a buttoned-up attorney, but also a woman who could let loose and have unstructured fun sometimes.

"Forget the costume exhibit," he said. "I have a better idea."

They left the city and drove the windy roads out into the forests. Matías checked the address on his phone one more time and asked Claire to pull over in a small patch of dirt.

"Where are we?" she asked as they got out and he led them toward the trees, their red and gold leaves rippling in the breeze.

Matías pointed to a painted wooden sign: Welcome to Anything You Want.

"A professor in my department inherited acres and acres out here," he said. "But instead of building on it, he decided to make it an art collaboration. Any artist is welcome to come onto his land, anytime, to create. The only restriction is you can't harm the plants or wildlife. I've been meaning to come out here but hadn't had the chance."

They found a narrow, worn footpath from the dirt pullout that led deeper into the property.

"So this place is called Anything You Want? What does that mean?" Claire asked as they walked through the thicket of trees—some with delicate, pale orange leaves, and others broad, in crimson hues.

"Literally anything you want to make here, you can," Matías said. "Like that."

He gestured into the woods to the left. There, bristly square doormats made of coconut fibers had been dyed black and something close to white, and they were laid up and down the hilly ground like an uneven chess board. Three- to six-foot-tall chess pieces made of copper wire stood on some of the squares—stumpy pawns, regal knights on horseback, bishops with hollow bodies except a solid cross at the heart.

"Oh my gosh, look!" Claire laughed, pointing at a wire figure behind a particularly stout tree trunk. "There's the king!"

Matías laughed, too. Because the king was cowering behind the tree, only his crowned head sticking out, and just a few yards away from him, a queen stood on her coir doormat square, her wire body mounted on a pole so she spun around and around in circles, as if searching for him.

"Checkmate," Matías said.

"Definitely." Claire grinned and linked her arm through his as they continued down the path.

They passed a long wooden shed with a sign over the doorway that read: Tools of Imagination.

Farther down the path, there was more: A dragon made entirely of bicycle gears, suspended on a zip line in the canopy above.

A single platform with a glass-covered plate—inside was a marble apple, waiting for Snow White. Little fairy houses nestled in fields of wildflowers, and colorful glass wind chimes in the tree branches. A gold statue of Aslan the lion. A topiary of a dancing couple. A fallen, lightning-struck trunk carved into a totem pole in repose.

When they came upon a low stone bridge over a creek that had dried up, Matías's chest swelled in the same way as when inspiration struck him for a new painting.

"There," he said.

"There what?" Claire looked at the bridge and all around it.

"Stay right here. I'll be back in a few minutes."

He ran through the woods, along the twists and turns of the various dirt paths, until he found the wooden shed with the Tools of Imagination. The door was unlocked, and inside, Matías found what he'd been hoping for—paint and brushes and tarps—as well as all sorts of art supplies he didn't need now but might use another day.

"What is all that for?" Claire asked when he returned with several canisters of spray paint.

"We're going to decorate the stone bridge," he said.

Her eyes grew wide. "Like, graffiti?"

Matías smiled. "Sort of. I know it's not in your comfort zone to deface something like a bridge, but since we do have the professor's permission to create anything we want here, do you want to give it a try?"

She bit her lip. Her fingertips did their cute, unconscious fluttery thing. Then she took a deep breath. "Okay. Let's do this."

In the end, they didn't scrawl their names over the rocks or anything resembling the art that graced the city's alley walls. Instead, Claire wanted to paint faces on the round stones. Dozens and dozens of happy little faces.

She beamed at their work when she was done.

Matías beamed at *her*.

"It's only a small rebellion," she said, "and technically it isn't even a rebellion because we were allowed to do it. But somehow, it still feels like it counts."

"It definitely counts," he said, spinning her toward him and kissing her.

The smell of paint lingered on her skin, and she tasted like sun and salt. Claire's hair had come undone from its bun, the strands dancing around her face in the wind.

He liked Claire in the city, where she had everything beautifully orchestrated.

He also liked Claire in the forest, with a lightness in her eyes from letting a little of her control go.

He backed her up against a smooth tree trunk next to the bridge and kissed her harder, letting his tongue find hers. His hand slipped into the waistband of her jeans.

She pressed her body against the length of his, and he could feel the urgency of her wanting, as much as he wanted her.

But then she said, between kisses, "Not here."

"We won't get caught," Matías said, already hooking his finger into the side of her panties. "There's no one else here."

"But they're watching . . ." Claire said.

"Who?"

Claire glanced sideways at the bridge. Matías's gaze followed.

"You mean . . . the stones?" he said.

She giggled, then fully cracked up. "Their cute little faces . . ."

Laughing, Matías hoisted her over his shoulder. He carried her farther into the forest, where there were no paths and no other art installations.

Then he lay her down on a bed of autumn leaves and they made love under a canopy of trees, the dappled sun on their naked skin, on someone else's property. And that was how Matías helped Claire achieve her second small rebellion of the day.

CLAIRE

WHEN CLAIRE ARRIVED AT THE HOSPITAL THE NEXT MORNING, there was a heated argument going on outside Matías's room between Aracely and possibly the most beautiful woman Claire had ever seen. She had huge Ana de Armas eyes and thick black waves of hair. Her bold floral maxi dress dipped low at the neckline, then hugged the curves of her chest before billowing around her feet like rippling waves. Every man in the hospital ward was transfixed by her; every woman both hated her and wanted to be her at the same time.

Except Aracely, who seemed like she just hated her as she pointed repeatedly toward the elevator.

"¡Las visitas son solo para los familiares!" Aracely declared, practically shouting.

"Pero yo casi fui parte de la familia," the woman said.

"Exacto, 'casi.' Tomaste tu decisión y le rompiste el corazón a mi hermano. Por eso él salió del país; no le dijiste nada después."

A nurse behind the beautiful woman motioned with her hands at Aracely and whispered something in Spanish that Claire assumed meant *Please keep it down!*

"Hola, Claire," Luis said, slipping next to her. "You are just in time for the show."

"Who is that, and what's going on?"

"That is Vega Castillo, Matías's ex. She wants to see him, but Aracely won't let her."

Oh. Vega. Matías had mentioned her name a couple of times, but he didn't like talking about her. Claire knew that he and Vega had met in art school and been together for a little while, but he'd never said what happened to them, only that the past was the past.

Was it, though? Because Vega was beginning to cry. She fell to her knees onto the linoleum, begging as she sobbed.

Aracely rolled her eyes.

"Vega is very dramatic," Luis said in a conspiratorial voice to Claire.

But Claire saw actual pain in the woman's posture as she reached out and clasped Aracely's hands. Vega's body trembled, not overly exaggerated like someone fake-crying, but in the way that Claire had experienced herself on the plane flight to Madrid, when her emotions were so frayed it felt as if all the nerve endings in her body were exposed and even a puff of air could send her into shock.

But Aracely wrenched her hands away and planted her feet even more firmly in front of Matías's door.

"Would giving her a few minutes hurt?" Claire asked Luis.

Luis sighed. "Matías asked Vega to marry him when they were only twenty years old. She said yes but would never commit to a wedding date, no matter how often he tried to set one. When he received the invitation for the visiting professor position in New York a year and a half ago, he asked her again for a wedding date so she could go with him to the United States as his wife, but Vega gave him back her ring and told him to go alone."

What?

Claire clutched the back of a nearby chair. Matías and Vega had been engaged for fifteen years? And presumably together for longer than that? Claire had thought it wasn't an important relationship since she knew so little about it.

But looking back, she realized she'd only thought that because Matías never talked about Vega. Which wasn't all that weird because Vega was, after all, an ex—not exactly the most popular topic to discuss with your current girlfriend.

Yet Claire's chest tightened as she compared the lengthy history Matías had had with this beautiful artist to the eleven months and one week he'd had with boring, tight-laced Claire. And the fact that he had hardly ever mentioned Vega meant the opposite of insignificance. Other than the last year Matías had spent in New York, Vega had been a part of all of his adult life.

Did he still love her?

Oh god . . . Was the engagement ring Claire found in his dresser the same one that Vega had once worn?

Feeling suddenly nauseous, Claire looked away from Vega kneeling on the floor. Even desperate, Matías's ex-fiancée was painfully beautiful.

"Aracely will never forgive Vega for breaking Matías's heart," Luis said. "And she definitely will not let Vega into that room."

The nurse who'd been imploring Aracely and Vega to keep the volume down had finally given up on them and called hospital security. The next time the ward doors opened, two very large men in uniform stepped through.

They strode over to Vega and said something quietly to her.

She answered them, loud enough to carry across the room.

"¡Ay, por favor!" Aracely said, throwing her arms in the air.

Even though Claire didn't want to look, it was impossible not to. "What happened?" she asked.

Luis shook his head at the scene; one of the security men was crouching to scoop Vega up into his arms. "Vega says she is too weak with grief and must be carried. As I said—very dramatic."

Vega draped herself elegantly across the guard's body, as if she were aware of the picture she was creating. Every man—except for Luis and his father—leaned a little bit forward, like they were hoping this might become one of those human chains, where, in order to help Vega, she must be passed from one man's arms into another until she reached safety downstairs.

But all Claire could think about was how Vega used to drape her body all over *Matías*. Whereas Claire had never been so performative or clingy. She prided herself on being independent, but looking from the outside in, she saw how stiff she must be compared to Vega.

Why would Matías have ever chosen me when he could have had a woman like that? One who lived her life as large as he did?

The guards took Vega into the elevator. As the doors shut, the men left behind exhaled their disappointment all at once.

Aracely, though, leaned her head against the door of her brother's hospital room and closed her eyes. When she opened them again, she saw Claire and gave her a weak smile.

"Come on, Claire. *You* are welcome to see Matías."

Claire took a step in that direction, but then she realized something, which she honestly wished she *hadn't* thought of.

With a sigh, she glanced back at the elevator.

"I'll be right back. Unfortunately, I need to have a word with Vega."

———

"Perdón," Claire said as she caught up with Vega in the hospital lobby, where she now had no trouble walking on her own.

"¿Sí?" Vega turned around and looked straight at Claire with her huge eyes, mesmerizing even though they were smudged with eyeliner.

"I'm Claire Walker, Matías's, um . . ." Suddenly she felt shy claiming him when he had been Vega's for so much longer.

"No hablo inglés," Vega said. She pulled out her phone and opened a translation app, turning on the mic and holding it up to Claire.

"I am Claire Walker. Matías's girlfriend."

The app said in a slightly robotic voice, "Soy Claire Walker. La novia de Matías."

"Ah," Vega said. "Aracely te mencionó." She stuck out her hand matter-of-factly. "Mucho gusto conocerte, Claire."

Claire shook Vega's hand. "I wasn't expecting that."

The app translated for her. It was so much better than the basic one Claire had been using since she arrived in Madrid.

Vega shrugged and spoke into her phone, which said, "I may regret my choice to break up with Matías, but I made it. And women do not need to be enemies simply because they love the same man, do they?"

Claire flinched at Vega's use of the present tense. *Love the same man.* Claire had hoped that when Matías said the past was the past he'd meant it. But apparently Vega still loved him, even though she had let him put an ocean between them. And Claire had no idea whether Matías still had feelings for Vega, since he'd never really mentioned her.

But she couldn't deal with those kinds of thoughts right now. She'd run down the stairs to reach Vega for a reason. And if they had to keep passing a translation app between them in order to achieve that, Claire would deal with it.

"I agree," Claire said. "Women shouldn't be enemies because of a man. And that's actually why I'm here. I was wondering if you could tell me what Matías's life was like when he was still in Madrid."

Vega tilted her head. "Sí ¿pero por qué?" *Yes, but why?*

"I guess I'm just scared of losing him. I'm greedy for the details of his life."

The real reason was because knowing the places Matías worked and lived—where he bought groceries or liked to grab a bite to eat—might help Claire figure out how to find him again. She couldn't count on Matías just appearing anymore. She had to be proactive, even if it meant facing another woman he'd loved—and perhaps loved *more*.

But of course she couldn't tell Vega *I'm hunting for Matías's soul*.

Vega sighed heavily, then spoke into the phone. The robot Spanish woman said, "How about if I show you, instead of tell you? I would not mind revisiting my memories of him, either."

THE MALASAÑA NEIGHBORHOOD APPEARED TO BE THE ARTSY part of Madrid. Vega led Claire past Bohemian vintage clothing shops, a used bookstore whose front window display was a collage of old punk zines, small cafés that looked like they were all venues for live music or open mic poetry readings, and mysterious doors painted in riotous colors that Vega explained were the entrances for clubs with some of the best DJs on the continent.

"That," Vega said as she pointed across the street at a window full of paintings, "is the art supply store Matías and I like. They have the best paints for him, and clay for me. I am a sculptor.

"Next door," she said, waving toward a bar that didn't open till later, "is where I got so drunk as a freshman that Matías had to carry me back to my apartment."

Common trick of yours? Claire wanted to ask, thinking back to Vega at the hospital.

But there was no reason to be rude when Vega was taking time out of her day to teach Claire about Matías's past. Plus, they'd agreed that rivalry between them would be . . . what? Immature? Moot because Vega had broken up with him? Unnecessary because Claire was the one Matías was with now?

Yes to all of the above, and yet Claire couldn't help feeling insecure in her ponytail, plain T-shirt, and jeans, next to an artist who oozed sex and confidence with every sway of her hips and swish of her skirt.

At that very moment, someone whistled at Vega and shouted, "*¡Qué guapa!*" How pretty! Claire didn't need the app to translate that.

Vega just laughed and waved the man off, like this happened to her all the time. But then, it probably did.

Not that Claire wanted random guys whistling at her in the street, but no one would ever even think to do that to her. Her best trait was her intelligence. Otherwise, Claire was goodlooking enough to get by, but never to stand out.

Maybe that was why Matías preferred Claire: He didn't have to fend off other guys like he must've when he was with Vega.

Yay. One point for Claire. What a depressing victory.

They walked several more blocks before Vega stopped in front of a bakery with a bright yellow tiled storefront that read La Mantequilla y el Huevo. She rattled off several sentences into her app. "This is The Butter and the Egg, our favorite place for breakfast. He liked sweet and I liked savory, so he ordered magdalenas or churros con chocolate. And I would order a tortilla. But by the end of the meal, he always ended up feeding me one of his churros dipped in hot melted chocolate." She closed her eyes and made a small moaning sound.

This might not be an *entirely* friendly trip down memory lane on Vega's part.

Claire's heart twinged. She'd thought that churros and chocolate was something special that Matías liked to make just for her, but now here was another woman—one he'd been with for more than a decade and a half and had wanted to marry— making not-so-subtle comments dripping with innuendo, and Claire felt so . . . stupid.

And small.

Plain Claire, an orphan and foster kid from Florida who thought she could change who she was by moving to the big city and dressing herself up in fancy lawyer duds. But underneath, she was still Just Claire.

Sure, Yolanda would argue that Just Claire managed to snag Matías de León, so who cares about the sultry artist who used to sleep with him?

But the problem was that Claire now had to win Matías over again. She had to not only find his soul but also make that version of Matías fall in love with her. What if this time she couldn't tap into whatever had attracted him to her in New York? Here in Spain, Claire wasn't a dynamo lawyer, she had worn the same two pairs of dirty underwear for several days before she managed to pull herself together to buy new ones, *and* she was illiterate! And what if—

Oh god.

What if Matías's soul also appeared to Vega? He was tied to his life in Madrid from a year ago. She would have already broken up with him by then, but still . . . If he still loved her before he left for New York, if he would've been willing to take her back . . .

But how could Claire ask? If Vega's answer was no she hadn't seen Matías's soul, then Claire would sound like a delusional fool. But if Vega's answer was yes . . . Maybe *she* was the one who could bring Matías back.

"I . . . I think I'll return to the hospital now," Claire said. "Thanks for showing me around some of the landmarks of Matías's life."

Vega let her eyes flutter open slowly and looked at Claire through her lashes. "¿Qué?"

Claire took a deep breath and repeated herself into the translation app.

Vega cooed. "You do not want to see our apartment? Well, it's mine now, but we lived there together for many years."

Claire swallowed the bile rising in her throat. If Vega wanted to play mean, fine. But Claire didn't have to take it. And she swore to herself that *she* would be the one to reconnect Matías to reality.

"I'm good. Thanks." Claire pivoted on her heel.

"His studio is still here in the neighborhood," Vega said, her tone suddenly softer. Sadder. The app didn't convey that, but Claire heard it clearly.

"It is?" She turned back around.

Vega nodded. "The landlord had a crush on him, so she let him keep the space rent-free while he was in the United States. He couldn't pack all of his pieces, and this was her way of ensuring he would come back after two years. The landlord, by the way, is eighty-six years old."

Despite herself, Claire laughed.

"The studio is three blocks that way," Vega said, pointing in a direction they hadn't ventured yet. "Armando probably has the key, if you want to visit." Vega had a faraway look in her eyes, as if she were remembering a time when she could come and go from the studio whenever she pleased, without Matías's family as the gatekeepers. When she could see and touch and immerse herself in his imagination.

But Vega's time with him was past, and Claire was not going to invite her into the studio when she got the key. Not after that churro story.

More important, though, Claire hoped that she would find Matías—or, more accurately, his soul—at the studio.

After all, he'd said he needed to pack up his paintings and get ready to send them to the Rose Gallery in New York, right?

CLAIRE

⌒

"Thank you for coming out here," Claire said. "I didn't expect to end up in Malasaña when I chased after Vega."

"It is no problem," Armando said. "It was not my turn to sit in Matías's room anyway, and I understand why you would want to visit his studio, especially if you are already in the neighborhood."

Together, they walked up to the sleek white building that housed a number of artist workspaces. It was only one story, but tall and long, and when they stepped through the gated entry, Claire was surprised to find a sunny garden full of orchids and ferns. All the studios had floor-to-ceiling windows that looked out onto the plants; if Claire had to guess, the windows were all north facing, to let in the best light. It was something Matías had missed in his studio in New York, where—without the right sort of windows—he'd had to rig his own artificial lighting with photography lights and reflectors.

"Matías's studio is at the end," Armando said, pointing in the direction of a cluster of yellow orchids. The shades on his windows were drawn, though, so Claire couldn't see inside.

Armando scanned a key fob and let them into the building, then down the corridor. The doors were all white, too, with nameplates or signs on them to indicate who worked there.

"Is it only painters here, or other kinds of artists?" Claire asked.

"Only painters," Armando said. "The landlady says potters and sculptors are either too messy when they work with clay or too loud when they work with stone. Do not worry. You will not see Vega here."

Claire bit her lip, thankful that he'd understood her insecurity without her having to express it out loud. Then she realized she'd been silly to even worry about Vega. If her studio was here, too, she wouldn't have seemed sad about not having access to the building.

When they reached Matías's studio, though, Claire's thoughts of Vega faded. Because the sign on the studio was his familiar signature, Matías de León, in elegant, looping penmanship with the accent marks somehow expressing exuberance in the way he dashed them upward, longer than necessary, like fireworks shooting up into the sky just moments before bursting. Seeing his autograph made Claire smile and want to cry at the same time.

Armando unlocked the door and held it open for Claire. She stepped in, expecting to see tubes of paint everywhere, half-finished work on easels, used rags and still life models all over the floor, and the general chaos that surrounded Matías's process. But instead of chaos and the usually ubiquitous stink of solvent in the air, it was mostly empty.

Some old drawings were taped to the walls, with blank panels of wood stacked beneath them, but there were no partially used tubes of oil paint scattered anywhere. It still smelled like solvent and linseed oil, but the scent was faint. Eleven months old.

Claire stared open-mouthed at the pristine space.

"It's strangely . . . tidy."

"He took much of his work with him to the United States," Armando said.

"I guess so." Claire walked slowly through the studio. There were two glass-topped taborets—worktables—one close to the door, and one deeper inside, both with old coffee canisters filled with various paintbrushes. Four wooden easels—all sturdy but of varying sizes, because most of Matías's pieces were "normal" dimensions, but he also liked having a huge, long-running project going on at the same time as whatever else he was working on. Shelves with jars of gesso, PVC, foam brushes, and other lesser-used supplies.

"Do you mind if I open the shades?" Claire asked.

"As long as we close them before we leave, go ahead," Armando said.

She walked over to the wall of glass and pulled down each of the blinds—they would seem upside down to most people, but that's because realist painters often liked to block the sun from the bottom part of the window so light streamed from the top, down onto their models at an attractive angle.

There was a gray couch along the windows; Matías liked to brainstorm lying down, which sometimes meant he accidentally fell asleep, but that wasn't necessarily a bad thing, because his ideas often clarified themselves in his dreams. As Claire passed the sofa, she ran her finger along an armrest, speckled here and there with paint. She wondered which piece each color had come from—red from the thimble-sized alien in the painting of a woman and her book? Orange from the monk offering the world in his hands? Yellow, green, blue, purple, black, and white from other paintings Claire had been lucky enough to see? Or did they belong to work that had come and gone long before he'd met her?

With sunlight streaming into the studio, the space felt even more like Matías now. She looked through a stack of wooden panels against a nearby wall; they were all prepped with rabbit skin glue and gesso, but they were still blank. Like Armando said, Matías had shipped most of his work with him for gallery shows in New York.

But then Claire noticed what looked like one of Matías's enormous panels in the back of the studio, propped against the wall. A bedsheet was draped over the painting. She strode over.

Armando turned just as she reached it.

"Claire, do not—"

Too late. She was already lifting the sheet.

Oh.

It was a self-portrait of Matías and Vega, done in Matías's signature realism, although this one had more than a touch of the surreal. In the painting, he and Vega faced each other in this very studio, but both their figures were unfinished; if this were a photograph, it would be a shot of two artists in the middle of creating their work. Matías held a brush in his hand, painting Vega in front of him, as if inventing her in real time. Her body was fully rendered—with all those sensual curves that Claire couldn't help imagining his brush caressing—but Vega's face was still a work in progress, much of it purposefully left as a hazy ébauche, an outline where you could only see a blurry shape of what was to come, including the brown transfer lines from the original drawing. Matías's brush was in the process of painting her lips.

At the same time, Vega was sculpting *him*, creating Matías

out of clay. His head and arms and torso were complete, but her bare hands stroked the part that would become his pelvis.

A wave of nausea roiled through Claire's stomach. She dropped the sheet over the painting and staggered back.

"It is truly in the past," Armando said quietly. "That is why Matías left that painting here."

"Right. Of course," Claire said.

But how could you leave something that passionate behind for good? Matías and Vega had been together for more than fifteen years. They were both artists, kindred spirits, and he had dreamed of being with her for the rest of his life.

Maybe Claire had just been a rebound. She had been in the right place, at the right time, when he came to New York. The fact that she was Vega's opposite in personality—a lawyer who lived by her calendar, who didn't understand a thing about art— might have been exactly what he thought he needed.

Then they'd just gotten stuck in the progression of a relationship, with one thing leading to the next, until faced with the fork in the road where you had to decide whether to break up or stay together. And Matías, who was a hopeless romantic, had chosen the path of proposing less than a year after meeting Claire. The road where he could be married and have that fantasy "happily ever after" where he had once slotted Vega.

Claire cleared her throat and tried to look stable, even though she still felt like she was going to throw up. She used a tactic that was reliably helpful as an attorney when faced with difficult situations—she pivoted and changed the topic.

"Armando, do you ever paint here?"

He watched her for a moment, assessing whether she really was okay after seeing such an intimate rendering of Vega with

Matías. But if Claire was good at anything, she was good at putting up a shield of unflappability and strength when others would panic; it's why her clients trusted her to run their make-or-break deals.

She pulled off another convincing job, because Armando answered her question. "Matías told me to consider the studio mine while he was gone, but I still work on my watercolors at home."

"Why? This is such a great space."

"Yes, but . . . how can I explain?" Armando smiled. "Okay. Imagine you have a little boy. He has a corner of his bedroom where he plays with all his stuffed animals and toy cars. He is a generous child, so he says to you, 'Mommy, when I go to school, you can play in my corner.'

"Do you do it? Probably not. Because in your mind, that corner belongs to your son. As a parent, that space is sacred to you because it is his.

"In the same way, I can never consider this place as mine. This is Matías's studio. I do not want to change anything about it, even if it is only using a corner of the room."

"*Vale*," Claire said softly. It was a word she'd heard the de Leóns use when they agreed with each other, which was quite often. What Armando said made sense, even in the context of his son's just going overseas for a couple of years. But now that Matías was in a coma, it seemed even *more* important to preserve everything that Matías had ever touched, every room he had ever graced.

"I am going back to the hospital." Armando gave her the key to the studio. "You will come back soon?"

"Of course," Claire said. "I just want to be here for a little while, if that's okay?"

Armando nodded. "I understand. The studio is like being with Matías, but in a different way."

CLAIRE WATCHED THROUGH THE WINDOW AS ARMANDO LEFT. When he had turned the corner, she hurried outside to a café across the street and parked herself at a table on the front patio. She hoped that Matías would come to the studio because he'd said he needed to pack up his paintings to ship overseas. But she couldn't already be *in* his studio when he appeared. That would set off all sorts of alarm bells in his head. She already had a strike against her, given how desperate she'd acted last night after the Sorolla Museum closed.

New tactic: Play it cool.

I just happened to be at a table at a café that has an unobstructed line of sight to the front door of your studio building. No, that's not weird at all. Total coincidence.

Claire would've made a terrible spy.

But what else could she do? She didn't have any better ideas for intercepting Matías. Yesterday, her careful strategy of being at the park's drink kiosk at the same time as she'd previously seen him was a bust, but then he'd suddenly appeared later, outside a lingerie store she'd never stepped foot in before. He wasn't predictable. So being here, close to the one place he'd said he would be, seemed like the best option.

That was, assuming souls actually followed their own plans.

Given that this was Matías, who—in corporeal form—had a hard time sticking to his calendar, the chances were not great.

And yet, Claire stayed.

She stayed through three cups of coffee.

She stayed through an order of toast with pomegranate jam, then an order of huevos rotos.

She stayed as her sunscreen wore off, and her skin began to scorch.

No Matías.

Was he not coming at all? Could she have missed him and he was already upstairs in his studio?

Or was Matías with Vega?

All that coffee Claire had drunk threatened to come back up her throat.

Don't think about Vega!

Claire took the key to the studio from her pocket and passed it back and forth between her fingers for a few minutes.

Then she got annoyed at herself for being impatient.

When the proposal hadn't happened as Matías hoped, he'd declared in his diary, "I will be patient. Because I think we are worth waiting for."

He was more than right. So Claire would stay here at the café, waiting for him, for as long as it took.

But god, she missed him. It was a constant, burning weight in the center of her chest. Not sharp like heartburn; more like she had a piece of charcoal embedded inside her, and the embers never went out.

She closed her fist around the key, crushing it to her palm.

Matías appeared at the café entrance. He walked right past Claire and inside, as if he was going to order something.

What? How?

Claire gawked after him for a second. Then her eyes went down to her fist. She uncurled her fingers, where the key to the studio lay directly on top of where Matías had kissed her before he left New York.

I'll be right here with you, he'd said.

"Oh," Claire whispered.

The first time, when he'd shown up at her hotel, she had just pressed her lips against her palm.

The second time, at the drink kiosk, she had had a bunch of coins cupped in her hand. But he hadn't come to the park yesterday because she'd already known which euro was which by then, so she hadn't poured them all out. Claire had just plucked them straight out of her wallet with her fingertips.

The third time, she'd been clutching a handful of underwear.

And now, the key . . .

But it couldn't be as simple as anything touching her palm. Claire carried things all the time. If that's all it took, Matías would be with her almost nonstop.

So what was the other common thread?

Claire had to drop the thought, though, because Matías re-emerged from the café.

She wanted to jump up and run over to him, but she'd already done that yesterday, and Claire didn't want him to feel like he was a rabbit who'd just sprung a trap—even though, truth be told, she had been lying in wait for him here.

Act nonchalant, she reminded herself. She picked up her phone from the table and put it to her ear, pretending to be on a call, while angling herself so he would see her.

He was about to pass her. And he was quietly talking to himself, which he did when he was lost deep inside his own thoughts, often working out an idea for a new painting.

Matías was going to walk right by her and not even notice.

Claire silently apologized to the waiter for what she was about to do.

She knocked her empty coffee mug onto the cement. The cup shattered, sending ceramic shards in all directions. "Oh my god!" Claire leaped up from her seat. "I'm so sorry," she said to the waiter who was hurrying over. And the whole time, Claire made a point of being in a position where Matías could see her face, but she didn't make eye contact with him; it was important that *he* notice her first this time, if this setup was going to have any chance of being credible as a coincidence.

"Please," Claire said to the waiter. "Let me pay for that mug." She did her best to play the role of loud American tourist, making a fuss as she got her wallet out of her purse, all the while using big arm gestures that Matías surely couldn't miss. She might as well be trying to help a plane land.

"Claire?" Matías said. "Is it you again?"

She faked being too flustered to recognize him for a moment, even though it was difficult not to stare, because when he stepped out of the shade of the building and back into the sunlight, it was obvious that he wasn't transparent anymore, but translucent. His body didn't go gauzy in the sun, but maintained all its color, just in a washed-out way that blurred at the edges.

Why the change? Was being with her slowly making him more solid as she strengthened his soul's connection to her?

But Claire had to keep up her act, so she squinted and said, "Oh gosh, Matías. I'm so embarrassed for you to see me like this. I'm not usually clumsy. It's just that this phone call—" She waved her cell in the air before realizing it was the home screen, with no active call.

Shoot.

Claire pasted a puzzled frown on her face. "I think my client hung up on me."

"For breaking a coffee cup? Tough standards."

Matías smiled, and Claire's breath stuttered.

After waiting for him for hours, now she just stood there, stunned by his easy charm, which was both familiar and new all over again.

"What are you doing in Malasaña?" he asked.

She exhaled. Claire had a prepared answer for that. "I figured that if I'm working in Madrid, I should try to see more of it than just my hotel and my client's office. All the recommendations online say this is a great neighborhood to check out, so . . . here I am. Working, but it's a victory because I'm outside of a conference room."

"Did you try the café's almendrados?"

"No," Claire said. "What are they?"

"Here, try one," Matías said, making the motions of opening what might be a paper bag, but just like his cellphone the other day, she couldn't see it. He held the invisible cookie out to Claire. "They're made from almonds."

"You really like sweet almond things, huh?"

"Actually, yeah. How'd you know that?"

Claire blanched. She *shouldn't* know that, at least as far as *this* Matías was concerned. On their first real date in New York, he'd brought those little glass jars of bienmesabe canario, his old family recipe. But that hadn't happened yet, not in his timeline.

"Just a guess," Claire said with a squeak. "I love almond sweets, too, but I'm going to pass for now, thanks. I'm really full from breakfast."

"Your loss, but more for me." Matías grinned as his fingers worked to close the bag of cookies that Claire couldn't see.

They had reached a critical juncture in the "chance" meeting. He could walk away. She could prevent it from happening by inviting herself to his studio. But that might give off the hunter-tracking-prey vibe again, as well as making her look pathetic. And Claire was sure that being pathetic wasn't the reason Matías had originally fallen in love with her, so it certainly wasn't going to work as the hook this time, either.

She decided to try reverse psychology.

"Well, it was great seeing you again, Matías."

"Oh. Uh, yes. Great seeing you, too." He hovered for a moment, then turned to walk away.

Patience, she thought.

She *knew* Matías. The same part of his brain that loved finding new hobbies also liked being a contrarian. If someone said, *You can never learn tennis well as an adult,* Matías would buy a tennis racket and rent court time to prove them wrong. If accepted opinion said coffee and cheese don't go well together, he would spend an entire weekend in the kitchen until he made a recipe where they did.

Not that Claire was just a hobby, but she understood his mind well enough to predict that if she gave him the brush-off, he ought to at least pause.

The question was, was she enough of a draw for him to come back?

He took one step. Two, three.

On his fourth, he turned 180 degrees.

"Claire?"

"Hmm?" She looked up from something that was supposedly important on her phone.

"Yesterday, at Museo Sorolla, the way you looked at the paintings and talked about them—How do you understand art so well? Did you grow up with it, or study it in university?"

"No," Claire said. "I didn't used to get art at all. But then a . . . friend taught me how to appreciate it. How to see beyond the surface. Now, one of my favorite things is discovering new painters I didn't know before."

"Really?"

"Yeah."

Matías hesitated for just a split second. Then he asked, "Would you be interested in coming to my studio to see my work?"

"Oh no, I couldn't intrude. You're busy; I don't want to get in your way."

"You wouldn't! I have to pack up my paintings anyway, so if you want to look at them while I'm doing that, it's not really any extra time."

"Are you sure?" Claire asked, already standing up and putting her phone into her purse.

"Absolutely. In fact, my studio is just across the street."

"No way," Claire said. "What an amazing coincidence."

MATÍAS UNLOCKED THE DOOR—OR HE *THOUGHT* HE DID—AND just walked through.

But the real—solid—door was still closed in front of Claire.

"Welcome to my studio," she heard him say from inside.

Shit! She fumbled for the key in her pocket.

Claire unlocked the door and slipped in while Matías was saying, "I'm sorry it's a mess in here. I'm not the neatest person, and it's worse now because I'm about to move across the ocean." Claire had just propped the heavy metal door open—so she wouldn't have the same problem upon leaving—when he turned to look at her.

"Well, what do you think?"

Her eyes widened. The studio *she* saw was nearly empty, since Matías had packed everything a year ago. But what *he* saw was probably something akin to what Claire had expected to see when she came here with Armando—tubes of paint and palette knives and brushes scattered across the taborets, rulers stained with paint, and rags and tarps and discarded drawings and color studies all over the floor.

She hadn't thought through the gap in their timelines when she'd accepted his invitation to come see his work.

"That bad?" Matías asked.

"No, it's just . . ." Claire riffled through her brain for how to respond. Luckily, being a lawyer, she had some practice in vague, noncommittal answers. "I'm hyperorganized to a fault. I like being reminded that there are other personality types out there."

"That was a very nice way to say 'You're a slob, Matías.'"

"No, it's not what I—"

He laughed, and it lit up his entire face like he was emanating pure sunshine. Claire swore the temperature in the studio rose by a few degrees.

Of course, being in proximity to Matías also had that effect on her in general.

"Anyway," he said, "you're here to look at paintings." He dropped his invisible bag of cookies on the end of the closest taboret, then gestured at an empty space in the middle of the room. "This is the one I've been working on since I received the invitation to go to New York. It's nearly finished. Just a few more small touches."

Based on the height of where he was pointing, Claire assumed he was looking at a painting on an easel, although there was no easel there at present that she could see.

But *what* was the painting of?

"It's breathtaking," she said, hedging. "What else are you thinking of adding?"

"I think there needs to be a bit more light reflected off the girl as she looks into the puddle. The cliché approach would be to put the sparkle in her eyes as she's looking at herself as a bumblebee. But I want to highlight the wonder in her *face*. Like in that Sorolla portrait from last night, with the woman in black in the drab room."

Claire teared up as she looked at the space where Matías's New York skyline and sunflower painting was supposed to be. It had been the first work of his she'd ever seen, in the window of the Rose Gallery. I want *that,* she had thought. That kind of surprising joy in the midst of normal life.

Matías turned to her. "Claire, are you all right? You're crying."

She tried to smile, while swiping the tears away. "It's stunning, Matías. Truly. A surreal delight."

He knit his brows together for a second. "Did you just say 'a surreal delight'? That's what I was going to name my exhibition."

"Unbelievable." Claire smiled fully now.

"Yeah. Wow." Matías shook his head. "Anyway, I want to show you more. Come this way." He darted left of the worktable, expecting her to follow. But moving around a studio where she couldn't see anything was easier said than done. How would

Claire know if she was running straight into a chair or another easel that wasn't in the same place as the ones she could see? Or if he'd left mahl sticks or big metal safety cans of used solvent in the middle of the floor?

But did it really matter? She would walk right through the things that weren't really there now. It would be fine as long as Matías didn't see her do it.

Still, she tried to keep on his heels without getting weirdly close.

Matías stopped in front of the eastern wall. Claire came up beside him.

"I want to take these with me," he said.

"Mm," Claire said, because she had no idea what they were looking at.

"But my sister, Aracely, says I shouldn't because they will only make me homesick."

Ah. Claire suspected this was his "Homage to Spain" series. Part of the exhibit at the Rose Gallery had been dedicated to it: the chef sprinkling tiny hearts onto paella. A flamenco dancer on a beach who, instead of castanets, performed with clacking seashells. A matador extending a bouquet of flowers rather than a sword at a black bull.

"I think," Claire said, "that your home country will always be with you, whether you have the paintings or not. Living in the States will never change that."

He crossed his arms as he contemplated both the work and what Claire had said. Since she couldn't really see the paintings— other than in her memory—she watched *him*. And what she saw, she'd never noticed before. There was a sadness in Matías's eyes, like part of him was reluctant to leave this place. By the time Claire had met him in New York, he'd been there a week already and had thrown himself with the usual Matías enthusiasm into experiencing everything there was to offer there. Any hint of regret never showed.

But right here, this Matías hadn't left yet, and that meant the future was a vast maw of the unknowable. At the same time, his heart was still raw from Vega's breaking off their engagement and telling him to go ahead and move to the other side of the planet without her.

"You should definitely bring these paintings with you," Claire said. She knew he would anyway, because she'd seen them at the Rose Gallery. But it also seemed like the right thing to say as he stood on the cusp of a monumental change in his life. For Matías, art had always been both wild exploration and security blanket. She knew what having a piece of home with him would mean.

He nodded slowly. "Thank you. I think I *will* pack these."

Matías showed her around the rest of the studio, identifying the other pieces he had selected for his first exhibit in New York. Talking about art animated him, and Claire relished seeing Matías so vibrant, his eyes like fire, the tanned muscles of his arms flexing as he pointed out this and that in his paintings.

He was so different from his pale, drugged and battered counterpart at the hospital who was growing thinner and weaker by the day.

Lost in thought, she didn't notice when Matías veered to the right to avoid something she couldn't see.

"Claire, no!"

Matías lunged toward her, knocking her away from whatever it was he saw there. Momentum threw them against the wall, but her head didn't hit, because Matías instinctively cradled his arm around her and took the impact.

He held her pinned like that for a long moment, chest to chest, her face tucked into the crook of his neck. She could feel his quickened breath across her hair, his heart pounding against her body.

Claire gasped.

She wasn't supposed to be able to feel him.

Matías was not exactly solid, but he wasn't *not* there, either. His touch was the *impression* of him, like when Claire had closed her eyes and pressed her lips to her palm and it had felt like Matías was truly there. She'd been able to imagine the pressure of his mouth so viscerally—the velvet of his lips and the strong lines of his jaw—that it had felt almost real.

Just like right now. He was holding her, her back against the wall, and she could feel the phantom weight of his body against hers. He was warmer than the air in the rest of the studio, and that heat made Claire flush with the memory of other times when they had held their bodies so close.

In the humid greenhouse of the New York Botanical Garden. Pressed against a stone arch at the Met Cloisters. Behind a cotton candy stand on Coney Island.

But in the privacy of a studio, they could do even more. She wanted to kiss Matías's neck, run her hands down his back, slide them down and unbuckle his belt, and do the things she knew would make him have to brace himself on her shoulders.

"Claire," he whispered.

"Yes?"

He tilted her chin up with a finger. She met his molten gaze.

And then his lips met hers, his kiss a summer storm. If she closed her eyes, Claire could feel him, like wind and sun grazing her mouth. She recalled the taste of his tongue from their first kiss—almonds and brown sugar—and as she kissed this version of Matías who was not yet hers, she also missed the one who was, and tears streamed down her face, mixing salt with the memory of sweetness.

But then she remembered where he really was—in a coma, surrounded by never-ending beeping, an empty chair by his bed, waiting for her.

Suddenly, he pulled back, breathing hard, and brought his hand to his forehead.

"Matías! Are you okay?"

"I'm just . . . light-headed."

The blood drained from Claire's face. What if Matías had noticed that he was touching her, but couldn't quite feel her? If his soul realized something was off, it might sever his connection to this world.

"I think I'm going to lie down for a moment."

Claire moved to help him, then jumped away. She shouldn't touch him anymore. Professor Hong had been wrong about the ability to feel him, and now it was obviously having some kind of bad effect . . .

As Matías staggered to the couch and lowered himself onto it, Claire's phone rang.

The caller ID said *Aracely*.

No no no . . . Had something happened at the hospital because Claire touched Matías's soul?

The timing was too on point for it to be mere chance. But she couldn't answer the phone here, not in front of this Matías, not when it could be about Comatose Matías's condition. Claire couldn't let this Matías know about the accident.

What was she supposed to do? If Matías was in danger at the hospital, she had to get to him. And yet, his soul needed her, too. If Claire abandoned him in this state, what would happen?

On the couch, Matías moaned.

"Can I help?" Claire asked.

"I don't know," he said, his voice sounding thin. "It just hit me all of a sudden."

She came closer and noticed tiny beads of sweat at his temples. *Oh . . . could it be . . . ?*

"Matías, any chance you have issues with your blood sugar? Maybe you're a little hypoglycemic?"

Of course, Claire knew the answer was yes. Often, when Matías got too caught up in his work and forgot to eat, a wave of weakness would suddenly wallop him. He'd feel light-headed and clammy and start sweating.

"Uh, yes, actually, I do," Matías said, slowly sitting up. "Do you think you could grab the almendrados?"

Claire hurried to the worktable near the door and swept both her arms together in the area he had set the invisible bag of cookies earlier. She held her breath in hope that she'd actually picked it up with her awkward swoop.

As she returned to the couch, Matías reached out and seemed to take something from the crook of her right arm. "Thank you."

She exhaled in relief as he opened the invisible bag and popped an invisible almendrado into his mouth.

Her phone rang again.

Aracely.

Shit . . .

Claire's heartbeat pounded in her ears.

"Do you need to take that call?" Matías asked.

She shook her head.

"Are you sure? Because you don't have to babysit me. I'm already starting to feel better."

"I'll stay until you finish all the cookies," Claire said. At home, a hit of sugar usually solved his hypoglycemic episodes pretty quickly. He'd have to eat something more substantial afterward, but at least he wouldn't feel ill anymore.

Matías made a big show of eating the rest of the almendrados and then tipping the crumbs from the bag into his mouth. At least, that's what Claire thought he was doing. She couldn't actually see.

Her phone chimed with several text notifications, and then it rang again.

On the couch, Matías looked nearly solid now.

"Claire, take the call."

"Are you all right?"

"I'm fine. See?" He rose from the sofa and remained steady on his feet.

Her phone was still ringing.

"Okay. Then sorry. I have to go!" Claire ran toward the open door, taking a route along the perimeter of the studio to make sure she wouldn't plow through anything invisible.

But by the time she hurtled out of the building, Aracely had hung up.

Claire punched at her phone to call her back as she sprinted toward the subway.

She had to get to the hospital.

She had to know if, by recklessly touching Matías's soul, she'd stepped over an uncrossable line.

CLAIRE

~

SHE GOT ARACELY ON THE PHONE STEPS BEFORE THE SUBWAY entrance.

"Claire—"

"What happened?"

"We don't know! Luis and I were sitting with Matías and his brain and heart activity had been elevated again, in a good way. We thought maybe it was a sign that he would come out of the coma. But a few minutes ago, his heart rate shot up, past what it would even for someone who was sprinting, and all the alarms went off. The nurses kicked us out of the room and the doctors are coming."

"Oh god."

"Claire, you have to get back to the hospital."

"I just left Matías's studio. I'll be there as soon as I can."

THE SUBWAY RIDE FELT INTERMINABLE. IT SEEMED LIKE THE conductor stopped at every station longer than he had to, and just when the train was about to depart, a tardy passenger would inevitably come stampeding down the stairs, and do-gooder passengers would hold the doors open for thirty more precious seconds.

Come on, come on, come on, Claire thought. She paced the length of the car, constantly checking the subway map on the wall as if she could possibly will them to the next stations faster. But every time she did that, the train would inevitably slow down in the middle of the tunnel. Or it would take its sweet time cruising into a stop, and then just sit there, and sit there, and sit there. Probably waiting for some unseen traffic ahead to clear, but still.

She crammed in her earbuds and tried to listen to a Spanish language lesson. But Claire's mind would not focus. Verb conjugations and new vocabulary fluttered from the phone to her ears and then straight out into the train stations, not bothering to stick around in her head for even a second. Sentences she had understood at the end of the previous lesson yesterday at Matías's bedside now sounded like gibberish to her.

No, even less, because she hardly even registered the sounds; the worried chatter of her thoughts drowned all the Spanish out.

When they finally reached her stop, Claire flung herself out of the train and ran all the way to the hospital, shoving through people on the sidewalks, yelling "¡Perdón!" over and over while not really meaning it, because she didn't care how they felt. All she cared about was getting to Matías, and it had taken way too long.

She burst into the hospital and almost crashed into an orderly in the lobby. She barely managed to avoid him as she hurried onward, into the elevator, up to the third floor, and down the hall past the other wards.

As soon as she ran through the doors of Matías's unit, Soledad and Aracely descended on her, both crying, both gathering Claire into their arms.

"Oh god. Is it bad?" she choked out. Claire both wanted and *didn't* want to know what the doctors had concluded while she was stuck on the subway.

"We still don't know anything," Aracely said.

Tears spilled over onto Claire's cheeks, and she sagged against Soledad and Aracely. It wasn't relief, because they did know something had happened to Matías's heart. But at least it wasn't the awful news that Matías was dead.

Yet.

A pair of cardiologists emerged from Matías's room. The entire mass of the de León family surged toward them.

"¿Qué está pasando?" Armando asked.

The woman doctor spoke in rapid Spanish. Claire stood helpless, only able to scan the faces and body language of those around her to try to figure out what the doctor was saying. This was not the time to ask Aracely to explain.

Soledad crossed herself. Armando squeezed his eyes shut. Aracely held herself rigid, fighting to keep her composure. Luis walked away.

The rest of the de Leóns reflected the same range of reaction. But what was missing were relaxed sighs or people going to sit back down. Everyone remained on their feet as they began to ask the doctors questions.

Claire looked all around, hoping someone could explain what was going on.

But everybody around her was talking all at once in Spanish.

She turned and located Luis, who had separated himself from the crowd and was sitting with his head in his hands.

Claire sat down beside him.

"What's happening?" she asked quietly.

Luis didn't lift his head. But he let out a long exhale and said, "Matías might have had a heart attack."

"What?" Claire's own heart clutched.

He slowly looked up, as if it took great effort to peel his face from the hands. "They need to do more tests. I'm sorry, I don't know what they're called in English."

Claire let out a sob. "Why didn't I work harder at Spanish months ago, when I had the chance?"

Luis shrugged, just a sad, minute movement. "It probably would not make a difference. I started learning English when I was four years old, and I still don't know how to translate these medical things for you."

Claire gasped. *Translate.* She snatched her phone from her purse and began searching the app store for the translation program Vega had used this morning.

"Here," she said, holding her phone toward Luis. "Tell me what the doctor said. Please?"

He squinted at her phone. "What is it?"

"An app that does immediate speech translation. Vega showed me this morning."

"Huh. I didn't know that existed. But I guess Vega would know, so she could sell her work internationally. Her English is shit."

Claire sat back for a second. She knew Aracely detested Vega, but this was the first time Luis had spoken about her so strongly.

Luis pressed the record button and repeated what the doctor had reported. A moment later, the app said in English:

"Various measures of Matías's heart appeared abnormal. It could have been a heart attack or it could be something else.

They need to run more tests to figure out what happened. A nurse is going to do an EKG soon, and a lab tech will come to draw blood to check troponin levels. They are also going to send him in for an X-ray, and maybe a CT scan if the other tests don't show anything definitive."

"How long will all that take?" Claire asked.

"At least two hours, maybe more," Luis said. He studied the translation on the phone and nodded, absorbing the new terminology. "The EKG will be the fastest, but everything else takes time. Even if they get the blood soon, the lab must run the test."

Claire slumped in her seat. *She* had done this, by kissing Matías. Or kissing Matías's soul.

What was she going to do? Professor Hong had said Claire had to get Matías's soul to fall in love with her. Yet when they touched, it seemed to hurt the part of Matías she was trying to save.

But what if Professor Hong was wrong? After all, Claire's body hadn't gone straight through Matías's, as the professor had said it would.

She was an academic, her knowledge accumulated mostly from the anecdotal reports of others who had interacted with astral projections, because it was impossible to set up scientific studies on the subject. So everything Professor Hong said was conjecture. A well-educated guess, but still a guess.

How the hell was Claire supposed to know what to do then?

She wanted to punch something. But just as Claire began to ball her hand into a fist, she froze.

Could she bring Matías's soul here and reunite it with his body with simply the press of her palm?

Claire whirled and stared at the door to his room, which now hung open, the doctors having left to take care of whatever needed to be taken care of, and the de León family back in their seats in the waiting area, hugging each other. Soledad, Armando, and Aracely were nowhere to be seen, though; they must be inside with Matías.

But Professor Hong had explicitly warned Claire that she could not tell Matías's soul about the accident until he was ready. Even though Claire was no longer sure that the professor was right, that part still made sense—it would be a huge shock to Matías's soul to suddenly expose him face-to-face to his own battered body, covered in stitches and bruises and splints and casts for the thirty-seven broken bones.

And Claire could not risk that discord breaking the tenuous threads that connected Matías's soul to reality. Without the soul, Matías would die.

So Claire uncurled her fist. She just had to keep hold of hope and let the doctors run their tests and do what they could.

She took a shaky, deep breath and walked toward Matías's room. She kept her left hand splayed open and held away from her body, no longer making contact with anything. Just in case.

SOLEDAD KNEELED AT MATÍAS'S BEDSIDE, PRAYING. ARMANDO stood behind her, his hand on her shoulder. And Aracely sat in a chair, glaring at Matías. The nurses would probably let the three-visitor rule slide for a little while.

Claire assumed her place in the chair on the opposite side of the bed, the one the family always kept open for her. Guilt stabbed at her as she sat down, aware that the seat had been vacant too long. Matías needed her here. She knew that. But he also needed her out there, with his wandering soul.

For now, though, Claire settled in, intending to be at the hospital until visiting hours ended.

She cocked her head at Aracely. "Hey. Are you okay? Why are you . . . scowling at him?"

"I am angry at him for scaring us," Aracely said, her voice hot, but also shaking.

"Oh."

"He's my big brother. He is supposed to be strong. He is always supposed to be there, and I am supposed to be able to take him for granted. But look . . ." She glared harder at him.

Claire understood. When her parents had died, she'd been mad at them, too, in completely irrational ways. Mad that they'd been so eager to go on that stupid RV trip to Carhenge. Mad that they'd died without clearing it with her calendar first. Mad that they wouldn't be there to send her off to law school, to see her get married, to meet their grandkids.

Mad that they had left her all alone, again, in the world.

"I get it," Claire said to Aracely. "Sometimes, pain masquerades as anger, because you can *do* something about anger. Pain by itself just chips away at you until you're pockmarked with sorrow and regret. It's better to yell and kick and punch things instead."

"I feel like the doctors might be unhappy if I punched Matías," Aracely said with a grim laugh.

"I can find you a spare pillow if you want," Claire said.

A lab technician came in wheeling a mobile cart full of vials, needles, tourniquets, and other supplies. She said something in Spanish—Claire assumed telling the family she was going to take Matías's blood—then began the process of cleaning the bend of his elbow, one of the few places not covered in bandages and casts.

Claire bit her lip. Matías's skin there was mottled purple from all the times they'd poked him. She'd asked on the first day why they couldn't just insert an IV and take blood from there, but the answer was that some tests required sterile collection and that meant they had to be able to clean the skin first. Claire still wasn't sure why IVs weren't considered sterile, but she'd seen lab techs come and go in the days since, sometimes drawing blood through an IV, and other times from the very same beaten-up site that was being used right now.

She looked away during the process. She wasn't squeamish about blood itself, but watching them draw the literal life force from Matías's already weakened body was too much. He seemed so much smaller in the hospital bed; it was shocking how quickly muscles lost their tone, how swiftly a patient could lose weight.

As the lab tech was leaving, a nurse came in with a portable EKG machine. Aracely stood. "I can't be here anymore. I'm going to get some fresh air."

When the nurse opened the front of Matías's gown, Claire let out a cry. It was the first time since being at the hospital that she'd seen that part of him exposed. She knew there had been surgery to stop the bleeding in his internal organs, but now she could see the red welts and the thick black stitches from the incisions. The undignified patchwork shaving of the hair on his torso to clear his skin for the surgeries and heart monitor stickers, like a lawnmower had gone berserk. The slackness of his usually taut abs.

Oh god, Matías.

The rest of the afternoon went like that—nurses and lab techs in and out as more tests were ordered. They took X-rays. Couldn't see anything obvious. Ordered a CT scan of the heart.

The chief surgeon—Soledad and Armando's friend—returned with the cardiologist from before. Aracely and Luis were permitted in the room, even though it was crowded, to hear the results of what they'd found.

"Sus niveles de troponina están elevados, lo que indica estrés en el corazón," the cardiologist said.

Luis, who had learned the cardiac terminology from Claire's app earlier, translated quietly for her. "Matías's troponin levels were high, which means there was some kind of stress on his heart."

Claire felt the blood drain from her face. "¿Es malo?"

"Todavía es difícil de decir," the cardiologist said. "Su electrocardiograma también fue un poco anormal, pero la radiografía no mostró nada preocupante."

"It's still hard to say," Luis translated. "His EKG was also a little abnormal, but the X-ray did not show anything worrying."

"Yes, but that doesn't mean it's fine, does it? X-rays are hard to see. Isn't that why they ordered a CT scan?"

He asked the question. The cardiologist neither confirmed nor denied, just said they needed to wait for more information.

Soledad threw her arms into the air. "¿Por qué estamos esperando? ¡Su corazón podría sufrir daños irreversibles! Dale algún medicamento o algo. ¡Por favor!"

The surgeon—their friend—gathered Soledad into her arms, where Soledad broke into tears. The doctor explained that Matías's levels were all down to his coma baseline now—heart rate, blood pressure, pulse—so they didn't want to give him anything like a beta blocker that might suppress his heart too much. Cardiac medications were very powerful, but they also came with potential side effects. They didn't want to overshoot and cause him more harm than he had already suffered if they didn't have to.

Claire hadn't taken her eyes off Matías the whole time since the doctors arrived, even when she was asking questions. He really did look like his body couldn't take much more; she understood why the doctors wanted to balance precaution and care.

Still, the limbo of waiting was horrible.

Her phone buzzed. A text from Yolanda. It was around lunchtime in New York. Checking in. How are you?

Claire sighed. She desperately needed to hear from a friend. But Yolanda would have to wait.

At the hospital, Claire typed. Call you in a few hours?

Yolanda wrote back immediately. Ok. If I'm on another call, I'll drop. Something is happening here. We need to talk.

Matías

◡

Five Months Ago

Matías stood in his studio surveying the fortune cookie still life he was almost done with. He wanted to surprise Claire with this piece to celebrate their six months together, which would be right when she returned from the business trip she was currently on. The painting wouldn't be completely finished by then—it would still need to dry fully for a couple of months before he could varnish it—but at least she would get to see the gift now. He would build a custom frame for it, too, in whatever style she liked.

He picked up his palette and a mahl stick to brace his hand because he was going to do detail work today. The painting was of a fortune cookie split in half, connected by the white sliver of paper inside. He was going to add miniature versions of himself and Claire sitting on the fortune, having a picnic of Chinese takeout.

Matías referenced the sketch he'd taped up on the wall behind the easel, then grabbed several of his smallest brushes and wedged them between different fingers of his left hand. He could work faster this way with multiple colors of varying darkness—deep red for Claire's dress, rich brown for her hair, and a glowy peach for her face.

As he began to paint her, though, an unwelcome memory

also floated to the surface. Years ago, back in Madrid, he had done an enormous painting of him and his then fiancée, Vega. They had known each other since they were eighteen and starting art school, and Matías wanted to capture their journey of growing together as artists, as a couple, and as people. So he'd painted a piece where he was bringing her from faint ébauche to full color, and she was molding him out of clay, each forming the other as they themselves were being formed.

Matías cringed at the thought of where he'd put Vega's hands in the painting. The sex between them had loomed as such a significant part of their relationship because he'd been so young when he met her, and there was nothing that took up more space in the brain of an eighteen-year-old man than sex. But looking back now, he could see how their unrestrained physical passion blinded him to Vega's selfishness, her inability to give more than she took.

Vega was gorgeous, and she'd wielded that like a demand. She expected to be cut to the front of every line, to be given free drinks at every bar. If Matías wanted to go out, it was always on Vega's schedule, not his. And if she called him at four in the morning drunk at an all-night party she hadn't invited him to, she still expected him to get out of bed and come pick her up.

Claire, on the other hand, was beautiful in a quiet way. She did not use it as a weapon. Her beauty was there, but it wasn't the most important thing to her, and *that*, Matías thought, made her even more beautiful.

He brushed the oval of her face onto the painting. The tumbling chestnut waves of hair. Then he drew her body in a burgundy dress, and as the tip of the brush stroked every curve—breasts, waist, hips—his pulse quickened.

But unlike Vega, it wasn't just Claire's body that made Matías's heart race. It was the way she lit up when she saw him at the end of a long day. The way she always touched him when she walked by—just a light brush of the fingertips on the back of his neck or a hand pressed momentarily on his shoulder.

It was in how she made little moans of appreciation whenever he cooked, and how she'd bring him small gifts each time she saw something she thought he might like—a novel, a handbound sketchbook, a single stem of a beautiful flower.

It was how she listened to him. How she kept him from forgetting his appointments.

It was, most of all, her love.

CLAIRE

⌒

"HEY, HONEY, HOW'RE YOU HOLDING UP?" YOLANDA ASKED AS soon as they were connected on video. Unlike Claire, Yolanda was put together—cream-colored silk blouse, matching gold necklace and earrings, and I'm-a-powerful-woman red lipstick. She sat in her spacious office with Central Park views; Yolanda had been promoted to partner in Windsor & Black's employment law practice last year.

"I have only been worse one other time in my life," Claire said, slumped on her bed in the hotel. The camera shot an unflattering angle from her lap straight up her face, so that it looked like she was all double-chin and earlobes. She did not care.

Yolanda shook her head. "I'm so sorry. Does that mean Matías isn't getting better?"

"Possibly worse. Still unconscious, and he might have suffered a heart attack today. They don't know yet, though. The CT scan wasn't done early enough for the cardiology imaging team to read it, and after they do, the cardiologists themselves still have to weigh in. So we won't know anything until late tomorrow morning, at the earliest."

"Oh, Claire."

"Yeah."

They just sat on the video call without saying anything for a minute, doing what girlfriends did best—being there for one another, even if nothing could be fixed.

Finally, though, Claire broke the heavy silence. "Distract me. You said something was happening. I presume at our office? What's going on?"

Yolanda toyed with her earring, which was a tell Claire was all too familiar with.

"That bad?" Claire asked.

"Maybe, maybe not," Yolanda said. "It's just that, there's been some grumbling among the partners about your sudden departure two weeks before the Intelligentsia deal is about to close."

"What?" Claire sat straight up in bed. "I'm in the middle of an emergency! Even then, I logged in and answered questions from the team as soon as I could after I landed here. I've tried to check in once a day, and I've only been gone a few days!"

"I know," Yolanda said, sighing. "You are a human being, and everything you're saying is logical and should be more than sufficient to excuse your absence. You shouldn't *have* to log in and do any work, either. But you know how Big Law is. The only acceptable excuse to be away from the office is if you're on maternity leave, and even then, the assholes talk about you. I mean, remember what happened to Gemma Tanaka?"

"I still can't believe they fucking put in her review that they questioned her 'commitment to the firm' just because she decided to start a family."

"Me, neither, and yet I wasn't surprised at all. She spoke openly to our mentor before she went on maternity leave, musing about how life would change with a baby. But she was naive to think that women could be honest with the people who are supposed to be guiding their careers."

"Well," Claire said. "At least she came back from leave with a vengeance and showed them."

"Yeah, but she had to work twice as hard to 'earn back' her reputation. Jason keeps asking when we can have a baby, but I'm terrified that there's never a good time. A lot has gotten better for women in the workplace, but there is still so goddamn much to be done."

"Hear, hear."

"But enough about that," Yolanda said. "This is about you. I'm worried because I've seen how hard it is to bounce back once the partners start muttering about you."

Claire sagged into the pillows again. "What am I supposed to do, though? I can't run the merger from here. I need to be with Matías. Fuck, Yolanda! Less than a week away from the office, and they're already stabbing me in the back? Which partner is it? Not Bill. Tell me it's not Bill."

Bill Nguyen was the senior partner on the deal. He was a rainmaker for Windsor & Black; his client list included big hitters in the tech world like Intelligentsia. He had also been the one who recognized Claire's talent for project management in her very first year out of law school. It was under Bill's wing that she'd been given the opportunities to rise to such high esteem at the firm.

"Not Bill, but he's not the only partner involved in the merger. Mitch Tahir is putting up a huge stink about your bailing on his deal, and it's making the firm nervous that they'll lose him as a client."

"They didn't defend me? They didn't tell Mitch why I left?"

"It's a personal matter. It's up to you whether to disclose it to Intelligentsia."

"Shit." Claire pounded her fist on the bed. "I'll email him right after we're done."

But it wasn't only that. Claire—like all attorneys in the harshly competitive world of Big Law—knew that showing any sign of weakness would be interpreted as a character flaw. Like right now: Her career was in jeopardy because her boyfriend had dared to get in an accident. She was supposed to be able to handle both flawlessly, as a sign of someone good under pressure. It was inhumane.

Claire clenched her jaw as she thought of how she'd bent over backward for the firm. No, she'd done the equivalent of legal triple backflips—getting up in the middle of the night to lead calls with Intelligentsia subsidiaries based in India, waking up early to coordinate with the European law firms working on regulatory approvals, and sometimes not going home at all and dozing for just a couple of hours in a sleeping bag under her desk so she could be available for crucial, time-sensitive documents that had to be reviewed and turned around as soon as they hit her inbox.

"I didn't *bail*," Claire said.

"I know," Yolanda said.

And that was the crux of it. Facts didn't matter. Reasonability didn't matter. In the cutthroat world of prestigious international law firms, the partners lived in terror that their high-paying clients would leave them. Hence, the beginnings of talk about Claire and her departure during the apex of the biggest corporate deal for the year for Windsor & Black.

All of her hard work for a decade could spiral down the drain in the span of a few days. She was *this* close to making partner. But it had hinged on successfully leading Intelligentsia's billion-dollar acquisition of Einstein Corp.

Claire swallowed. "Are they trying to replace me?"

"Mia Kovač is gunning for your role."

"She's not even *on* this deal!"

"She's a shark."

"And she smells my blood in the water." Claire slid all the way down into the covers. Her computer fell off her lap and face-planted onto the bed.

"Claire?"

She righted the laptop, the camera now showing a close-up of her squished face half blocked by the duvet. "I wish you could run the deal for me."

"Me, too," Yolanda said. "But I'm a specialist, not a general corporate maestro like you. They wouldn't let me helm the Intelligentsia merger even if I begged. I'll do what I can for you among the partnership, though. Not sure how much they'll listen, since I'm a brand-new junior partner. But you know that Bill and I will stand up for you."

Claire closed her eyes, wanting to just go to sleep instead of deal with another problem.

But being an attorney in Big Law meant you had to be "on" all the time. You had to be superhuman, with thick armor to block any emotions that might try to attack you. And she had worked too hard and for too long to lie down without a fight when she was on the cusp of finally grabbing the brass ring of partnership.

She opened her eyes, pushed away the covers, and sat up.

"I guess I'd better log in, then, email Mitch, and catch up on what's going on," Claire said.

"You shouldn't have to," Yolanda said.

"Agreed. But *shouldn't have to* is different from *don't have to*."

CLAIRE

⟿

From: clairewalker@windsorblackllp.com
To: mitch.tahir@intelligentsia.tech
RE: Personal Update

Dear Mitch,

I'm sorry that you've been kept out of the loop. I thought the firm would let you know why I've been less available, but they didn't do so for privacy reasons.

The short version is, my boyfriend was in a terrible accident, and he is currently in a coma. I'm at his bedside in the hospital in Madrid.

Although I may not be able to respond to messages immediately, I am still here to help make sure the closing of your merger runs smoothly. I value my work with you and Intelligentsia, and I want you to know that you can count on me.

—Claire

From: mitch.tahir@intelligentsia.tech
To: clairewalker@windsorblackllp.com
RE: Personal Update

Claire,

I am so sorry to hear what you are going through, and I apologize for my irascible behavior.

I recently went through something similar with my wife. Thankfully, she recovered, but I know that watching a loved one suffer is one of the most difficult things you will ever encounter.

You should not even be thinking about work right now. But of course, I would never prescribe advice that I could not follow myself; I understand how work can sometimes be a comforting distraction. But just remember that at the end of the day, it is only stacks of paper, not life.

Do take care, and I will keep your boyfriend in my prayers.

—Mitch

Matías

~

As soon as Matías walked into his apartment, Claire popped her head out of his bedroom.

"There you are!" She was dressed impeccably in a black sheath dress with her hair up in a sleek bun. "Where have you been?"

"I was playing volleyball on the sand courts." He tried to dart in for a kiss, but she dodged.

"Matías! Your shoes!"

He looked down. "What?"

"You're tracking sand all over the place. I thought we were taking our shoes off at the door."

"Oh, right." He backtracked to the entrance and kicked off his shoes. More sand flew out. Claire sighed, even though this was *his* apartment and he didn't care about the sand. But she wanted things to be nice for him, and he understood and actually appreciated it. It was just that she had so many little rules about everything, and it was hard to remember them all.

"Volleyball wasn't on your calendar," Claire was saying.

"I know, but as I was leaving my studio, Lawrence called and asked if I wanted to play, so I thought, why not?"

"Why not?" Claire threw her arms in the air. "Because my firm is hosting its big summer welcome dinner for the law school interns at Le Bernadin tonight, and it starts in half an hour!"

"*Coño,*" Matías cursed. "I forgot. I'm so sorry. I'll change quickly and—"

"No, you can't go like that. You're covered in sunscreen and your hair is all sweaty. Matías . . ." Claire's voice shifted then from angry to desperate. "I'm up for partner soon. I can't . . . You can't . . ." Her whole body trembled.

"Hey, hey, churri, shhh. It's okay. I know. I messed up, and I'm sorry." He stepped toward her to hug her, but then remembered he was in his sandy workout clothes.

Claire hung her head, still shaking. "I have to go. Just . . . please shower and look nice and come as soon as you can, okay?"

Matías tilted her chin up so she was looking at him. "I will. And I'll make this up to you, I promise."

HOT WATER CASCADED OVER MATÍAS'S BODY AS HE SHAM-pooed his hair as fast as he could. He had to rein himself in. At the start of their relationship, Claire had been patient with his impulsiveness and tendency to forget appointments, but now that they'd been together for ten months, he knew that that part of his personality was beginning to wear on her.

He didn't want Claire to get annoyed at him, like his sister did when he was still living in Madrid and she would have to check up on him to make sure he hadn't disappeared into his work and abandoned his other responsibilities. It was one thing for Aracely to feel that way, because she was related to him by blood and couldn't leave him. It was another thing entirely if he was starting to irritate Claire.

Because he wanted to spend his life with her. He'd known it early on, but as time passed, he'd only grown more sure. They were opposites, but they were beautiful together, like the moon and its reflection in a lake.

Unlike Vega, who'd been much more like Matías but amplified a thousandfold.

In retrospect, he never should have stayed with Vega that long. But after being engaged for well over a decade, Matías had just accepted that that was how his life looked. Vega was tempestuous and self-absorbed, but that was also what made her sculptures unique. A lot of artists were egocentric and prone to excess.

But when Matías was invited to come to the United States, and Vega reacted not by finally committing to marry him, but by sliding the black onyx engagement ring off her finger, Matías finally saw her clearly. Vega did not support his career. Vega would never sacrifice her own wants for his. And Vega's penchant for burning things down in an outburst of melodrama was the opposite of what Matías needed, because he, too, could sometimes become so absorbed in the art coming to life in his head that he disconnected from reality. He needed someone with two feet on the ground, and Vega wasn't it.

"Keep it," she'd said of the onyx ring. "Maybe you can reuse it for a nice American girl."

Matías's heart had been broken and stomped on, but he'd known he would never hold on to that ring, that he'd never give it to someone else. He asked Carlos to sell it for him, and Carlos had taken care of it the next day. Then Matías and his friends went out and spent all of Vega's ring money on enough beer to drown his sorrows for a week.

But that was then, when Matías had felt his entire life in flux. Now he had Claire, who was like a steady clock keeping time, helping Matías from getting too lost as he flitted around in the world.

She was drifting away, though. He had to find a way to bring her back.

I'll propose, he thought as the hot water rinsed the shampoo from his hair. *Why wait? I want to spend the rest of my life with her.*

Immediately, he began to design the ring in his head—a sparkling sun made up of a round diamond in the center and tapered topazes around it like flames, because he would give Claire all the stars from the sky if he could, but at the very least, she could have the sun.

It would be perfect. They were planning to visit Spain next month. She would meet his family in person, and also his best friends. He would show her all the best places in Madrid, just like she'd introduced him to New York. And then, while on the Teleférico—the cable car that crosses the city with panoramic views from above—he would get down on one knee and ask Claire to marry him.

And hopefully, she would say sí.

CLAIRE

CLAIRE STARTLED AWAKE AT THE SOUND OF HER PHONE RINGing. She had fallen asleep on her keyboard—when was that, 4:30 A.M.? Five?—and for a moment, she didn't know where she was, because waking up from a late night of work in a hotel room was par for the course for her job, and she could have been in any city, working on any deal.

But the second ring of her phone jolted her back to Madrid, 9:30 A.M.

Matías!

She lunged for her cell, barely glancing at the screen before answering. "Aracely?"

"It was not a heart attack."

"Oh, thank god." All the air in Claire's lungs rushed out in a relieved gush. "So his heart is okay?"

"The CT scan looks fine, and they just did another EKG and that is also fine. They are going to continue to monitor him. Something caused stress on Matías's heart. They don't know what it was, but his heart is stable for now."

It was me, Claire thought. *I caused stress on his heart by kissing him.*

But maybe it was just like the other times when she was with Matías's soul, which raised the heart activity in the real Matías.

It was just that the touching—the kissing—was *too* much stimulation, and it had crossed the line from good elevation to something that worried the doctors.

So she couldn't touch him again.

Yet there was something else to consider, too. Matías's soul was getting progressively more solid every time Claire met him.

It must be working. She was connecting with him, and it was strengthening his attachment to this world.

But now that she knew the physical part of Matías was stable at the hospital, Claire would need to find his soul and apologize for running out of the studio yesterday. She also needed to come up with an excuse for why they couldn't touch.

"Claire, are you coming to the hospital?" Aracely asked. "My mother is asking about you."

"I'm sorry, I just woke up," Claire said. "There's something I need to take care of this morning, but I promise I will be there later."

CLAIRE WENT BACK TO THE SAME CAFÉ FROM YESTERDAY, where Matías had appeared. She also sat at the same table on the patio. Sameness hadn't worked at the drink kiosk, but Claire was running on fumes, and it was the best she could come up with.

A waitress came over, and Claire—who knew she had to practice speaking Spanish if she wanted to get better at it—took a deep breath and said slowly, "Buenos días. Un café con leche, por favor."

"Vale," the waitress said. "¿Y algo para comer?"

Claire replayed the question in her head, parsing out the

words. She got three out of four, and thankfully, they were the critical ones.

Y = and. *Para* = for. *Comer* = eat.

Unfortunately, she wasn't literate enough yet to read the menu, and she didn't want to order churros con chocolate because, try as she might, Vega's description of Matías feeding them to her was too vivid for Claire to fend off before she'd had coffee. However, she had learned another trick from her language app—a lot of English words ending in -tion sounded almost the same in Spanish, except they ended in -ción.

"¿Una recomendación?" Claire asked the waitress. "Una sorpresa, por favor." *A recommendation? A surprise, please.*

The waitress smiled. "Okay," she said, which needed no translation.

The coffee came a few minutes later, and Claire sipped it while looking out onto the sidewalks and the street, although she didn't actually see any of it; her thoughts were on Matías.

What should she tell him about touching?

Maybe she could say that there was something in her past that made her shy? It was true, in a sense. After her parents died, Claire couldn't stand to be hugged or for anyone to express affection for her. Love and strong arms were the purview of family, and since Jim and Sarah had been taken away from Claire, she didn't want anyone else to taint the memory of their tenderness. It had taken all three years of law school for her to get over it, but finally, when she graduated, she'd felt sufficiently re-armored to go back out into the normal world. Her law school roommate had given her a hug that day, and Claire hadn't felt like throwing up.

But while this was information she could share with *her* Matías—actually, he already knew it—it was a lot to drop on the *other* Matías, who was still quite new to her. Besides, no one wanted to be with someone who showed up to their second date (or fourth run-in) with all their baggage already opened and dumped across the floor, right? And the point of this was for Claire to get him to fall in love with her, so he would feel compelled to rejoin this reality to be with her, and then Matías would wake up.

Or *was* the goal to make him fall in love with her? That had been one of Professor Hong's assumptions. But the professor had not anticipated that Claire's spending time with Matías's soul would make him more and more solid, to the point where Matías could throw her across his studio, pin her to a wall, and kiss her.

What if Claire didn't have to make Matías fall all the way in love with her? What if she just had to spend enough time with him that their link grew stronger? After all, that seemed to have had beneficial results so far, other than the kiss, which was admittedly getting Claire hot just thinking about it. No wonder it had sent Matías's heart into overdrive.

The waitress returned to the table with a steaming plate. "Migas," she said, pointing at the dish.

Claire smiled. She knew migas—fried cubes of bread, chorizo, bacon, and garlic—because Matías had made it for her before.

"Delicioso, gracias," Claire said as the plate was set in front of her.

"¿Más café?" the waitress asked, gesturing at the empty coffee mug.

"Sí, uno más, por favor."

Claire took a moment to savor the smell of her breakfast. There was nothing like a rich, hearty meal after a long night. For a lot of people, this would be hangover food. For Claire, it was post-working-till-5 A.M. food.

She moaned at the first bite and closed her eyes. The flavors melded on her tongue—rich meatiness and spice and garlic and olive oil—tossed together with the crunch of the croutons. Even though Claire had never been to Spain before, this food tasted like home. It was one of many things Matías cooked for her, and she missed it, missed him. She wanted to eat in slow motion, linger over every mouthful.

Her eyes flickered open. *That's it!*

"I want to take it slow."

That's what she would tell Matías. She knew that if she said something like that, he would respect it. He was the kind of man who cared and listened.

The progression would be the opposite of how their relationship in New York had started, with impulsive, fiery love made on the law library floor. Claire hoped she would be enough of an enticement without that kind of physical passion. She hadn't wanted to think about Vega, but the fact was, this version of Matías was coming off a breakup with his fiancée of fifteen years.

Hell, the Matías who had fallen in love with Claire in New York had been, too.

But I can't touch him without risking his life, she thought. *So I have no choice.*

This would have to do.

As she finished eating her breakfast, she thought over the

plan of telling Matías she liked him but needed to go slow phys-ically. It wasn't what she *wanted*—Claire would replay that kiss in the studio over and over in her mind for the rest of her life—but what she wanted even more was for her real, corporeal Matías to wake up and heal and be with her again.

"Okay," she said as she polished off the last of the migas and drained her second coffee. "I'm ready. *Lista.* Let's do this thing."

She steeled herself with a calming breath, then pressed her fingers to her left palm.

Business continued as usual on the street. There was nobody she knew.

Claire frowned. She flexed and unflexed the fingers on both hands, then tried again, holding the pressure on her palm in place.

She sat like that for five entire minutes, scanning the side-walk and the entrance to the café the entire time, to no avail.

Matías? she thought, trying the visualization technique that some of Yolanda and Jason's art world friends swore by. (Lawyers usually didn't believe that woo-woo stuff, but that was before Claire began dating her boyfriend's soul.)

Still, no Matías.

Claire's gaze darted around the tables nearby. There was an elderly gentleman reading a print newspaper. A couple of moth-ers chatting while rocking their babies' strollers back and forth. A businesswoman in a suit, typing into her phone.

No one to judge Claire as she brought her open palm to her lips and kissed it . . .

She thought of Matías' mouth, soft and hot at the same time, on hers.

Of his hands, roving over her bare skin.

ONE YEAR AGO IN SPAIN | 219

Of the way their bodies crushed closer, as if they could never be near enough, as if there were a way to occupy the same space.

She let the kiss and the daydream linger for a long moment, like the feeling of sun on your skin after a summer day.

Then she opened her eyes, expectant.

There was no one there besides the people from before. And the old man with the newspaper was looking at her now in grandfatherly concern, his two bushy eyebrows raised.

"Shit," Claire said. Why wasn't it working? Matías had always appeared before when she pressed on that spot on her hand.

She stayed at the café for another hour, repeating the process of pushing on her palm. She tried pouring coins in. Cradling another cup of coffee. Stabbing at it with a pen she borrowed from the waitress.

But no Matías.

Finally, Claire had to give up so she could get to his bedside. If she couldn't be with Matías's wandering soul, then she needed to be with his stationary body.

Claire choked on the thought of him as just an unmoving mass of flesh and bones.

No, he's more than that. So much more.

She threw down more money than she owed for the breakfast and hurried over to the hospital.

IN HOSPITALS, BORING IS GOOD. AFTER THE TERRIBLE EVENING over Matías's heart, it was a sad but welcome relief for Claire just to sit next to him.

Tía Juanita and Tío Victor rose from their places on the opposite side of the bed. They had been there for an hour, and Abuela Gloria had been there for an hour before that, singing to him; it was someone else's turn now. Claire marveled at the dedication of the de León family. For every minute of visiting hours, there were people in this room, making sure Matías could feel their love and know that, on this side of consciousness, plenty of people cared and longed for him to return.

She had never had a big family. Claire didn't even remember her biological parents, who'd died before she had memories that stuck. And then her new family had been small. Brimming with love, but just their little trio.

What would it have been like to grow up surrounded by so many relatives? To know that if you fell, so many hands were ready to pick you up again?

Traitor, Claire thought. She had been lucky to have Jim and Sarah. Some of the other kids in her foster home never got a permanent place to stay, let alone became adopted. They bounced from house to house, year after year, until they turned eighteen and were spit out into the world still completely alone.

At least Claire had had a family once.

Aracely and Soledad stepped into Matías's room. Claire smiled upon seeing them.

Soledad did not smile back. "Where have you been?"

"I . . . I had to work late because of the time difference," Claire said. "So I overslept. And then I had to take care of something before I could get here. I mentioned it to Aracely."

Soledad dropped into her seat heavily, arms crossed. "You should not be working while you are here."

"I know. But my job—"

"Americans are married to their jobs. But a job is not a life."

Claire pursed her lips. She knew that. Everyone knew that. But she also loved her job—the excitement of working on deals that made headlines, the adrenaline spike of juggling so many expensive balls in the air at once and not dropping them, of knowing that without you, none of it would be happening. That you were the wizard behind the curtain.

It's true that Americans were often workaholics to the detriment of other facets of their lives. But Claire also knew that she didn't want the fantasy that so many others dreamed of—sitting around with nothing but leisure time. She would drive herself (and Matías) bonkers within a month if she didn't have a high-intensity goal to work toward.

But Claire didn't want Soledad and Aracely to think she was absent just because of work. They were the only family she had right now—even if she wasn't officially part of them yet—and she needed them to understand that she *was* trying to help Matías.

Would they believe her?

She didn't know. But she had to try.

"I've . . . been spending time with Matías's soul," Claire blurted. "Outside the hospital. That's why I haven't been here."

Aracely and Soledad looked blankly at her.

Claire swallowed and tried again. "I think . . . his consciousness is detached. But he came to me at my hotel, and I've talked to him. So that's why I haven't been here. I feel like I need to spend time with Matías's soul, to try to get him to reconnect with this reality—"

"Enough," Soledad said. "I don't want to hear such nonsense excuses."

"But, I—"

Aracely shook her head. "This is a rough time for all of us, Claire. I know it's hard, and I'm sorry. But if you want to help Matías, you have to get yourself together."

"He is right here," Soledad said. "Not a ghost at your hotel."

Claire's eyes stung. "I didn't mean that he was a ghost. I'm not making this up—"

"Tomorrow morning," Aracely said, giving Claire a sad look like she was sorry that Claire was losing her mind, "we are all going to a gathering to remember Carlos and Diego—*el evento conmemorativo*. They were like brothers to Matías. He was always at their homes, and they were always at ours. They have been around for as long as I can remember, and they were like brothers to me."

Claire swiped at the tears threatening to spill over. It had been a long shot to tell Aracely and Soledad about Matías, but they hadn't even given her a chance. They had written Claire off as easily as someone shrugs off the tall tales that little kids tell, and she felt more like an outsider than ever.

And yet Claire had to stay in their good graces. Soledad and Aracely controlled access to Matías.

"Evento conmemorativo tomorrow morning," Claire repeated. "Of course. I'll be there."

"No," Soledad said. "You will be *here*. In that chair." She jabbed her finger where Claire sat.

"Oh." Claire's body shook as she tried to hold on to her pride while also bending to Soledad's will. "Um, okay. I thought Aracely meant she wanted me to come to the evento conmemorativo, but of course I'll stay with Matías."

"He is your life," Soledad said, shaking her head. "You were supposed to come to Spain *with* him. You stayed in New York for your job instead. But he was going to ask you to marry him. Did you know that, Claire?"

"I did . . ." In her shock at being scolded so harshly, Claire hadn't been prepared to lie.

Aracely let out a tiny gasp. "You did? And you chose not to come?"

Claire looked down at the linoleum. "I made a mistake."

"And you are still making mistakes," Soledad said. "My Matías is here, suffering, every minute, every second. The rest of the family is here, every minute, every second, that we are allowed. But where are you? Working? Sleeping? Visiting an empty studio and looking for a ghost?"

"I—"

"I do not know what you are searching for, Claire," Soledad said, "but it is not out there."

CLAIRE

As soon as visiting hours were over, Claire fled the hospital and the watchful eyes of Soledad and Aracely. The de Leóns had not invited her over for dinner, even though her Spanish was decent enough after being immersed here for almost a week to understand—very generally—that they had been making plans among themselves.

Not that Claire would have wanted to go. She desperately wanted to be part of their family, but she also needed to get far, far away.

Oh, Matías, she thought. *This was not how I wanted it to be the first time I met your family. I'm sorry for screwing it up. I'm trying really hard, though . . .*

If only you were here to help me navigate all this. You could tell me what to do, and you could translate into proper Spanish because I feel like I'm missing nuances.

And there is so much you wanted to show me of your hometown, but now I'm here by myself. I don't know what to do in my off-hours when I'm not with you.

I'm just . . . alone.

Four blocks after Claire left the hospital, Matías suddenly appeared by her side.

"Holy fuck!"

"Sorry, didn't mean to scare you," Matías said.

"You . . . I . . . Never mind. I'm, um, fine," she said while glancing at her hand.

Her fingers were curled up, the nails pressing hard into her palm.

So it had worked now, but not before. Why?

But Claire also didn't care. She exhaled and let the tense muscles around her shoulders relax a little because Matías was here. His soul hadn't disintegrated after she kissed him and left him on the sofa in his studio.

And his presence also meant she could *do* something other than get chastised by his family. She *could* help bring Matías back, for all of them.

"What were you doing at the hospital?" he asked, walking beside her as she headed toward the subway station.

"Um . . . I was visiting . . . a colleague. He fell ill."

"Will he be okay?" Matías asked.

"I hope so."

"Were those the phone calls you got in my studio and why you ran off?"

Claire bit her lip and nodded. Sure, why not? That was a reasonable explanation, even if it was based on the lie she'd just told.

"Good," Matías said. "I mean, not good that your colleague isn't well! I am very sorry to hear that. What I meant was I thought maybe you left yesterday because I kissed you and made it awkward . . ." He smiled shyly at her, and warm shivers tremored through Claire's body because it was the same hopeful smile he'd given her on their first date in New York, when he'd showed up at the firm with dinner. Part of what made Matías so damned irresistible was the combination of his broad-shouldered ruggedness with his ever-buoyant, boyish charm. Even having been with him for almost a year, Claire still melted now, and it helped her shift from the hospital mode of being beaten down to the hope that there might be a future for Matías.

"It was a *great* kiss," Claire said, blushing. "But . . ."

"Uh-oh."

"I like you, Matías. A lot. And I want to get to know you more while we're both still in Madrid, if that's okay. I don't want to wait until you move to New York. But I want to do it the old-fashioned way—a slow burn if you will."

"So I can't kiss you right now?" he asked. "Because the way the lamplight is hitting the angles on your face, it makes me want to paint you."

Claire laughed. "That is a terrible line! Do you use that on all the women?"

Matías grinned. "I blame my English for the bad joke."

"Your English is perfect."

"Not when the jokes are bad. Then it's a translation problem, for sure."

Claire laughed again. God, it felt so good to do that, and with her favorite person, too.

"To answer your question," she said, "I *want* to kiss you, but I prefer if we don't. I think there's something romantic about old movies, where the guy and the girl go on dates and fall for each other's minds and personalities, rather than just their bodies. Where the women wear gloves and collars up to their chins, and no one touches until the very end of the film."

She knew this was the opposite of how they had started, making love impulsively on the law library carpet. And the opposite of the very carnal relationship he'd had with Vega, if the painting in his studio was any indication.

But it was the only way she could think of to keep his interest while not breaking that tenuous connection from his inbetween state to her reality.

"Hmm," Matías said, running his hand through his hair, leaving the waves a mess. Just the way Claire loved it.

"I seem to recall," Matías said, "that in those olden days, even seeing the back of a neck or the skin on ankles was scandalous. Maybe we don't have to go *quite* that far? Because I do like you in that ponytail today."

Claire's hand instinctively went up to her hair and the nape of her neck.

He winked.

She felt her skin flush again.

"Fine," Claire said. "But when you do fall for me, it better be for my mind first."

"Deal," Matías said. "And maybe then you'll let me see your ankles?"

She snorted, then covered her mouth at the noise. "Pretend you didn't hear that. So, uh, what are you doing right now?"

"Taking a beautiful woman to see Madrid at night, I hope."

With the late sunsets of summer, the Palacio Real— the official residence of Spain's royal family and the largest palace in Continental Europe—basked in soft evening light. There were some tourists here and there, but most must not have realized that although the interior of the palace was closed at this hour, the grounds surrounding it were open until 10 P.M.

"I can't believe people actually live in a place this grand," Claire said, admiring the columns and sculptures of the baroque palace.

"I hate to shatter your fantasy, then," Matías said. "The Palacio Real is mostly used for ceremonial functions."

Claire frowned. "But the sign at the front said it was the royal family's home."

"Official residence in Madrid," Matías said. "But they rarely live in this city."

"Ah. So many castles, so little time."

Matías laughed. "I would not be upset to have that problem."

She shook her head. "I don't think you'd like owning so much real estate. Too much of a logistical headache. Think of the property maintenance and annual gardening fees for several castles. I mean, look at this place." Claire swept her arm in an arc around her, at all the carefully manicured trees and hedges and flowers.

"You haven't even seen the palace gardens yet," Matías said.

"My point exactly! You'd need to employ an army of gardeners. Ugh, and if I start to contemplate the international tax implications—"

"Who looks at a palace and immediately wonders how much tax is owed?" Matías said, the corners of his eyes crinkled up in laughter.

Claire snorted again, and this time she didn't bother trying to cover it up. "I can't help it. I'm a lawyer through and through."

Matías stopped in the middle of the plaza and just looked at her.

"What?" Claire said.

"Nothing."

"No, really, what?" She glanced over her shoulder, but there was nothing there. He was definitely looking at her.

"You are very down-to-earth," Matías said. "Different from most of my friends and . . . other people I know."

Claire was pretty sure he was referring to Vega, who at this point in time for him would be a very recent ex-fiancée.

"I can't help it," Claire said. "I am who I am."

"It's not a bad thing!" Matías said. "I probably need more of it in my life. I am the kind of person who will forget the basics if I'm in the middle of painting. When I was young, my mother or my sister, Aracely, would knock on my door at mealtimes and I would be shocked to find out that ten hours had passed since the last time I ate. But now that I'm an adult, I can lose entire days if I am inside the flow of painting."

Claire nodded but closed her eyes for a moment. Because she already knew this about him, and even though she was enjoying herself on this date, it was also painful because *he* didn't know that they already knew each other, already loved each other, already had so many memories.

She already knew that Matías was brilliant and talented but absentminded with no sense of time. She would ask him to do something like take out the trash, and he would earnestly say "in a minute," but then four hours later, it would still be overflowing while he was sketching out a new idea or picking out a new tune on his ukulele or playing a seventh game of online chess.

It had been driving her crazy the last few months. But here in Madrid, knowing that he might die, it was so clear that *she* had been the one who was wrong. Just like Claire couldn't help being hyperorganized and having a brain that was mapped onto a calendar grid, Matías couldn't help that he hurled himself into whatever he was doing. It's what made him a beautiful, successful artist. But the same ability to leap into a deep pond of his imagination when painting also meant that he leaped into everything else as fully—chess, sketching, playing the ukulele—and small mundane concerns like trash sometimes got forgotten.

Every person had a price of admission. Claire had read that in a relationship advice book years ago but hadn't understood it until now. The price of admission for being with Claire was putting up with her type-A need for control. The price of admission for being with Matías was accepting he could *not* be controlled.

She opened her eyes and smiled at him. "I don't understand how you can forget to eat—because I literally write meals onto my calendar—but I like that you can be so into what you're doing that it completely transcends basic needs."

He smirked. "I don't think my mom and sister would agree with your assessment of me, but thank you. That's a very generous way of interpreting . . . me."

"I think the world would be a better place if we all interpreted each other a little more generously."

"Including ourselves," Matías said.

They walked around the Palacio Real, through the wide-open plazas, and eventually made it to the Sabatini Gardens. Funny how it had originally been on Claire's list of "things to do," but it only happened when she didn't plan for it. The sun was setting now, and a long reflecting pool mirrored the palace and the pastel sky like a deeply saturated watercolor. "It's so beautiful," Claire murmured, turning back and forth between the shimmering image in the reflecting pool and the actual Palacio Real and sky.

"This was one of the earliest scenes I painted when I was in grade school," Matías said. "I didn't know anything yet about mixing colors or technique, but I still remember how every brushstroke felt like magic, you know? At first, there was only blank white paper in front of me. But then I sketched out the shape of the palace and the long, rectangular pool and the silhouettes of the trees, and then I added paint—layers and layers of it until the paper was warped from the moisture and weight. It was a childish rendition of a Palacio Real sunset, but painting it was a pure experience."

"Unfettered joy," Claire said, thinking that that was also a perfect description for Matías himself.

"Well, that used to be my philosophy for what life should be," he said as he started walking into the gardens. "But now I think that sometimes, guardrails are good."

"Oh?" Claire followed him along the path.

"Yes. You cannot live in the pursuit of hedonism alone. You cannot run over everyone in your way and rearrange everyone else's lives to suit your own." He whacked lightly at a hedge. "There must be compromise."

Vega, Claire thought.

"But joy and hedonism aren't necessarily the same things," she said. "I think you can shoot for unfettered joy while still being responsible."

Matías thought that over as they continued deeper into the gardens toward a large fountain. "Perhaps you're right. But it is like playing with fire. If you are going to do it, you should be sure to have some water nearby."

Is that what I am? Claire thought. *The water to his fire?* Maybe he and Vega had both been flames, and two together eventually burned out of control. Maybe that was why, when Matías moved to New York, he had been drawn to someone as reined in as Claire.

I am an excitement killer, she thought. *Awesome.*

And yet it was the closest she'd come to a reason why someone like Matías would be with someone like her.

When the sun dipped below the horizon, Claire asked, "What are we going to do next?"

Matías wrinkled his forehead. "What do you mean?"

"You said you were going to show me Madrid at night. And now it's dark; therefore, officially night."

"Ah, excellent point. Well then, let's see. Are you hungry?"

"No!"

She couldn't let Matías take her to a restaurant. What would he do, eat ghost food while she ate real food? But even if he didn't notice that he wasn't actually eating, it wouldn't escape his notice that she was only ordering enough food from the waiter for one person. She certainly wasn't going to order an entire bottle of wine just for herself.

And oh god, even the moment of walking into the restaurant, if the host asked whether she was a party of one . . .

"That was very emphatic," he said. "But are you sure? I thought I heard your stomach growling back by the hedge maze. We could stop for tapas."

"I'm not hungry at all," she lied.

No dinner. Absolutely not.

"Okay, if you're not hungry," he said, "have you ever seen flamenco?"

She shook her head.

"Perfect. I know the best theater."

To make sure that Matías wouldn't try to walk up to the box office, Claire insisted on buying the tickets on her phone, claiming she could charge them to her client as a business expense. (A lie, but Matías wouldn't know that.) She bought two tickets, of course, to make sure that someone wouldn't try to sit in the seat next to her and *on top* of Matías. But it was a single QR code for both, and when they walked in the theater doors, the usher just scanned her phone and waved her in; Matías, being invisible, obviously didn't register.

The theater was quite intimate in size, and they found their seats easily.

"What do you know about flamenco?" Matías said.

She thought of his painting of the dancer in the ruffled red gown, dancing on the beach with seashells as castanets.

"It's a passionate art form," Claire said, remembering the focus and ardor of the face of the dancer in the painting. "The dresses are beautiful and part of the performance because the movement of the fabric contributes as much to the dance as the movement of the body. And rhythm is very important."

"Muy bien," Matías said. "I'm impressed. Are you sure you have never seen flamenco before? You describe it like a Spaniard."

It's only because I've been in love with a Spaniard for eleven months and one week, she thought. But who was counting?

Claire was. Because with Matías in the hospital, she suddenly understood that every hour, every day, every week mattered.

"Flamenco," he said, "has a long history and many forms, but this kind, in the theater, is one of my favorites. It is like emotion rendered physically. The rhythm—from the castanets to the lightning-quick, stomping feet—is the beating heart. And each dance tells a story. Sometimes of strength, sometimes of love or sorrow, but always with deep spirit."

Soon enough, the lights dimmed. For a minute, the stage was completely black and the audience silent.

Then a single guitar began to strum. The curtains parted. The spotlight turned on.

And a woman in a red dress swayed to the melody.

The audience breathed.

The next hour passed in a storm of swirling dresses, fiery footwork, and hot-blooded songs. There was a dance about jilted lovers and vengeance. A story about impoverished immigrants and the sacrifices they made for their children. A duet about a flower that fell in love with a fish, and the impossible rivers and mountains that separated them. Matías whispered the plots to her as they watched, and Claire sat on the edge of her seat the whole time.

For the final dance, a woman sauntered onstage in a dress designed to look like an hourglass, with grains of sand trailing from the bodice to the skirt and the train. "*Soy La Señora del Tiempo,*" she said.

"I am Lady Time," Matías translated, his mouth so close to Claire's ear that it sent goosebumps prickling across her skin.

"*Y todos estáis a mi merced.*"

"And everyone is at my mercy."

Claire shivered again, but not from wanting. She noticed the dancer's dark makeup and contouring, almost as if her face were meant to resemble a skull, or a mask of death.

"Please no," Claire said to herself. But apparently, loudly enough because Matías asked, "Are you all right?"

"I . . . I don't know if I can watch this one."

"Okay. Do you want to go?" Matías, always willing to sacrifice himself for what Claire wanted, didn't even ask her why.

She nodded and leaned down to gather the program, which she wanted to keep, and her purse, which she had set on the floor. But just as she was about to rise, a fog machine began to blanket the theater in mist, and all the other dancers from the troupe streamed onto the stage. A handful wore billowing black costumes and Xs painted over their eyes. The other half wore suits and dresses in all white.

The audience around them was rapt. And they completely surrounded Claire and Matías.

"We can't leave now," she said.

"Shh!" The man next to her scowled. The woman in front of her turned and glared.

Claire clutched her purse in her lap and hoped this wasn't going to be a dance about dying.

But in the first few seconds, it became clear that it was. A projector cast a background of a cemetery on the left side of the stage, behind the black-clad dancers, shadows in the afterlife. Alternately, a colorful backdrop of nightlife in Madrid played behind the white-clad dancers, those who were still alive.

Claire expected the black shadows to chase the white souls, to grab them and tow them into the underworld. She wished she could reach over and hold Matías's hand, his strong grip an assurance that as long as they were together, everything would be okay.

But they weren't together, were they? Not really.

Onstage, the dead did not chase but instead danced with the dead, and the living danced with the living, each with their own impassioned style, but to the same song. They were like a black ocean on one side and a white one on the other, the bodies bending and curving into each other like waves. In a strange way, it reminded Claire of how, late at night in New York, Matías would sometimes pull her into the empty streets to dance, as fluid and carefree as the performers onstage.

But then Claire shoved the memory out of her mind. Because she could *not* think about the obvious analogy that followed—her, living, dancing with Matías, dead.

As if picking up on her exiled thought, though, some of the shadows began to dance slowly through the fog and took living people as their partners. The border between the black and white onstage started to blend into gray.

But even though those metaphorical souls were being coaxed into the afterlife, it was with an enthusiastic splendor as only flamenco could demonstrate, a new kind of duet that celebrated both the living and the departed.

The man next to Claire sniffled. But he wasn't grieving; he was smiling as he wiped away a tear.

More and more dancers crossed the line from life to death, and as the souls crossed over into the land of shadows, the dancers dramatically ripped off their white costumes, revealing sleeker black ones underneath.

And still, they danced, and still, their movements were beautiful, possibly even more beautiful than when they were alive.

As the melody faded to only a single guitar, and then to nothing, the souls also danced as one, united in a final, coordinated stomp. The peace of death.

The dancers bowed together, and then the fog of the stage swallowed them whole.

The audience burst into raucous applause. Furious clapping. Whistling. Plenty of tears of awe.

Except for Claire. Claire, who had lost her parents in a car accident on a day that was supposed to be a celebration. Claire, who had a comatose boyfriend in the hospital, and his wandering soul beside her.

She understood the message the dancers were trying to convey—that death didn't have to be sad. That Lady Time would come for everyone in the end, but you could make your life before that worth it, so that when your time was up, it felt less like you were being stolen from the world and more like you were *dancing* into the afterlife.

That probably was how Matías's soul would do it. Matías certainly lived every minute to its exuberant fullest potential.

But what about the people who were left behind after their loved ones died? There was no waltzing to the funeral home, no flamenco dance of happiness on their graves. When Jim and Sarah had died, it had been a tragedy, plain and simple.

If Matías died . . .

"Can we get out of here?" Claire asked.

"Of course," Matías said. "I'm sorry. I didn't expect the show to be so philosophical. And with your friend in the hospital . . . I'm sorry."

"It's not your fault. The show was incredible, really. I just—"

"Yeah."

When they got outside, Claire gulped air like it could cleanse the grief and fear away. It didn't; it wasn't that simple. But after a few minutes of walking, she did feel a little better.

"How are you feeling?" Matías asked.

"I'm . . . okay," she said. "Steadier now."

"Do you want to talk about it?"

"Maybe someday," Claire said. "But not tonight."

He nodded. "All right, then. Do you want to keep exploring Madrid? Or if that's too much and you want to go back to the hotel, I understand."

"No, let's keep going." She wasn't ready to be alone again. And she also didn't want to let go of Matías, especially with the imagery of souls dancing into the afterlife.

CLAIRE

⌇

MADRID WAS BEAUTIFUL IN THE DARK, ITS LANDMARKS ILLU-minated like glowing beacons, and Claire and Matías walked and talked all the way until dawn. He never touched her, although she could tell he wanted to—a reach here, a lean there, before he remembered her request to be old-fashioned, and then he'd pull back with a sheepish, lopsided smile on his face.

As the sun rose, Matías sighed happily as he watched the sky shift slowly from purple to pink. "I love this time of morning. It's like you can feel the world turning."

Claire smiled to herself. She knew exactly what he meant, but in a different way. She was closer to his soul than she'd ever been before—even in New York—and it felt like something in their universe was shifting. Slowly, but in a good way.

As the sky grew brighter, they slipped into El Retiro, a vast green park in the middle of the city that used to be the private playground of the royal family but now belonged to all of Madrid. It was huge, one of the classic-style European parks on which New York's Central Park was modeled. Claire would spend forever here with Matías if she could keep him. There was a lake for rowing boats, a building made entirely of glass called the Crystal Palace, and innumerable paths and gardens galore.

"If it were later and the boathouse were open, I'd take you out on the water," Matías said.

"Can't. I get seasick," Claire said. Besides the fact that she couldn't let him row a boat, because he couldn't hold the oars. "Do you think we could find a place to sit down for a bit? My feet could use a break. I don't think I've walked that much since . . . ever."

In truth, she probably could have fallen asleep standing. Claire sometimes pulled all-nighters at the firm, but even then, she was in a chair or she could curl up on the sleeping bag she kept under her desk for a minute or two. But it was worth it to walk all night if it meant keeping Matías close.

"Let's go to los Jardines de Cecilio Rodríguez," he said. "It's like a fairy tale garden. And there are peacocks there."

Claire arched a brow. "Really?"

"Yes, really. But you don't have to believe me. You can see for yourself."

The entrance to the Cecilio Rodríguez gardens portion of Retiro Park was like a vast, tiled checkerboard, and Claire smiled, recalling the time Matías took her to the art collective in the forests outside of New York. There she'd felt like Alice crossing into Wonderland, and the sensation was magically similar here, too. Straight ahead of them was a path flanked by ornate iron lamps and tall cylindrical hedges. On either side of that were pergolas with rows and rows of white columns swirled with deep green vines of ivy.

As soon as Claire stepped onto one of the checkerboard tiles, a sapphire blue peacock crossed the path right in front of her. It stopped to look at Claire, its jeweled plume like a cascading bouquet; then it tilted its head and looked straight at Matías.

"Buenos días," Matías said, grinning.

Claire didn't laugh. Could the peacock see him?

It strutted off before she could scrutinize its gaze further.

"Bench or grass?" Matías asked.

"Definitely grass," she said. The benches were made of stone, and after having stone and tile and concrete beneath her feet all night, she wanted something squishy to dig her toes into.

They found a spot and Claire sighed happily as she pulled off her shoes. The grass was still cool from the night and a little damp from morning dew, but she didn't mind at all.

"Ohh, that feels *so* good." She lay flat and stretched her arms over her head, elongating her spine and moaning at the satisfying little pops and cracks of releasing the tension from her back.

Matías, on the other hand, stared at the exposed strip of skin between the hem of her blouse and the top of her jeans and made a small noise of his own.

"Dios mío. Las cosas que te haría si pudiera . . ."

She laughed and pulled her top down to cover her stomach.

His eyes went wide. "Did you understand what I just said?"

"I know a little bit of Spanish." She didn't tell him that he said those very words to her every time before they made love. *My god. The things I would do to you if I could . . .*

And she would always answer, *Puedes.* You can . . .

They held each other's gaze, and the unseen ribbon that connected them tightened just a little.

Matías flushed. "I'm sorry. That was not very gentlemanly of me."

Claire sighed, still lost in the memory. But then she gathered herself and turned toward him, smiling. "It's okay. It was probably what Mr. Darcy was thinking all those times when he looked at Elizabeth Bennet."

Matías chuckled. "So I am forgiven?"

"Just this once."

"I will be on my best behavior from now on," he said, putting his hand over his heart.

That's too bad, she thought. But it was also necessary.

They lay side by side on the grass for a while then, almost but not quite touching and watching the sun rise. People often thought of a sunrise as the launch of the day and the sunset as the end of one, but for Claire, last night's sunset had been a start, and this morning's felt like another, different start. Time with Matías was full of continuous beginnings.

"It's beautiful," she said, both of the sky and the idea that Matías somehow made the world never-ending.

Until she thought about how he was in a coma. And how things could definitely come to an end.

"You're frowning," he said.

"Yeah . . . um, it's nothing." She forced a smile. "Tell me something good. What should we do next?"

"You're not tired yet?"

"Only a little," Claire said, even though her eyelids felt as if they weighed ten pounds each. "Are you?"

"Not at all," Matías said. She wasn't surprised, though. He didn't have the constraints of a physical body that demanded sleep.

He turned his face back up to the clouds. "Have you ever been skydiving?"

"God, no."

Matías laughed. "You seem very sure about something you've never tried."

"I . . . like control," Claire said.

"You should give it up."

"What?"

"Control." The corner of his mouth curved up a little.

She knew that look. One part amusement, one part dare. It was how Matías prodded her limits. In the early days of their relationship, she'd given in, but in the past few months, she'd dug in her heels for her stable status quo. After all, one of them had to be the practical partner.

And if she had come on the original trip to Spain with Matías, she could have insisted that he and his friends not drive the speedboat like Hollywood stuntmen, or hell, not even get on the thing at all.

"Skydiving is out of the question," she said.

"Why?"

"It's too dangerous."

"Not if you go with someone experienced," Matías said. "Besides, if you think watching the sunrise and sunset from the ground is beautiful, *free-falling* as the sun goes down is a masterpiece. You *must* try it."

"Matías—"

"Tonight, 9 P.M. We'll fly with Nubes Aladas, Clouds Like Wings, at Ocaña Airport. They have the best instructors and you can dive tandem with one of them. And I will be right beside you."

"No."

"Think about it."

"I did. The answer is still no."

Matías sighed. "You're missing out . . . But I think I will go, regardless. Now that we've talked about it, I realized I want to do this one more time before I leave Madrid. I'm sure the sunsets in New York are nice, but there is nothing like the Spanish sun. If you change your mind—"

"I won't."

"You know where I'll be."

Claire thought about lecturing him on the dangers of dropping out of a plane from thousands of feet in the sky and banking your entire life on a flimsy, fluttery piece of tarp. But then she remembered that it didn't matter, because the real Matías was *already* in life-threatening danger, and a soul couldn't be hurt by clouds and air.

She'd have to go back to the research she did on her computer for activities she and Matías's soul could do that didn't involve her jumping out of an open airplane. In fact, maybe she could remember her list now. Her brain was foggy from lack of sleep and food, but if Claire just closed her eyes, she might be able to envision what she'd written . . .

Soledad

⟳

SOLEDAD SAT IN THE DIM, CANDLE- AND FLOWER-FILLED LIV-
ing room with Carlos's and Diego's mothers, and the many other
mothers and aunts and grandmothers of the neighborhood. The
rest of the de León family was scattered about the house—the
children on the back patio racing the toy cars Luis had brought
for them, the young people in Diego's bedroom listening to CDs
from his teenage years, the fathers and uncles and grandfathers
in the kitchen halfheartedly playing dominoes and drinking.

The entire neighborhood mourned because Carlos Garcia
and Diego Ramirez and all the other boys had grown up in each
other's homes. Sometimes Matías was at Carlos's apartment
down the street with Diego and a handful of other kids, helping
his mom fold empanadas and eating half of them as a reward.
Sometimes they were all at Soledad's house, making a joyful
mess with Matías's paints. But more often than not, they were
here at Diego's, because he had an Xbox *and* a PlayStation, and
an older sister who had cute friends.

"I cannot believe they're gone," Guadalupe said. "I keep expecting my Diego to walk in the door at any minute, carrying his
twin girls in either arm."

"I hallucinate the same thing," Lucia said. "Last night, I
thought I heard Carlos knocking at the door. It *was* Sofía and

Carlos, Jr. But I could have sworn it was the pattern that Carlos used to rap." She knocked three times fast, then two slow on the end table.

"Their poor babies," another mother said.

"And their wives."

Everyone sat with their heads hung for a minute. But then Guadalupe clapped her hands and said, "*Suficiente*. We wanted to gather everyone today to share our best memories of Diego and Carlos. We will pray for their souls, but then we must also celebrate their lives."

Soledad nodded, barely holding back tears. Not only because Carlos and Diego were dead, but because she still had Matías, and the guilt twisted in her gut, even though it was no fault of her own and no one here would hold it against her. On the contrary, they were tender toward her, as they were for Leo's and Facu's families who were still in Valencia with them. No one wanted more of their boys to die. To lose two was already too many.

The women closed their eyes and held their hands before them as Lucia led a prayer.

"Lord, Carlos and Diego are gone now from this earthly dwelling, and have left behind those who mourn their absence. Grant that we may hold their memories dear, never bitter for what we have lost nor in regret for the past, but always in hope of the eternal kingdom where you will bring us together again. Through Christ our Lord."

"Amen," they said in quiet unison.

The candles guttered all around them. The heads of all the flowers seemed to bow a little more.

But after another minute of silence, Lucia opened her eyes

and gave everyone a brave smile. "Now, let us please tell stories about happier times. Many of you have known our boys for a long time, and we would love to hear how they touched your lives, in any small way."

Soledad wiped away a tear. "I would like to begin. If that is all right?"

Guadalupe and Lucia nodded. These stories about their sons were as much for them as they were for the practice of honoring the dead.

"This happened before many of you moved to the neighborhood," Soledad said, "but a few of you will remember. It was May, when Carlos, Diego, Leo, Facu, and Matías were seven. Just old enough to think they were the most brilliant minds on the planet, and still young enough to believe that no one would notice their scheming."

Everyone in the room smiled a little.

"They had decided that they wanted to assemble their own gifts that year for el Día de la Madre, and what do moms want the most for Mother's Day? Sweets. At least that was their conclusion. But rather than bake their own using the ingredients in the kitchen, like their smarter sisters would have done, what did they decide to do?"

Lucia started snickering because she remembered exactly what had happened. Guadalupe was smiling, too.

"What?" one of the other women asked.

"They decided they would steal from the local bakeries," Soledad said. Half the room gasped, and the other half tutted.

"But, as I said, they were seven years old, and clever enough to know that they would be caught if they tried to steal entire trays of cookies for their dear mothers. They thought, however, that if they nicked just a small piece or two from each panadería, no one would notice. I don't know whose brilliant plan this was—"

"It had to be my Diego," Guadalupe said. "He was always the most reckless of an already fearless bunch."

"The plan *does* have Diego's fingerprints on it," Lucia said.

"As did the cookies," Soledad said, and the room burst into more laughter—the borderline hysterical kind that comes with grief, when everything is sadder and funnier and too raw, all at once.

"So," Soledad said, trying to talk through her teary laughs. "The boys enacted the plan for Saturday, the day before el Día de la Madre. But there were five mothers to gather sweets for, and only five bakeries within the radius they were used to traveling. Therefore, they needed a schedule, so they could pop in through the back doors of the panaderías at different times throughout the day in order to grab a couple of cookies. They figured that by the end of the day, they would have collected enough."

Lucia shook her head, a small smile still on her face. "That part sounds like Carlos. My boy was always the organizational ringleader. We were not surprised when he grew up to be a logistics manager."

"It's amazing how much you can tell about someone's personality from childhood," another woman said.

"Yes," Soledad said. "It was a pivotal point in Matías's life when he realized that finger paints were more fun to draw pictures with than to eat."

The room erupted in another wave of sorrow-tinged laughter.

"Did you each end up with a big box of cookies for Mother's Day?" one of the older ladies asked once everyone had calmed down again.

"Quite the opposite," Soledad said. "First of all, seven-year-old boys may understand that their mothers like cookies, but they do not think about how important it is for those cookies to be whole."

"What do you mean?"

Lucia chimed in. "She means that my Carlos may have had an early aptitude for scheduling, but he had not yet grasped the finer details of project management. He didn't plan for any boxes for the cookies they stole."

"They put them in their pockets!" Guadalupe said, snorting.

"Oh no!" someone said.

"Oh yes," Soledad said. "What cookies they managed to snatch were crumbs by the time they reached us. But do not think that they went from cookie theft straight to their mothers—the plan was not executed so smoothly! Because the second thing we must remember about seven-year-old boys is that they are not as stealthy as they believe they are.

"Their early-morning walk-bys were successful because the panaderías were very busy at that hour. It was easy enough for a scrawny boy to dart in through the delivery door, grab a couple cookies from the extra racks in the back, and slip back out.

"The late-morning thefts were also, apparently, successful. But their third round—in the noon business lull—was when their arrogance caught up with them.

"It so happened that Lucia, Guadalupe, and Leo's and Facu's mothers—Pilar and Carmen—were at my apartment for our usual Saturday coffee and gossip when my phone rang. It was the baker at Pastelería la Favorita, who said, 'I have a little thief here who says his name is Matías. Does he belong to you?'"

The women in the room tittered. Being mothers, too, they were not unfamiliar with juvenile mischief.

"I asked the baker to hold," Soledad said, "and I told Lucia and Guadalupe what the call was about. And then, to no one's surprise, the call waiting on my phone beeped. It was Lucia's husband, Esteban, calling to say that a baker at El Pan Dulce had caught Carlos pocketing cookies. We told him we would call him back soon with instructions on what to do. And then Guadalupe's husband, Salvador, called to report that Diego was being held at Panadería Corona for the same offense.

"By this time, it was clear that this was no coincidence. Therefore, the Council of Wise Mothers—Lucia, Guadalupe, Pilar, Carmen, and me, of course—deliberated, and we decided that the best gift we could request for el Día de la Madre was to have a little fun with our sons."

The eyes of the women next to Soledad widened, and those on the farthest couch leaned forward to better hear.

"We asked a policeman to pick them up. And he brought a priest with him."

"¡No!"

"¡Dios mío!"

"¿De verdad?"

"Yes, really," Soledad said, grinning. "One of Carmen's friends is an officer. He was off-duty, but he got into uniform, picked up Father Perez along the way, and then stopped by each bakery to retrieve the boys. He told a white lie—that he could arrest them, but that Father Perez had begged for mercy for them instead.

They were taken to the church and 'charged' with community service for the afternoon instead of prison time."

Guadalupe giggled. "We were terrible mothers to scare them like that."

"But they were much smarter about the trouble they got in from then on," Lucia said.

"Exactly," Soledad said. "Also, the church was very clean ahead of Sunday mass."

Everyone in the room laughed appreciatively.

"And we still got cookies at the end of the day!" Lucia said. "Crumbled and stolen, but with love."

"To be clear, we *did* pay the bakers," Soledad said. "Well, the boys did, along with handwritten apology letters."

Guadalupe and Lucia smiled beneath their tears.

"I have a story to share," said Isabella, one of their oldest friends. "Leo's and Facu's parents cannot be here because they are in Valencia by their sons' bedsides, but I know they would want me to tell this."

The crowd murmured their approval.

"It was the summer when the boys were sixteen. The five of them had known every aspect of each other's lives until that point. But with hormones come changes, and while Carlos, Diego, and Matías were busy looking at girls, Leo and Facu had begun stealing glances at one another, although only when the other one wasn't looking.

"While most young crushes pass relatively quickly, it was different for these two because they were already best friends. Un-wittingly, they had fallen in love with every detail of each other—how Leo loved books so much he talked about the char-acters as if they were real. How Facu had an encyclopedic mem-

ory for fútbol statistics. How Leo spoiled his little sister, buying
her little gifts whenever he passed by a store window with something he thought she'd love. How Facu was always the first in
video games to offer himself as a sacrifice to the monsters, in
order to save the rest of the team.

"But Leo and Facu didn't want to ruin their friendship by
revealing their feelings, because what if the other didn't recipro-
cate? And they certainly did not want to destroy the dynamics of
their group, because it had always been the five of them since
their mamás met at the park when they were barely crawling.

"So one day when Facu was busy and couldn't hang out with
them, Leo confessed to Carlos, Diego, and Matías. And then
just a few days later, when Leo was occupied elsewhere with his
sister, Facu came to Carlos, Diego, and Matías, and also poured
out his heart, wondering what to do.

"Well, those three did not even hesitate. They told Facu he
should tell Leo. While they could not reveal Leo's feelings
themselves, they made it clear that they would help Facu in
whatever way they could.

"That weekend, it was Leo's birthday. The boys set up a scav-
enger hunt for him, and the first clue led Leo to the library. But
only Carlos, Diego, and Matías were with him.

"'Where's Facu?' he asked.

"The boys shrugged. 'He said he'll show up later, but that you
should go on without him.'

"Leo's shoulders drooped, his disappointment evident. But
the four of them walked into the library, where he solved riddle
after riddle, collecting scraps of paper hidden in books. Each
paper contained one word, the message scrambled:

Have. I. Tell. Secret. You. A. To.

"'I have a secret to tell you?'" Leo asked.

"At that moment, Facu stepped out from between the library aisles. He clutched one more piece of paper in his hands, and, shaking, he held it out to Leo.

"Leo unfolded the scrap, and gasped. 'I think I love you,' he read in a whisper.

"Facu smiled. 'I think I love you, too.'"

The room was silent for a moment with tears—of sorrow and of pride. These were their boys. They had lived hard, and loved hard, and they had done it all together.

"They were very sweet boys," Guadalupe said. "A handful, but wonderful. We were lucky to have them."

Matías is a very sweet boy, Soledad thought, at the same time ashamed at how traitorous the thought was in the midst of Carlos and Diego's evento conmemorativo.

She looked around the dismal room full of candles and the cloying sadness of flowers. Her poor friends. Parents should not outlive their children; it is a cruelty of the worst kind.

Soledad choked back a sob.

And she prayed that they would not soon be holding un evento conmemorativo for Matías, too.

CLAIRE

⌣

WHEN CLAIRE WOKE, THE SUN WAS HIGH IN THE SKY. HER SKIN ached like she'd been roasted, and a peacock was staring her in the face.

"Ack!" Claire jerked back.

The peacock squawked back in equal surprise.

Claire scuttled backward, in case startled peacocks got aggressive like the geese in New York.

The peacock, though, just shook its head at her, like it was judging her an idiot before it stalked away.

Claire expected Matías to start laughing. But when she looked around the grass, he wasn't there.

"Dammit!" she muttered. She hadn't meant to fall asleep, but jet lag and sleep deprivation seemed to be ganging up on her this week.

Claire pressed her left palm to her mouth.

Of course, nothing happened.

Why did he show up sometimes and not others?

She tried a couple more times, but it clearly wasn't working.

Her stomach growled. Her clothes were rumpled and grass-stained, and she was sure her breath smelled exactly like the thick, white, pasty bacterial colony that had grown in her mouth overnight.

And then she looked at the clock on her phone.

"Fuck!"

She had promised Soledad and Aracely that she would be at Matías's bedside all morning while the family attended Carlos and Diego's evento conmemorativo. She had sworn Matías would not be alone, that she would be in that chair.

And now it was well past noon, and they would be arriving at the hospital soon, if they weren't already there.

Claire leaped up and ran.

When she reached the hospital ward, Claire exhaled in relief. The waiting room was empty of the de Leóns. They must still be at the evento conmemorativo.

Claire began to walk toward Matías's room, past the nursing station.

"Disculpe," a nurse behind the desk said.

"¿Sí?" Claire didn't recognize her.

"¿A quién está buscando?"

"I'm sorry, could you repeat that more slowly?"

The nurse wrinkled her forehead, not understanding.

"Lo siento," Claire said. "No entiendo. Más lento?" *I'm sorry. I don't understand. More slowly?* That had been part of the "useful phrases" primer in the lessons she'd been studying this week in Matías's room. Not that it would help if the response was still words Claire didn't know.

"¿A quién está visitando?" the nurse said, obligingly at half speed.

Ah, Claire could decipher that. It was a pretty basic grammatical construction.

Quién = who. *Está* = is/are. And then the action verb.

Who are you visiting?

"Matías de León," Claire said.

"¿Cómo se llama?"

"Mi nombre es Claire Walker."

"¿Y su relación con el paciente?"

"My relationship with Matías? I'm his girlfriend. Soy su novia."

The nurse arched a brow at Claire, then shook her head. "No. Su novia ya está aquí."

Su novia = his girlfriend. *Ya* = already. *Está aquí* = is here.

"What?" Claire said. "No, that's—*es imposible.*" She pointed at herself. "*Yo soy su novia.*" *I* am his girlfriend.

The nurse pointed at her visitor log.

On the first line for today, as soon as visiting hours began, the handwritten entry read:

08:00 Vega Castillo

As luck would have it, no sooner had she read the name than the doors to the ward opened behind Claire. Aracely walked in, followed by Soledad and the rest of the de León clan, all wearing black.

Seeing Claire at the nurses' station, Soledad asked, "What's going on? Is Matías okay?"

No no no no no. This was *not* happening.

She watched helplessly as Soledad, taking Claire's disheveled state as an indicator of her son's, rushed past everyone to Matías's room.

Soledad flung open the door, took a step inside, then froze.

When she turned around, it was in furious slow-motion.

"What. Is. *She*. Doing. In. There?"

Implied but not spoken aloud was the other half of the question: And what are *you* doing out here?

Claire swallowed hard.

"What is my mom talking about?" Aracely said.

"Er . . . Vega . . ." Claire whispered.

Fire flashed in Aracely's eyes. Behind her, Luis shook his head. Armando crossed himself.

Aracely grabbed Claire by the arm and dragged her across the ward to Matías's doorway.

Vega sat huddled up next to Matías, stroking his matted hair. She blinked up at Claire, Aracely, and Soledad with red, swollen eyes.

"Estaba solo," Vega said meekly. *He was alone.*

Guilt squeezed Claire's insides. "I'm sorry."

"Where *were* you?" Aracely spat. "You knew we were going to be gone this morning. You knew Matías would need someone by his side."

"I messed up."

"Again. You messed up *again*. Don't you understand how important it is that you're here for him? His friends, Leo and Facu—the ones who were in comas in the hospital in Valencia—guess what happened just half an hour ago? They woke up."

Claire gasped. "They did?"

"Yes," Aracely said. "At the exact same moment. Because they're in love and they were in the same hospital room, and even when they were deeply unconscious, they were still together. I spoke to Leo's sister; she said that just before the two of them woke, their heartbeats started to pulse in sync . . ."

Soledad wiped at her welling eyes.

"But," Aracely said, "Matías doesn't have that. The woman he actually wants, *you*, not *her*"—she jabbed her finger in Vega's direction—"seems unable to be here by his side. I can't believe Matías told us you were reliable," Aracely said, "that if we ever couldn't reach him in New York or if there was an emergency or anything at all, we could call you and count on you. We were all so *relieved* back then, because I love my brother, but god knows he can lose himself from reality if he's too into his work or whatever new hobby he's discovered. We thought that he had finally found someone who could be his counterweight, to keep the balloon of his whimsy tied to the ground. But instead, it's *Vega* who is here when he needs someone. And you're not doing anything for him at all—"

"I am!" Claire shouted.

"Shh!" Soledad glared at her.

"I am!" Claire said more quietly. Tears spilled down her face. "I tried to explain . . ."

"Not that ghost bullshit again."

"I'm telling the truth!"

Abuela Gloria pushed her way into the room. "¿Qué está pasando?" *What's happening?*

Soledad said something to her in rapid-fire Spanish.

"Get out, Claire," Aracely said.

Claire gasped. "No. Please."

"I mean it," Aracely said. "And don't come back until you get your shit together. We're all suffering, Claire, but the rest of us still show up here. We've taken leave from our jobs. We sacrifice sleep. We don't make excuses."

Claire turned to plead with Soledad. "You have to understand . . ."

Soledad crossed her arms and turned away, facing the wall.

Abuela Gloria frowned, her eyes vanishing beneath her
wrinkles.

"Go, Claire," Aracely said.

Claire started to cry harder. She took a step toward Matías to
say goodbye, but Aracely moved in her way.

The tears were so thick Claire couldn't even see by the time
she ran past the nursing station and hurled herself into the elevator.

MATÍAS

⌇

TWO WEEKS AGO

MATÍAS SAT ON THE EDGE OF HIS BED, SHAKING. CLAIRE HAD just left, after telling him she wasn't going to Madrid with him, and while he'd put on a brave facade while she was there, now his shoulders crumpled. It was too much an echo of Vega, deciding against coming to New York with him.

Could I have done more for Claire? He racked his brain. He loved Claire with his entire soul and tried to be the man that she wanted him to be. He had started using his watch to record reminders for himself so they'd automatically create a to-do list for him that he saw anytime he turned on his phone. He remembered never to put his wallet or keys on the dining table or kitchen counters, because those were clean surfaces for food, and money and keys were definitely not clean. He was even in the habit now of removing his shoes as soon as he stepped in the door. No more sand tracked across the apartment floor.

There's nothing else, he thought. Matías was willing to do everything and anything for Claire, but he couldn't think of what he'd missed. She wasn't like Vega, who had been an open book of demands for gifts and attention and compliments.

Sometimes Matías couldn't see inside Claire at all. There were still pieces of herself that she kept locked up. In fact, it seemed that the more she fell in love with him, the more she also backed away. They no longer went wandering through his professor's art collaboration to make love in the middle of the forest. She let her work hours bleed later into their time together in the evenings, so that sometimes he was reading on the couch while she typed on her laptop in a separate armchair. And although he did video calls once a week with his gregarious family, Claire had never shown him a photo of her parents. All he knew was they had died on the day she graduated from college. He didn't even know their names.

Matías had hoped this vacation together to Spain would bring them closer. That he would propose, and an engagement would open Claire up again.

But now she wasn't coming, and he didn't know how to reach her.

He let out a long exhale and rested his head in his hands.

All Matías could do was keep being himself, and hope that she would eventually open herself up and let him in completely.

CLAIRE

⤳

CLAIRE HAD NOWHERE TO GO BUT THE HOTEL. SHE STUMBLED into her room a tear-soaked, snotty mess and collapsed on her bed, which was still pristinely made from the previous day because she'd spent the night wandering through Madrid instead.

Her computer dinged from the desk.

Every muscle in her body clenched. The last time Claire had been on her computer, it had been because Yolanda warned her that some of the partners were doubting Claire's abilities. So she had spent all of *that* night putting out fires on the merger, trying to deputize the other members of the team to take over her parts.

But that was over thirty hours ago.

Still. Fuck it.

There were more important things going on right now.

And yet . . . Claire could do nothing about the other things. Work, though . . . That was something she could still control. It was a world where people listened to what she had to say. Her whole life might be cratering, but that part was crumbling slower and she might still be able to fix it.

Claire peeled herself off the mattress, stopping at the mini-bar for two little bottles of cheap wine before she sank into the chair at the desk. She woke her computer screen as she cracked open the screw-top on the chardonnay.

There were over two hundred new, unread emails. And god only knew how many Slack messages.

But if something *really* bad had happened, Yolanda would have texted her, right? And Claire hadn't gotten any messages from her.

She glanced at her phone. The battery was dead.

Oh no.

Claire jammed a charger cable into the phone. But it would take at least a few minutes before it had enough juice for her to check her texts, and meanwhile, all those emails and Slack messages were lying in wait . . .

She chugged the first bottle of wine, then opened and drank the other one, an equally bad cabernet so sharp it made her wince.

Claire took a deep breath and clicked on the Slack window.

Where are the notes from the call with Atwood IP counsel about the renegotiation of the 416 patent license?

What do the pale pink boxes on the corporate contract spreadsheet mean? Are they different from the medium pink and the dark pink? What about the different shades of yellow?

I can't find the flowchart that tracks the assignments of all the different contracts from the Singapore subsidiary to the Italian subsidiary. And how did the Finnish parent holding

corp relate to that? Was the German sister company also
involved? Why would Einstein make corporate structures so
complicated that even their own people don't understand
what is where and how it all connects???

There was message after message like that. When Claire was
at the helm of a deal, everything ran smoothly because her milita-
ristic organizational system meant she could find anything anyone needed immediately. Her color coding was so precise there
were thirty-eight different colors and shades, denoting not only
categories, but how things were linked, and the cross-references
were kept in separate tabs full of all her shorthand footnotes.

The problem was, no one else could decode her meticulous
system but her. She had made herself indispensable—partly out
of type-A control freak tendencies, and partly so the law firm
would *always* need her and would therefore have to promote her
to partner eventually. But now when Claire couldn't be there to
run the merger, it was like someone had stuck wads of gum into
the machinery and nothing was moving.

If she had been at home in New York, if life were still normal, she would have called Matías and he would have been at
her door as soon as humanly possible, with ready hugs and almond cake from Épicerie Boulud.

But here, she was so, so alone. Claire buried her face in her
hands.

"What am I going to do, Matías?"

"First, order room service," he said. "My mom always says
that a meal can't solve everything, but it *can* make things a little
easier."

Claire's hands flew away from her face.

He was sitting casually on her bed, as if he'd been there all along.

She gawked at him, then rubbed her eyes to make sure she was really seeing him.

But yes. Matías was here.

"How did you get in?"

He gave her a funny look and glanced at the door of her hotel room.

She, however, stared at her left palm. "Why are you here? I mean, why are you here *now*?"

"Whoa." Matías rose from the bed, shaking his head. "If you don't want me here, I can go."

Claire pressed her fingers into her temples. He was doing that thing again, evading questions if the answers didn't make sense. She couldn't push too hard or he might realize there was something off—that she hadn't let him in, that he hadn't been here just a minute before.

"No, I'm sorry, it's fine," she said. "I . . . work is blowing up and I'm having a rough time of it."

The expression on his face softened. "What can I do?"

She sighed. "Just be here."

He smiled and sat back down on the edge of the bed, only a couple of feet away. "I can do that. I'm here whenever you need me."

Claire's breath hitched.

Is that what it was? Matías appeared not simply when she touched where he'd left the kiss on her palm, but when she *needed* him?

The first time she'd kissed her hand in the hotel lobby, she'd actually said aloud, "I *need* you, Matías."

The second time he'd shown up, she was in a mild panic trying to get a simple Coke from the park vendor.

The third time, Claire had been buying underwear but freaking out that how many pairs she bought would somehow signify her faith in Matías's recovery and might jinx him.

As for last night, she'd just left the hospital after being lectured that she wasn't doing enough for him, and she had been clutching her purse, upset because she *was* spending her days doing everything she could to connect with his soul, to try to bring him closer so he could reunite with his body and hopefully wake up.

In each of those instances, Claire had shed some of the armor she usually wore. And in that vulnerability, when she pressed on her palm, Matías came.

Because he knew she needed him.

Her eyes welled up as she looked at him sitting on her bed. "How do I deserve you?"

Matías shook his head. "You don't have to earn *anyone*, Claire. Just be you."

"I doubt that's enough."

"I'm pretty sure it is."

Her stomach growled.

A grin crept onto Matías's face. "Now how about we order you some food?"

CLAIRE COULDN'T EAT MUCH BECAUSE OF THE ANXIETY OVER what was in her inbox, but after some bread and gazpacho, she at least didn't feel like she was going to pass out.

"I'm afraid to look," she said, turned away from her computer.

"Do you want me to read for you?" Matías asked.

"Yes," she said. "But no. I should do it."

She took a few more sips of Coke. Then, with no more excuses to procrastinate, she pivoted slowly to the computer and clicked on her inbox.

Claire skimmed the names of the senders. There were so many emails she would have to prioritize whose to read first. She skipped over the name of junior associates, and went right to the ones from Bill Ngyuen, her mentor and the senior partner in charge of the merger, to Mitch Tahir, Intelligentsia Tech's general counsel.

Reading the emails in chronological order, she saw they began as the usual firing squad type of questions Mitch asked daily to keep up to speed on the ten thousand moving parts of the merger.

But as Claire got to emails from the more recent hours—the end of the business day in the United States yesterday—she stopped seeing messages with Bill's name as the sender.

Instead, Mitch would copy her on things, with Bill's prior emails below. Emails Bill had cut her out of.

Until finally, a message from Mitch to Bill:

Is Claire no longer on this deal? Should I stop including her on emails, too?

"No . . ." Claire stared slack-jawed at the screen.

"What's happening?" Matías asked.

She didn't answer. Her hand shook as she started panic-scrolling through the next emails. Mitch had forwarded one to her with the message "I'm sorry, Claire," and below was an email from Bill:

From: billnguyen@windsorblackllp.com
To: mitch.tahir@intelligentsia.tech
Cc: miakovac@windsorblackllp.com
RE: Claire Walker

Mitch,

My sincerest apologies. Claire's work ethic is not up to Windsor & Black standards, and she is not fit to helm a deal as important as yours. But please be assured that Intelligentsia is my number-one priority. I am personally stepping in to handle all day-to-day matters on your acquisition of Einstein, with Mia Kovač as my second-in-command. (I am cc-ing Mia on this email.)

Give me a call when you have a chance. I am at your immediate disposal.

—Bill

What? Why had Bill written her off after only seven days away? Seven days when she'd checked in whenever she could, despite the paralyzing terror of losing the love of her life and despite choosing to *work* instead of get a few hours of sleep? Claire had worked so hard for Bill over the years; she thought she would have merited more respect from him. Not only that, but he hadn't even reached out to her *first* to let her know he was about to replace her.

"Fuck!" Claire slammed her laptop closed.

Matías jumped up from the bed and stepped toward her, arms outstretched to comfort her.

"Don't touch me!" she yelled.

He raised both hands in the air and backed away. "I didn't mean—"

"Sorry," Claire said, clenching her fists and beating on either side of her head. "It's not you. I just . . ."

"It's okay." Matías lowered himself to the carpet so he was sitting at her feet. "You're in shock. But I'm here for you."

She sagged in the chair. "I just got kicked off the deal I was leading. I've been working on it for the last eight months. It was supposed to be the feather in my cap, the one that would make me partner."

Matías frowned. "But aren't you here in Madrid for work? Why would they kick you off the deal?"

"I'm here for . . . a different client," Claire said.

"Well, then, that's not fair. If you have to work on something else, how can they blame you for not also working on the first deal?"

Claire laughed humorlessly. "Law firms are not exactly humane places to work, especially the top international ones like Windsor & Black. There are so many attorneys who would kill to be in a firm like mine—the prestige, the pay, the excitement of the power brokering we sometimes get to be involved with. And because supply outstrips demand, that means the firms get to abuse us however they want, because if I can't do the job, then Mia-fucking-Kovač is salivating to step in the second I falter. Which, apparently, was yesterday."

"So why don't you quit?"

She tilted her head at him, brows furrowed. "Because I'm really good at my job, and I like it."

"Even when they treat you like this?"

Claire bit her lip. "No. Not when they treat me like this. But they never have before. They've demanded everything short of me flying to the moon, but they always respected me until—"

"Until you dared to be human?"

"I beg your pardon?"

"I like you, Claire. And I haven't known you for very long, but it's weird because I feel like I do already know you somehow . . ." He ran his hand through his hair in that familiar way of his when he was working out a thorny problem.

Claire froze. Was this what Professor Hong had meant, about Matías's soul being ready for the truth? His edges were still blurry, but his color was more saturated now. Not entirely solid, but close.

"Maybe it's just déjà vu," he was saying, "or maybe I'm confusing it with things we've done together. But I already know that when you commit to doing something, you give two hundred percent. Like when I said I wanted to show you Madrid at night, you weren't in for just a few hours, you were in for the *whole* night. Or like the time before that when we ran into each other, and I said I was busy, but you insisted that we go out anyway.

"I get it. I'm the same way. My sister would tell you that I'm scatterbrained because there are so many things I'm interested in, but when I find something I want, I'm in all the way. That's how I paint; I give myself entirely to the work. That's how I love—my family, my friends, my . . . Well, anyway, my point is, I think I understand that about you."

"But I suspect it means you also give every single second of your life to your firm, if they ask it of you. You are the best kind of soldier, the kind who never shows weakness, who always says she can fight on no matter how depleted her resources or how impossible the situation. And yet, Claire . . . you're human. You have limits. If your law firm really did respect you, they would understand that."

Claire shook her head. "It's not that simple. Plus, I don't really have a choice. I love being in charge of high-profile mergers and acquisitions. I'm really good at it, too. Besides, it'll get better once I'm promoted from associate to partner."

"Will it?" Matías held her gaze, his golden eyes unwavering.

She looked away and at her phone instead. It had enough battery power now that Claire could check her texts, and sure enough, there had been several from Yolanda. The last one said, "I'm so sorry. There was nothing I could do."

Maybe Matías was right. It didn't get *that* much better once you made partner. You climbed to the top of the associate ladder just to be hoisted up to the bottom rung of the partner one. Sure, Yolanda made more money now, but she was still too scared to start a family because all the major clients were "owned" by the senior partners, and the juniors were basically just there to work for them. Not much different from being an associate, except with better pay.

"I like the substance of what I do too much to quit, though," Claire said. "I'll just . . . have to prove myself again when I get back to New York."

"Hmm," Matías said.

Claire raised a brow. "What is that supposed to mean?"

"Nothing. Never mind."

"It didn't sound like nothing."

Matías sighed. "I think you're probably better than that, Claire."

"Better than what?"

"Than letting other people walk all over you, then thanking them and going back for more."

"Wow. That . . . makes me sound pathetic."

"You're not—"

"No, thank you for that clarity. Do you have more hard truths to tell me? Because I seem to like that. You know, being cut down and then begging for more."

"Claire . . ."

"You know, Matías, not everyone can be born an artistic phenom. Some of us have to work for what we want."

"Excuse me? I *work*, Claire. Maybe most people don't understand it, because they think art is something any AI or child can do since everyone used to paint in grade school, too. But it's *not*. I have studied for years to master my technique and define my style. It takes me over five hundred hours to complete a single, standard-sized painting, and that doesn't count the months I wait for the paint to fully dry before I varnish the piece, or the time I spend custom-building the frames for each painting. When I'm in my studio and I forget to eat, it's not because I'm an empty-headed, flighty artist. It's because I am consumed by my work, because I care so damn much about making it right.

"You, on the other hand, confuse the love of what you do with the love of where you work. You think you're brave, Claire, for being able to take the shit your partners—your supposed future *colleagues*—heap on you. But there's a different kind of

brave, too, and that's the ability to face the truth, even if it's uncomfortable."

Claire scoffed. "Oh, that's rich, coming from you. You're not
even real."

He stared at her, brows furrowed. "I beg your pardon?"

Fuck. She hadn't meant to let that slip, to make a reference to
his soul's inability to deal with what was really happening. But in
the heat of the argument, it had slipped out. "Forget it."

Matías's hands tugged at his hair again, and Claire worried if
she'd gone too far.

But this Matías didn't get light-headed like he had when
she'd kissed him in the studio. Instead, he threw his arms up in
the air.

"No, I *don't* want to forget about it," he said. "I was starting
to fall for you, but maybe it's better that we say what we have to
say now. Then we won't have to waste time together when we're
in New York."

The blood drained from Claire's face. "Matías . . ."

"Actually, I think I have already heard enough," he said, getting up from the carpet. "It was nice meeting you, Claire. I'll see
myself out."

"Matías, wait!"

He walked to the door without looking back and vanished
through it.

"No, come back!" Claire rubbed on the spot on her palm. "I
need you, Matías! And you need me, too. You just don't know it,
please . . ."

The hotel phone rang.

"Matías?" she answered, full of nonsensical hope. Because
how could a soul call her on a real telephone?

"Señora Walker," the receptionist said. "I apologize for the disturbance. There is someone here to see you."

Claire still hoped it was Matías, wanting to apologize. But then she realized that it couldn't be him, because he'd just left. And the receptionist wouldn't be able to see him anyway.

Was it Soledad or Aracely, here to reconcile?

"Do you want to come downstairs?" the receptionist said. "Or should I send her up?"

"Who is it?" Claire asked.

"She says you'll know her as Abuela Gloria."

Gloria

One of the kind receptionists had helped Gloria into an armchair in the lobby, with her walker right next to her in case she needed it. Of course, the receptionist was being polite. Gloria would definitely need the walker—no "just in case" about it—because it had been some years since she could move around unaided.

She had left the hospital soon after Claire. The family usually doted on Gloria, but this time, they were too busy extracting Vega from Matías's room to notice when Gloria slipped away. They were probably working themselves into a frenzy now, but Gloria only chuckled at the thought. Her ninety-two-year-old body might be slow and creaky, but her mind was as sharp as it had ever been. As long as Gloria could sit—like in the taxi on the way here or now, in this plush armchair—she would be more than fine.

Besides, she had *had* to sneak away, because if Soledad or Aracely had known that Gloria was coming to the hotel, they likely would have tried to stop her. The de Leóns were legendary for how tightly they could hold on to grudges if someone hurt one of their own, and Claire had just joined Vega on their grievance list.

Claire emerged tentatively from the hotel elevator, taking

small, slow steps like she was walking into a panther's cage. Gloria didn't blame her, after the thrashing she'd been given by Aracely and Soledad at the hospital.

But Gloria smiled to ease Claire's worries. She was so young—an accomplished attorney and yet still only a fledgling adult. Most of the time, Gloria knew that young people needed to be allowed to stumble and make their own mistakes. But sometimes, like right now, she just wanted to help. She wanted to gather Claire up in her arms and tell her everything would be all right.

But how could she, when everything might never be all right again?

"Thank you for meet me," Gloria said slowly, reciting the English sentence she'd looked up on her phone on the taxi ride here.

An uncertain spark of hope creased the corner of Claire's mouth. "Hola, Abuela Gloria."

"I . . . sorry. English very bad." She wished it was better, but she couldn't change history. Foreign-language education was nonexistent during her childhood in the midst of the Spanish Civil War, and thereafter, Franco had become dictator and declared Spanish the only language of the country. All other languages were either banned or strongly "discouraged."

Claire waved away Gloria's concern as she sat into the adjacent armchair. "Está bien. Yo estoy—I mean, soy—una mala estudiante de español."

Gloria appreciated Claire's attempt to speak Spanish. It was little better than Gloria's English, but equally as earnest.

Claire took her phone out of her pocket, tapped on the screen, then said something rapidly in English.

"This is a translation program," a computerized voice informed Gloria in Spanish.

"Dios mío, qué útil," Gloria said.

The robot woman clearly translated her words into recognizable English, because Claire nodded. This would, indeed, be quite useful.

"Well, then," Gloria said with a smile, the phone automatically translating what she said into something Claire could understand. "I suspect you wish to know why I am here."

"I *am* curious," Claire said through the phone. "Especially given how the rest of the family feels about me now."

"They should not project their past experience with Vega onto you."

Claire sighed. "I don't think that's it . . . I haven't been at the hospital as much as they would like."

"From the moment the doors open until the nurses kick you out?" Gloria said with a wry snort. "The chair that Soledad designated for you is as much a prison as a gift."

Claire's mouth parted in surprise. She probably had not realized that Gloria had been observing her all the times they were in Matías's room together. But it had been quite clear to Gloria how much Claire loved Matías and wanted to help him, but also how trapped the poor girl was, under the well-meaning but heavy weight of Soledad's love for her son.

"Um, the family means well, though," Claire said, having gathered herself. "I understand why they're mad. But I have good reasons for not being there."

Gloria nodded solemnly. "I know. And that is the reason I came to the hotel. Please, tell me about Matías."

Claire let out a short laugh under her breath. "I doubt you'll believe me. I tried explaining it to Soledad and Aracely, and they didn't believe me, either. But then, why should they, when it sounds so crazy, even to me? I'm usually the most logical person in any room, and *I* wouldn't believe me." She slouched in her chair.

Gloria had spent enough time in the past week watching Claire to know that she was not a woman who folded easily. Matías's girlfriend was a fighter. She had been thrust into an unimaginably terrible situation in a foreign country and surrounded by the enormous, loving but sometimes overwhelming de León family, and she hadn't quit. She had tried to be there for Matías while also juggling her demanding job, and if what Soledad had said at the hospital was true, Claire had been stretching herself thin for Matías away from the view of the family, too.

"Tell me," Gloria said gently. "I will not judge." She reached out and patted Claire's hand, suddenly all too aware of the contrast between Claire's firm young skin and her own. When had she gotten so old?

But that was the price to be paid for experience, and Gloria was glad for all she had lived through. It was how—at the end of a life—one could find peace. "I have seen a great deal over the years, and I like to think it has made me a little wiser."

Claire exhaled deeply. Gloria wondered if this was what Claire did daily as a lawyer—steel herself to tell the truth, even if it scared her.

"You can do it," Gloria said. "I am listening."

"Okay . . ." Claire said. She still trembled, barely perceptibly, but her voice was strong. "Then here it is. I have seen Matías, outside of the hospital. That's why I haven't been at his bedside. I've been with him—at his studio, at a flamenco show, falling asleep in Retiro Park." She bit her lip, as if bracing for Gloria to chastise her as Soledad had.

But instead, Gloria said, "Like a ghost?" Soledad and the younger generations of the family may have drifted from what they thought were old-fashioned superstitious beliefs, but Gloria had grown up in civil war and Franco's Spain. She knew ghosts were very real.

"No, his soul. He's a little lost, and he thinks it's one year ago."

Gloria traced a button on her armrest as she thought about Matías's soul, detached from his body. It would be just like her grandson to go wandering off.

But Claire had said he was lost, so it wasn't curiosity driving his soul. "Hmm . . ." Gloria said. "That could make sense, if he is confused."

Claire's mouth dropped open. "Wait. You believe that I can see him? And that it's really Matías's soul?"

Gloria smiled sadly. "As I mentioned, I have seen a great deal in ninety-two years, and more recently, that has involved the passing of many of my friends. I have never been able to see their souls, but I have felt them the moment they leave their bodies. And—don't tell Armando—but sometimes, I can feel the seam where my own soul is attached. The threads have begun to unravel." It was not an alarming revelation for Gloria, just an observation, like one might notice that a well-loved coat was beginning to look thin at the elbows.

"Oh no, please don't say that, Gloria!"

She shook her head. "It is all right, my dear. I have had my time on earth." She had been through war, yes, but she had also seen the highs of being human—falling in love with her neighbor Pedro, bearing children and watching them grow, and then being there when they themselves fell in love and had their own children. Life always contained some traumas, but the most important things were the joys. And Gloria had had a lifetime's worth of blessings.

But Matías had not. He deserved to live, to marry Claire, to have babies and teach them how to ride bicycles and to paint and to cook. His friends' young lives had been cut off much too soon; Gloria could not bear for her own grandson to follow the same fate.

"Claire," she said, leaning forward in the armchair, even though it took great effort to pull herself from the deep, plush cushion. "I think there is still something that can be done. If Matías's soul is drawn to you, you are the one who can save him."

Yet at her words, Claire only slumped deeper into her armchair. "Or maybe it's not me. Maybe it's supposed to be Vega. His soul thinks it's one year ago, and a year ago, he was still in love with *her*."

Gloria scoffed. "Matías's soul has *not* visited Vega. Believe me, if he had, she would have been marching all around gloating, rather than desperately sneaking into his hospital room. And you are wrong that he loved her a year ago."

Claire looked confused. "But . . . weren't they engaged?"

"Yes, but they had been together for so long that it was simply . . . how things were. It was not movement forward; it was, in truth, holding them back. Matías and Vega were both artists with great respect for each other's talent. They lived in the same fickle world where most people don't appreciate the work they toiled to create, and it is difficult to make a living. Having a constant like a relationship made it feel a bit less risky for Matías.

"But as his abuela, I know Matías to his core. He is enthusiastic about trying new things, but he also craves stability. He grew up with a solid, loving family, and once he and Vega were together, I believe he assumed she would be his new foundation.

"However, Vega has a difficult time committing to anything. Matías may have many interests, but he is also able to focus intently on the projects and people he loves. Vega, on the other hand . . . She is not good at following through. Her studio is littered with unfinished sculptures, and she complains about impatient clients who think it unreasonable that a piece they commissioned five years ago is still not complete. She is not made to be tied down—although I do not think Vega understood that about herself when she accepted Matías's proposal, because they were so young then.

"But by the time Matías received the invitation to teach in New York, he and Vega had already grown apart. They lived together in the same apartment, but they were rarely there at the same time. He worked in his studio during daylight hours; she got her inspiration when it was dark. They loved each other in the way that one loves old friends—a deep, steady fondness that you assume will always be there, whether you see them every day or only once every few years.

"Their breakup was a relief to our whole family. I think even Matías was relieved. He is a man who keeps his promises, and he would never have taken back his proposal to Vega if she hadn't broken it first. But Matías needs someone to be a home base, someone who is reliable to ground him. Someone who can give back to him as much as he gives out.

"His soul chose *you*, Claire, not Vega. The conscious Matías knows you are his home, so his subconscious feels it intuitively—even if, I suppose, he doesn't remember you yet."

Claire sat up a little straighter in her chair, as if something important just occurred to her. Gloria frowned.

"Is there more about Matías's soul that you haven't told me?" Gloria asked.

"Well . . ." Claire blushed.

Gloria crossed her arms. It made her elbows crackle, but the stern posture seemed to have the effect she wanted on Claire.

"It's just that . . . Matías and I have kind of been going on dates."

"What do you mean?"

"I talked to a professor who specializes in astral projections, and she said that his soul needs to reconnect to reality in order for Matías to wake from his coma. So I've been trying to spend time with him—his soul—walking around the park, going to the Sorolla Museum, that sort of thing. It's the reason I can't always be in the hospital."

Gloria chewed it over. As a theory, it made as much sense as anything else. "Is it working?"

"I think so . . . The other day, he, um, kissed me."

Gloria could tell from the flush in Claire's cheeks that it must have been more than a quick peck.

"And the more time we spend together," Claire was saying, "the more solid Matías's soul is becoming. It used to be that if there was a beam of light, it would shine right through him and he'd go transparent. But now he's getting more and more opaque." She ended with a hopeful smile.

But Gloria sank back into the depths of the armchair. Because this brave young woman clearly thought she was helping

Matías, when—Gloria was quite certain—she was doing the exact opposite.

"Did I say something?" Claire asked.

"Oh, Claire . . ." Gloria let out a long sigh. "You did not mean to. It is true that you are strengthening Matías's soul, but I fear it is in the wrong way. The more time his soul spends with you in the unreal world of one year ago, the further he strays from his body and the less likely he is to return to it. And here, in our reality, Matías is slipping away."

"No!" Claire said. "I'm his anchor, and I'm trying to reel him in."

Gloria hesitated, then took a deep breath. She did not want Claire to feel guilty, because Claire's connection to Matías's soul meant she really was the only one who could save Gloria's grandson. But Claire also had to understand that what she was doing might well be killing him. "The doctors have said that Matías isn't getting any better," Gloria said. "He is actually getting much worse."

"Oh no," Claire whispered. "It's because we fought."

"When?"

"Literally seconds before you arrived and the receptionist called me."

Gloria shook her head. "That cannot be it. It took me a while to get here from the hospital." The taxi ride itself had been quick, but the walk down to the hospital lobby before that had been arduous. "Matías was already doing poorly before you two fought. He has become sicker ever since that episode we thought was a heart attack. All the time that you are spending with Matías's soul—the Matías in the hospital bed has been growing weaker and weaker."

"Oh god . . ." Claire looked like a small child who'd gotten lost in the woods, hoping that Gloria was here to guide her out.

But Gloria couldn't. Claire was the one Matías's soul knew.

"The doctors told us to start thinking about whether we want to bring Matías home. In Spain, we prefer not to pass away in the hospital."

"No!" Claire said. "It's too soon."

"Your time is running out," Gloria said. "The longer Matías's soul is separated from his body, the more his condition declines. It is no longer time for caution, Claire. You have to make up that fight you had with him, and you have to bring his soul back to this world."

"But I don't know how to do it!"

"Then you must figure it out. Because you are the only one who can save him."

Matías

One Week Ago

As they walked down the dock toward the speedboat they were renting for the afternoon, Diego punched Matías on the arm. "Okay, tío, you ready for this? I don't know if you've gone soft while living in America or if you can still handle us."

Matías laughed and gave it right back. "You talk a big game for someone who spends his days changing diapers and falling asleep at 7 p.m. in your kids' bed with stuffed animals all around you. Besides, haven't I kept up the last few days? I seem to remember being the least freaked out about scuba diving at night in the pitch dark."

"He's got you there," Leo said, holding hands as usual with Facu. The two were inseparable and proud of it, and it made Matías's heart ache a little, wishing Claire had come on the trip.

But she would have hated what they were about to do—not only because she got seasick on boats, but because Diego would be driving, and that meant speed, speed, and more speed. It wouldn't matter where they went or what they saw, as long as they went faster than anyone else around them.

They reached the slip where their boat was, and Carlos—who was rolling their cooler behind them—let out an appreciative whistle.

"Yeah, this will work just fine," Diego said, rubbing his hands together. He hopped onto the boat first and went immediately to the throttle controls, stroking the leather steering wheel and shifter like he'd never seen anything as beautiful in his life.

"Careful there," Facu said, "or your wife is going to get jealous."

"She doesn't need to know what goes on during our guys' trips," Diego said, and they all laughed because one, *everyone* knew how much Diego loved speed (he could recite from memory the maximum speed of every plane, train, and automobile that ever passed within sight), and two, Matías and his friends were all so unflinchingly loyal to their partners that there would never be anything they *had* to hide about a guys' trip. It just wouldn't occur to any of them to stray.

He, Carlos, Leo, and Facu climbed onto the boat. Matías tucked his backpack safely in a storage hold so it wouldn't get wet, but Carlos's cooler wouldn't fit into one of the compartments, so he just wedged it in the corner next to his legs. It wouldn't matter anyway if the cooler got a little bit of salt spray.

"¿Listos, tíos?" Diego said as he eased the shifter forward. The motor purred to life, and they sailed out of the marina, slowly at first, and then accelerating as they entered open water.

The wind whipped through Matías's hair, and he took a deep breath and let the warm, briny air expand his lungs. Next to him, Leo's hat flew off into the water, and Facu—out of loyal instinct—started to lunge after it. Leo caught him by the waist and Facu froze, stunned for a moment that he'd been about to leap into the water, until Leo tugged him back down onto the bench and said, "Gracias, bombón, but it's just a hat."

"I'll buy you another as soon as we get back to shore," Facu said.

"I know you will," Leo said, and kissed him.

Matías sighed wistfully. *That* was what he wanted with Claire. He just had to convince her to say yes to forever with him.

At the wheel, Diego whooped as he ran the engine at nearly full throttle. Carlos shouted something, but it was lost to the wind. Matías sat back and just beamed at his friends. They'd all grown up together and been so close, and he missed them. He loved his life in New York, but these guys would always be in his heart, and he was just so glad to be with them again.

They flew along the coast, heading south from Valencia toward Alicante. The plan was to enjoy hurtling across the water for a while, going wherever Diego's speed-loving heart wanted, then eventually dropping anchor near one of the many secluded coves to swim, snorkel, and have a little to eat and drink.

Half an hour into the trip, though, Diego spotted a red-and-white buoy bobbing about three kilometers away.

"How fast do you think I can get us there?"

"Tío, no," Matías shouted over the wind.

But Diego just grinned and jammed the shifter forward. The boat—which had already been flying—shot like a bullet over the water, going so fast that everything around Matías blurred. He clutched the edge of his seat, and salt spray flew at his face like a thousand tiny needles.

The bottom of the boat bounced violently every time it hit the top of a wave. Matías tried to read the speedometer, but the roaring wind and stinging water in his eyes made it impossible to see more than that Diego was close to maxing out their speed.

It might have been fine, if the path before them had been clear.

But then Carlos stood up. "Watch out!" He jabbed in the direction of a pod of dolphins just ahead of them in the water.

"¡Coño!" Diego shrieked, and jerked the wheel.

At the speed they were going, the sudden change in direction jarred Carlos's cooler free. It sailed in the air toward Diego's head.

Everything seemed to happen in slow motion then. Matías screamed, the sound filling his own ears like a timpani, as the cooler smashed into Diego, knocking him unconscious to the boat's floor. Carlos, who was closest to the controls, lurched toward the wheel and grabbed it, but too late. The momentum of Diego's fall had jerked the wheel even more off course, and the boat went airborne.

They careened toward the buoy, twisting as they flew.

The red-and-white metal—which had seemed so small and harmless when they were far away—now towered before them. It was also unforgivingly sturdy, made to withstand turbulent storms and salt rust and years and years of being moored deep in the harsh ocean.

As the boat flipped nearly upside down and hurled toward the buoy, the cliché Matías had always heard became true. The most important parts of his life flashed in front of him—a final montage of greatest hits before God came to take his soul to heaven.

The warm smiles and embraces of Mamá, Papá, and Abuelita Gloria.

Aracely on her first day of school, when Matías had held her hand as they walked together.

Cradling Luis as a baby, just hours after he was born.

And Claire—from the moment Matías first set eyes on her

at the Rose Gallery to the way she felt in his arms as he lay her down on the carpet of the law firm library floor. How in the mornings she wandered into the kitchen squinting because she hadn't put in her contacts yet, and how at night she snored like a small mouse but was too embarrassed to ever admit it.

The way she scrunched up her nose or bit her lip when she was working on a knotty legal problem. How, at the end of the day, she curled up on Matías's lap and nuzzled her head into the crook of his neck.

How he had never felt safer, more grounded, more *solid* than when he was with Claire.

And the diamond-and-topaz ring shaped like the sun, waiting for her. For *them*. For a future they might now never have.

In the final moment before the boat smashed into the buoy, Matías saw Claire's face ringed by the sunlight reflecting off the water's surface.

I love you, he thought. *I always will.*

And then the boat slammed into the buoy at 180 kilometers an hour, and everything went black.

CLAIRE

〜

"¿CUÁNDO MÁS TIEMPO?" CLAIRE ASKED THE TAXI DRIVER.

She wasn't sure if it was the right way to ask how much longer it would be until they reached Ocaña airport, but apparently it was close enough, because he said, "En diez minutos, señora." *Ten minutes.*

"Gracias."

The small airport that Matías had mentioned for skydiving was just south of Madrid. After his abuela left, Claire hadn't had any luck getting him to appear by pressing on her palm, so now Claire was on her way to the place where he said he would be at nine o'clock, whether she was there or not.

I can't believe I am voluntarily signing up for skydiving, she thought.

But at the same time, it was absolutely what she *should* do. Not only because she couldn't get Matías to show up at the hotel, but because in their relationship, he was always the one coming to her. It was Claire's turn now to come to him.

It had probably been her turn for a while, but she hadn't wanted to compromise in the past. She had wanted to keep her life exactly as it was—with her insane work schedule and her white-knuckled grip on control and most of all, the citadel wall she kept up to protect herself. All the family she'd ever had had died. All the men she'd dated in the past had eventually found fault in her and left. So Claire had subconsciously synthesized this to mean that if she didn't give too much of herself to anyone else, she wouldn't hurt as much when it ended.

But Matías had never wanted anything from Claire but for her to be herself. He had put forth an immense effort to fit himself into her life, memorizing as many of her tidiness rules as possible even though they were in complete opposition to his personality, making meals for them around her client calls, not being angry when she canceled their trip to Spain at the last minute.

And what had she given in return?

Order. Reliability. A "home base," was how Abuela Gloria had put it.

But still, it wasn't enough. Matías loved Claire, but he deserved not just a stable routine, but her true, vulnerable self. His soul was drawn to it; it was the reason he'd shown up for her here in Madrid, when she let herself need him.

And maybe that was where Professor Hong had gotten it wrong. Matías's soul hadn't needed to fall in love with Claire in order to connect with her. Instead, it was *she* who had to open herself up enough to be his guide back.

Ironically, being here in Madrid and caught up in these impossible circumstances had forced a slower pace to her relationship with Matías, unlike the impulsive whirlwind of their New York courtship. Because Claire had had to spend long stretches of time here without him—and because the threat of losing him forced her to see her need for him more clearly—she had fallen more deeply in love with him. Or, in a way, had *truly* fallen in love with Matías for the first time ever, rather than the last eleven months of holding up her protective walls, never giving in entirely to love because she was scared he would see her weaknesses and leave.

But instead, Matías's soul had shown up when Claire was at her most vulnerable, the least in control. And none of what she once feared had happened. He had seen the soft, scared person under her facade of control and, like his abuela, had not judged. So she had let him into her heart completely.

And that was possibly helping him to remember who he was. Who *she* was. Who *they* were together. Before their fight in the hotel room, he had paused, confused for a moment, when he felt like he knew her. Maybe it was because *her* Matías—the one in New York—had always understood Claire better than she realized. She hadn't needed to try so hard to hide her tender spots and imperfections from him. He'd already seen them, and he loved her—broken bits and all. So in the past week, each time Claire let herself need Matías's soul, she let him in a little more, let him see her whole self. And that was helping him to remember.

Though, if Abuela Gloria was right, it was also hurting him. The more time Matías and Claire spent together—the more his soul was drawn to her—the worse things got for him physically. Claire felt sick. Instead of guiding him back to his body, she'd been inadvertently luring him away from it, making a relationship with *her* feel more appealing than with the weak, broken body that awaited him in the hospital. And the more solid their bond grew—the more substantial Matías became around her—the thinner the ties holding him to his body became.

She hoped she could find him one more time, convince him to go back.

"Ya hemos llegado," the driver said as he pulled up to Ocaña Airport.

"Muchas gracias."

She got out and stood a bit stunned as the taxi drove away. This wasn't so much an airport as an airstrip. There was one small building that seemed to be the main one, and then a few hangars. That was it.

Claire swallowed hard.

I can do this, she thought. *If not for myself, then for Matías.*

After a couple of deep breaths, she followed the signs for Nubes Aladas, Clouds Like Wings. Claire was already shaking, and she was still on the ground.

"Hola," she said when she reached the front desk. "Quiero . . . jump out of a plane?"

Definitely a question, not a statement.

The man behind the desk grinned. "Your first time?" he asked in English.

Claire nodded.

"Okay. Do not worry. It is very safe, and we will take good care of you. The sunset dive is an incredible experience. I guarantee you will love it."

Without realizing what she was doing, Claire had been rubbing her right thumb over and over the middle of her left palm. She looked around, hoping that Matías would show up any second now to do this with her, but he was nowhere in sight.

Maybe it was because she was early. The plane took off at nine, but she'd wanted to get there with enough time to get in the mandatory training for first-time jumpers.

Or . . . maybe Matías wasn't here because he was too angry. He was a de León, after all, and he could hold a grudge like the rest of them. When Mia Kovać had talked shit about Claire at the law firm holiday party last year, Matías's eyes had immediately transformed from sunshine to white-hot lightning, and Mia very quickly decided she ought to leave the party early.

But Matías had never been mad at Claire for very long, and even when he was, he never lashed out.

Claire pressed her thumb into her palm harder while the man behind the counter, Javier, went through the skydiving package information with her. There was a short instructional video she would watch, and she would dive tandem with one of the crew members, just like Matías had said. She wouldn't have to worry about releasing the parachute herself or steering their landing if she didn't want to, because she literally would be strapped to an experienced skydiver.

It only made Claire 2 percent less nervous.

But she signed the waiver and paid. Javier showed her into a small room that held just a TV on the wall and a few folding chairs, two of which were already occupied by a middle-aged British couple so excited they were bouncing in their seats.

"You doing this by yourself, dear?" the man asked.

Claire looked around again, still hoping for Matías, but she was all alone.

"I guess so," Claire said.

"Were you expecting someone?" the woman asked.

"Sort of. I, um, didn't know if he'd show up."

The woman made a face. "Oof, sorry, love. Men can be so insensitive sometimes."

"With the exception of yours truly," her partner said. The woman swatted him playfully, and then Javier turned on the TV, so their conversation ended.

———

After the safety and instructional video, Claire put on the red jumpsuit Javier gave her and thought, *This won't be so bad*.

But then they walked out onto the tarmac.

"We're flying in *that*?"

Just like Ocaña Airport was so tiny she wasn't sure it actually qualified as an airport, the plane looked like an overgrown toy. It was bright yellow with propellers over the wings, a line of seats inside, and an open door that she wasn't sure ever closed.

Oh god. That's the hole I'm going to jump out of.

Into the fucking sky.

She stopped walking as the rest of the group proceeded down the tarmac.

A minute later, Javier came jogging back with a dark-haired woman in a yellow jumpsuit. "Claire? This is Esmeralda. She has done thousands of dives, and she will be your partner tonight."

"We are going to have fun," Esmeralda said. She was a solid woman, and she linked her arm through Claire's to coax her toward the plane.

Claire glanced one more time over her shoulder, but Matías hadn't come.

Maybe he *was* still upset with her. Or had she strayed too far outside of Madrid for his soul? Was the distance from his body in the hospital too great?

But it wasn't *that* far from the city . . .

She and Esmeralda reached the plane. If Matías wasn't going to be here, did Claire really have to go through with this?

Yeah, I do, she thought. Just like she had promised that she would learn Spanish no matter what happened to Matías, she had decided to come here as proof of how she was willing to put herself out there for him. And that was still true, whether or not he would witness it.

Esmeralda patted her on the back. "¿Lista, Claire?" *Are you ready?*

Claire clung to the doorframe for a moment. Then she said, "Lista," and ducked inside the pocket-sized plane.

THE DOOR OF THE PLANE DID ACTUALLY CLOSE. IT WAS LIKE A smaller, clear version of a garage door that rolled down once everyone was on board. The British couple buckled into the jump seats to Claire's left, and Esmeralda and the other instructors were buckled in across the narrow aisle. Although everyone else enjoyed watching the takeoff through the transparent door, Claire squeezed her eyes shut.

Not long after they were airborne, one of the instructors rolled the door back up.

Claire's eyes flew open. "We're already going?"

"No, no," Esmeralda shouted. "It is only to allow in some air. Otherwise it will be too stuffy while we wait to reach altitude."

"How high are we going?"

Esmeralda raised her eyebrows. "That was in the video you watched. Do you remember?"

Claire shook her head. Right now, she couldn't do anything other than cling to her seat. She certainly couldn't recall a specific number.

"Fifteen thousand feet," the British man yelled over the noise of the wind. "One of the highest offered in all of Europe!"

"That's why we chose this company," his partner said with an approving nod toward Esmeralda and the other instructors.

Claire shut her eyes tight again, every muscle taut, hands pressed together like in prayer.

I can do this on my own, *she thought*, but I don't *want to, Matías. I want to do everything with you.*

I want to wake up every morning and have breakfast with you. I want to spend each evening curled up on the couch, talking about our days. I want your opinion about my career. I want to watch you for five hundred hours while you craft miracles out of blank wooden panels and paint.

I want you to be able to tell me about Vega without being afraid you'll hurt me. And I want to tell you stories about my childhood and about Jim and Sarah, even if it makes me cry to remember that they're gone.

I want to give you all *of me, even the softest, most frightened parts that I usually keep hidden under chain mail and steel plates.*

You would do anything for me, Matías, and I want to prove that I'll do anything for you, too.

"This seems like a good start," Matías said, fully suited up in the jump seat next to Claire. "You're leaping out of a plane."

She let out a little cry. Esmeralda looked over, concerned, but Claire pasted on a smile and waved her away.

Then Claire turned toward Matías. He looked nearly solid—barely blurred edges, colors bright, his eyes that beautiful, molten gold she loved. She let her hair block her face so it wouldn't look like she was having a conversation with herself. The wind whipping through the plane obscured the sound of her voice.

"Matías, you're here!"

"I said I would be, didn't I? Whether you decided to come or not?"

Tears prickled Claire's eyes. He always kept his promises.

Luis had said the same of him, and it was one of the things Claire loved most about Matías. "I am so sorry about the fight in my hotel room," she said. "You were just trying to help, and I shut you down viciously."

"I'm sorry, too," he said. "Your career is important to you. I shouldn't have suggested you could simply walk away from your life's work. I would have reacted the same way to someone telling me to quit painting."

"You were only giving advice."

"I really like how dedicated you are to your career."

Claire sighed. "And I love you." The words flowed easily out of habit.

Matías, though, cocked his head.

Oh shit. She'd temporarily forgotten that this Matías had only known her for a handful of interactions.

Claire tried to look sheepish. "Pretend you didn't hear that? I think I'm just super nervous about, you know, hurling my body out of a flying tube of tin, fifteen thousand feet from the ground."

But instead of laughing, Matías frowned.

Then he ran his hand through his mess of black hair. "Would it be strange to say I feel like we've known each other in a different life?"

She had to bite back a sob.

Claire reached toward him. Her fingers fluttered, but she closed the last inch and grazed his hand.

It was so light, barely a touch. Even so, she could feel tiny sparks in the infinitesimal space between them.

Matías held still.

Could he feel it, too?

"Does this mean I have permission to touch you now?" he said.

She half laughed, half cried. "Yes. You do."

Across the way, Esmeralda rolled the plane door closed again. One of the other instructors turned toward Claire and the British couple. "We are close to altitude now, so we are temporarily shutting the door so you can hear about final preparations. Each of us will come by to check your harnesses, and then we will be ready to jump!"

Claire inhaled sharply.

"Don't worry," Matías said. "I will be out of the plane right behind you."

Esmeralda came over and double-checked Claire's gear.

"You look good. Goggles on and we're ready to go!"

Claire looked over at Matías. He gave her an encouraging nod before he lowered his own goggles over his eyes.

The crew rolled open the door again. The sun was setting now, and the air around them glowed as if on fire.

It would have been one of the most beautiful things Claire had ever seen if she hadn't been worried about jumping into it with just a scrap of fabric to slow her descent.

"Okay, get close to the door," Esmeralda said.

Claire inched forward but refused to look down.

"You'll love it once we're out there!" Esmeralda grabbed the top of the doorframe and finished strapping herself onto Claire's back—not the other way around, as Claire had initially thought. But this would be better, right? Even though Claire would have to see the ground coming at them first, it meant that Esmeralda would be in charge of pulling the cord for the parachute and steering it and everything.

"On the count of *tres*, okay?" Esmeralda shouted into the wind.

"You got this," Matías said as he climbed past them and

swung himself through the door, so he was holding on to the outside of the plane.

The outside of the plane? Claire's eyes went wide, but he winked at her. "I got this, too."

"Uno," Esmeralda said, beginning to swing herself and Claire in the doorway. "Dos, tres!"

They shot out into the sky.

Oh god oh god oh god . . .

Matías pushed himself off the plane a moment later.

Claire's stomach shot up to her throat. She hated falling. She'd thrown up even on the kiddie roller coasters at the county fair. Why would anyone sign up to do this over and over again?

A hand clapped over hers.

It wasn't Esmeralda's, so Claire looked over.

Matías had caught up to them, and he threaded his fingers with Claire's, his right palm clasped against her left. Like when he had kissed her in the studio, he was here but not, his touch a warm pressure against her skin.

She smiled at him, and all of sudden, her fear flew off into the clouds.

He squeezed her hand.

She squeezed back.

And then Claire looked straight down at the earth, at the sunset sky all around her, and she opened her mouth and let out a whoop of pure, unshackled glee.

Matías howled like a jubilant wolf.

And together, they spiraled through the orange and pink sky, holding hands all the way down.

CLAIRE

WHEN THEIR FEET HIT THE GROUND, ESMERALDA CONGRATU-
lated Claire, and Claire responded but didn't remember what
she'd said, because all she was focused on was Matías, wind-
blown and ruddy cheeked.

Claire couldn't stop grinning, even as they walked across the
field toward the hangar to return their gear.

"That was fun, wasn't it?" Matías said.

"It was. I didn't think I could like something like that. Thank
you."

"For what?"

"For helping me feel safe so I could let go."

Matías stopped in the middle of the grass, smiling shyly.
"Really? I did that?"

"Yeah," Claire said. "You were exactly what I needed."

AFTER CLAIRE CHANGED AND RETURNED HER GEAR, SHE MET
Matías outside the hangar.

"Well," he said. "The last time we spent an evening together,
I showed you Madrid. I think it's your turn. What are we going
to do next?"

Claire laughed because it was an echo of her demand after

they'd walked through the grounds of the Palacio Real and Sabatini Gardens.

But the smile fell quickly off her face because she knew what she really had to do.

"Matías . . . There's something I have to tell you."

"Shoot. Did I dump my green jumpsuit into the bin meant for purple ones? Or did I put my gear in the wrong cubby?" He started to turn back toward the skydiving office, then stopped short. "Wait. Why am I worried about that? I don't . . . I'm not the kind of person who even notices there are specific bins for each color."

Claire twisted her purse strap around and around her finger. "Yeah . . . That's kind of what I wanted to talk to you about."

He raised both hands, like he'd just been caught red-handed. "I did warn you when you came to my studio that I can be messy."

She smiled a little. "I know. Or, really, I *already* knew."

Matías cocked his head, confused.

"On the plane, you asked if it would be strange to say that you felt like we knew each other in a different life. Well, the thing is . . . we sort of did."

"What?"

"Maybe you'd better sit down for this." Claire pointed to a bench a short way off, in front of the empty airport parking lot.

So they walked over, and Claire told him, as gently as she could, about the accident. About how they had been together for the eleven months and one week before that. And about his injuries and how they were running out of time now. That Abuela Gloria had convinced Claire to tell him because he needed to return to his body.

When she finished, Matías sat with his head in both hands. He didn't say anything for a long while.

Finally, he exhaled. "That's . . . hard to believe."

Tears started to well in Claire's eyes. If she couldn't convince Matías to return to his body, he would die. Either *now*, because his soul would sever his connection to his body and no longer be tethered to this world, or *soon*, because Matías's body was nearing the end of its ability to hold on to life.

"But . . ." Matías said, and Claire's breath caught in her throat.

"Even if it's hard to believe," he said, "I *feel* it. When I kissed you in my studio, I already knew your mouth. I knew the shape of your body against mine. I somehow remembered—without ever having experienced it yet—the little sound you would make if I brushed my lips against your throat."

Claire involuntarily made that sound now.

"That," Matías whispered. "Yes, that."

They were quiet for a few minutes.

Finally, he asked, "So I'm really not supposed to be here with you?"

She bit her lip and shook her head. "No. Not like this."

Matías jammed his hands into his hair. But then he shook them out and instead, turned and cupped her face gently.

"I'm scared, Claire. What if try to go back, and it doesn't work? Or what if it does, but my body is too damaged to recover?"

"No," she said. "That can't happen. It won't."

"But it might." He swiped away a tear falling on her cheek. "So before I go, I want only one thing."

"What?" she asked, her voice barely audible.

"To make love to you, Claire. Just in case it's the last time."

———

CLAIRE FOUND AN AIRBNB CLOSE BY, AND BECAUSE 10 P.M. WAS not considered late in Spain, the landlord—who was just sitting down to dinner—approved the rental right away.

She and Matías took a taxi the short distance, and Claire didn't care if the driver thought she was drunk or delirious because it seemed like she was talking to herself in the backseat. He dropped them off at a beautiful stucco home surrounded by trees, with a fountain out front and stone paths leading to the front door and a wrought iron gate on the side.

"This way," Claire said to Matías, indicating the second path. "We have the studio bungalow in the back; there's a remote-entry keypad at the door."

She took his hand and led him past the house, past the patio and the garden lit with fairy lights, her heart pounding against her ribs.

He didn't let go of her as she entered the code on the keypad. She heaved open the thick wooden door, and they stepped inside.

"This is beautiful," she said. The room was cozy, with walls painted vivid cerulean and yellow. There were two leather armchairs and throw blankets in Spanish prints, and a small kitchenette stocked with cookies, a bowl of berries, and coffee, tea, and honey. A speaker played gossamer piano music, and in the corner stood a wood-framed bed topped with a cloudlike feather duvet.

"Look at this," Matías said, their linked hands bringing her with him as he wandered over to a stack of blank canvases and paintbrushes on a side table. "There's a note from the owner— 'Welcome to La Casita de la Inspiración. Please feel free to use these art supplies during your stay if you feel inspired.' Did you know this would be here?"

Claire shook her head. There hadn't been many rentals available in this area on such short notice. She'd chosen this one just because it was a standalone, private place rather than a room inside someone's home. "Kismet, I guess."

"Maybe so," Matías said, but he was no longer looking at the paintbrushes. He was looking only at Claire.

And unlike in the past, when she would be scared of his looking too close, she didn't hide anything and let all her emotions show. Her love. Her fear. But most of all in this moment—her want.

The warm sconces in the kitchen behind him lit Matías up like he was glowing, the black waves of his hair tipped as if aflame. He was like one of his own paintings, rendered in lush, accurate detail but for one small whimsy.

Matías de León, always a little more than reality.

Claire took two steps toward him, so they were mere inches apart.

He stilled completely.

"*Bésame*, Matías." *Kiss me.*

He leaned in and kissed her neck, his mouth ghosting against the sensitive skin at her throat as she gasped. Even if he wasn't entirely here, he *almost* was, and because her nerves had to work harder to feel him, their sensitivity was dialed up impossibly high.

Every look was starlight.

Every breath, the forerunner to a hurricane.

And every touch felt like fiery autumn leaves, skittering across her skin.

She let out a small moan, and he pressed his thumb, on her lips, gently until her mouth parted. Claire ran her tongue over the tip, and sucked, just once. Matías gasped.

"Dios mío," he said in a low rumble. "Las cosas que te haría si pudiera . . ."

The things I would do to you if I could . . .

"Puedes," Claire said. *You can.*

He led her to the bed. As she lowered herself onto it, he said, "Wait here."

Matías went back to the art supplies and scooped up the paintbrushes, or at least he thought he did. He didn't seem to notice that he hadn't actually picked them up; maybe he had taken the souls of them instead. Likewise, he went to the kitchen for the honey, bowl of berries, and some plates. He returned to the bed and set his invisible bounty down next to Claire.

"What are you going to do?" she asked.

"I am going to paint you," he said.

"Oh . . ." She didn't need to ask more. Because he had done this before, in New York. Made his own colors from strawberries and blackberries. Painted her like she was a masterpiece. Then kissed every inch of his work.

"I don't want my clothes to stain," Claire said, reaching for the hem of her shirt and taking her time lifting it up. First, she revealed her stomach, then the slight trim of lace on her bra. By the time she pulled the shirt over her head, Matías had stopped moving, nearly stopped breathing, just to watch her.

"You might want to be careful with your jeans, too," he said, barely audible. "Berries are notoriously difficult to wash out."

Claire rose onto her knees on the mattress and undid the top button of her jeans. Then the next. Slowly. And the next. Matías's breath came faster as she slipped the pants off her hips, then tugged them off completely, leaving her in only the panties she'd bought here in Spain, the ones with the tiny satin ribbon on the front.

"Your turn," Claire said.

He smiled, almost shy for a second, that hint of boyishness she loved that was usually concealed behind the man. But then he pulled his shirt off in one motion, and now it was Claire who couldn't breathe, taking in his broad chest, the muscled arms that had carried her across her apartment so many times, the dusting of golden hair below his stomach that matched his eyes, not his head. But even if that wasn't how he'd look in the future—if his body was weak and covered in scars from the accident and the surgeries—she would still love him, still want him. She would kiss every last one of those scars because they would be reminders that Matías had survived.

She watched as he made his paint, mashing phantom strawberries on one plate, blackberries on another. She couldn't see the colors themselves, but somehow she could smell them, a hint of fruit perfuming the air.

They shed the rest of their clothes simultaneously until there was nothing between them but summer heat and wanting.

"Lie down," he said.

Claire was used to being in charge, but with Matías, she didn't mind taking orders.

He sat on the side of the bed beside her and dipped a brush into one of the plates. The bristles skimmed her neck, where he had kissed her before, and Claire sighed into the scent of strawberries and closed her eyes to concentrate and feel the barely there touch.

The next, long stroke caressed the side of her throat, across her collarbone, then down and around the swell of her breast. She heard Matías pause and swallow to gather himself before he reached for a different brush.

With blackberry, he painted a mirroring curve. Then with both brushes at the same time, he swept down from just under each breast, across the softness of her stomach, and out to her hips, drawing spirals like the body of a cello.

She arched up, yearning for him.

"Not yet," he said as softly as the skimming of his paints.

He unscrewed the jar of honey, its sweetness blossoming into the air. When he touched his brush to Claire this time, it was to the inside of her ankle. And even though it wasn't real, the honey was warm and thick as the brush trailed up, along the side of her calf. Up, past her knee. Up, across the pale skin of the part of her thigh that rarely saw the sun but that was feverish now, burning, as the sweep of honey stroked the crease where her leg met her core.

Torturously, Matías painted her other leg with honey, too, and by the time he was done, she was begging him. "Please."

"Please what?"

"Please touch me. Everywhere. Make me yours."

He bent over her neck again and kissed her, hungrier now, tracing the swoop of strawberry down her throat, her collarbone, the heat of his mouth on her breast. He did the same to her left side, murmuring her name, ending with his tongue hot on her nipple.

In the background, the piano music sped up, no longer languorous. Claire's breath came quicker, too, matching the tempo.

Matías worshipped the curves of her stomach and her hips with his mouth. She arched toward him again as his lips completed the second cello swirl.

"Almost," he whispered.

Instead of kissing her ankles, though, he wrapped his hands

around both, his thumbs in the honey. Then he began to glide up, inch by slow inch, a massage along the interior of her legs that felt alive, like the buzz of electric against her skin. Ankle. Calves. Thighs.

Slowly higher and higher . . .

Until his thumbs met.

"Dios mío," Claire gasped.

He spread her open and slid himself inside.

"Oh, Claire . . ."

It didn't matter that he was only a soul. She remembered *her* Matías, and this version of him was not that far removed from the one she had met at the Rose Gallery, the Matías who had brought a picnic dinner to her firm, then made love to her in the shadowed law library. This soul—who was only one year removed from the present—was the same Matías who would later wake Claire up in the mornings with tender kisses and gentle entanglement in the sheets. He would also fuck her against the wall in his Greenwich Village studio. And on the paint-splattered floor. And one time, in the elevator with the emergency switch pulled.

So now, with eyes still closed, Claire blended her memories of the past with the man in the present, and she felt Matías's hands in her hair, her body pressed hard against his, her hips meeting his movements. She could feel the stickiness of the honey and fruit on their skin even though they weren't really there. The drumming of his heartbeat in his chest against hers.

Their muscles tensed.

Breathing synced, shallow and fast.

She bit his shoulder as the eddying storm inside them grew wilder and wilder.

And then the tempest unleashed, exploding in a beautiful fury of colors and shards of Claire and Matías, of blinding lightning and thunder so loud it rendered the world without sound. She was Claire, but she wasn't, because nothing as mundane as a mere person could exist in this moment. Even time seemed to hitch.

Afterward, she swam for a while in the drowsy bliss of its aftermath.

But eventually, her heartbeat slowed close to normal, and Claire's eyes fluttered open.

"Matías?"

But she was alone on the bed. In the room.

Claire bolted upright.

"Matías?"

He was truly gone.

Oh god.

Had he returned to the sleeping half of him? Could he?

Or was it already too late?

Claire scrambled for her phone and stabbed at the screen, failing several times before she managed to call a taxi. While she waited for it to arrive, she tried the hospital, but they wouldn't release any information to her. None of the de Leóns answered their phones, either.

As soon as the taxi pulled up, Claire flung herself into it before the driver could even park.

"Madrid," she said, her heart in her throat. "Hospital Universitario La Paz. ¡Rápido, por favor!"

CLAIRE

⌐

At half past one in the morning, the taxi pulled up in front of the hospital. Claire grabbed a handful of cash from her wallet and thrust it at the driver.

"Señora, esto es demasiado."

He tried to count out change for her, but she waved him off, already flinging open the car door.

"Keep it!" she shouted as she ran toward the hospital entrance.

But when she got there, Claire slammed into the glass door. What? Why wasn't it opening?

She looked for a handle somewhere, but no, these were sliding doors, ones she'd never even thought about on previous visits because they'd just parted as soon as she approached.

Claire tried to read the words etched into the glass. There was a range of times—8 A.M. to 8 P.M.—which corresponded with visiting hours. She didn't understand the rest, though, so she pulled out her translation app to scan it.

For Emergencies After Hours, Please Go to the Emergency Department →

She sprinted toward the emergency room.
There was a security guard at the entrance.

Why was a guard there? The main entrance never had a guard posted out front. Was it just because it was the middle of the night?

"Buenas noches. ¿Necesita ayuda, señora?" *Good evening. Do you need assistance, miss?*

"Sí," Claire said. "Quiero . . ." She had to think word by word to say things coherently in Spanish, and that was incredibly difficult since the only thing she could hear in her head right now was *Please be okay, Matías, please be okay, please be okay.*

"Quiero visitar a mi novio," she finally said. *I want to visit my boyfriend.*

"Disculpe, ahora no se puede." He shook his head. "Puede volver a las ocho." He pointed to his watch, then held up eight fingers.

"Eight o'clock? That's six and a half hours away, I can't wait until then!" Claire tried to look behind the guard, hoping she could get the attention of the woman stationed at the intake desk. "Um . . . es importante. Now . . . ¡ahora!"

He shifted to block her view of the emergency room and crossed his arms. "Señora. No."

"But it's an emergency!"

"¿*Usted tiene una emergencia?*" He pointed at Claire. *Do you have an emergency?*

Yes, she wanted to say. *My boyfriend's soul is trying to return to his comatose body, and I need to get inside to see if he succeeded or . . .*

"Mi novio está . . ." But Claire didn't know how to explain any of that in Spanish, nor did she want to use her phone to do it, because it wouldn't make sense anyway, would it? Soledad and Aracely had reacted to Claire's revelation about Matías's soul in the way any sane person would. Why would this guard be any different? Part of his job, Claire realized, was to keep hysterical people like her away from the patients who actually needed care.

She clearly was not going to get into the hospital through the emergency room.

"Um, okay. Gracias," Claire said, backing away.

The security guard eyed her suspiciously.

She held up eight fingers. "*A las ocho*. I will come back *a las ocho*."

He nodded once before she turned and went back toward the main hospital entrance.

But there must be another way in. Even though visitors could only be at the hospital for twelve hours of the day, the hospital itself had to run 24/7. They had patients to care for and to feed and clothe.

There's got to be a back entrance for food and linen deliveries, Claire thought.

THE LOADING DOCK AT THE BACK OF THE HOSPITAL WAS IN full swing. As with other organizations, the wee hours were the best time for deliveries to be made because it interfered less with daytime business. Crates of milk cartons and vegetables were being unloaded from a massive refrigerator truck, and a laundry truck was backed up to a separate loading bay.

In the bustle of work being done, Claire grabbed a patient gown from a rolling rack of clean linen and dashed in through the laundry door.

Inside, she ducked between two giant hampers of dirty clothes—holding her nose because the hospital gowns were soiled in a very different way from ordinary clothes—and quickly slipped the *clean* gown on. Claire tucked her purse into her waistband against her stomach. An actual patient wouldn't be walking around with a purse. But hers was small enough that if she hunched and let the gown's fabric hang in the front, it could just look like a stomach bulge.

Dressed "appropriately" for the hospital, she darted in and out between the hampers, toward a set of double doors that seemed to lead into the main corridors of the hospital. Twice, someone almost caught her, but she dove and found cover behind adjacent rolling shelves and bins.

Finally, Claire made it through the double doors. She branched off that hallway as soon as possible and found an elevator.

It got her to the third floor, but the elevator was on the other end of the building from Matías's ward. Claire was halfway there when a nurse exited one of the wards and frowned at Claire.

"¿No debería estar en su cama?"

Claire had no idea what the nurse had said, but Claire had already prepared her story while she was sneaking through the hospital. "Ejercicio," she said. *Exercise.* She had seen how the nurses encouraged the ambulatory patients in Matías's ward to walk laps in order to get *some* exercise during their hospital stay. The nurses beamed at the patients slowly shuffling around, because they understood how hard it was for any of them to move, and how much easier it would've been to just stay in bed.

"Es un poco tarde," the nurse said to Claire. That one, she understood: *It's a bit late.*

"Un poco más," Claire said. *A little more.* She pointed toward Matías's ward at the end of the corridor to indicate her destination.

The nurse hesitated and thought it over.

"Vale," he said, motioning her on.

Because what was he going to do anyway if Claire was already on her way back where she belonged? Make her stop exercising so he could go get a wheelchair for her? That would defeat the nurses' goal of encouraging their patients to move on their own whenever they could.

"Gracias," Claire said. "Buenas noches."

ONCE IN MATÍAS'S UNIT, SHE DUCKED DOWN SO THE NURSES wouldn't see her from behind their desks in the middle of the ward. Claire wouldn't be able to pull the "patient out for a stroll" trick here because the nurses would either recognize her from her visits or *not* recognize her but know that she wasn't one of the patients under their care. Claire removed her shoes and shuffled in her socks past ten different rooms before she reached Matías's.

But then she hesitated. Her heart battered her ribs, and her whole body shook as she crouched on the linoleum.

Please be all right, Matías. Please please please be awake and smiling . . .

She didn't want to open the door.

But she had to.

Claire took in a shaky breath, turned the handle, and slipped inside.

"No . . ."

Matías's skin was gray and slack, his eyes sunken. He had lost so much weight, his chest hollow and collarbones sharp, no longer resembling the athletic man she'd just made love to. Even the beeping of the machines sounded more resigned than when Claire was last here.

"Oh, Matías." She tiptoed to his side.

"I'm sorry." Claire brushed some of the matted hair away from his forehead. She ran her fingers across his jawline, a rough, patchy beard now.

She wished she could climb into bed with him. Instead, she lay her cheek down lightly on one of the sole spots on his chest that wasn't covered in bandages or monitor leads. "I am so, so sorry."

"For what?"

Claire jumped back.

"Why . . . are you . . . sorry?" he rasped.

She let out a small squeak because Matías had cracked his eyes open. Just enough that she could see the glimmer of gold.

"Matías!" She flung himself onto him.

"Agh . . . gentle, churri." He spoke slowly because his broken jaw was secured with wire.

"Oh god, sorry, sorry!" She immediately backed away.

"Please . . . stop . . . saying . . . you're sorry," he said, even though he was wincing from the pain she'd just caused.

Tears streamed down Claire's face. "You're awake."

He coughed, and she rushed to his side. "Do you need water? Or do you want me to prop a pillow behind you?"

Matías grimaced and touched his ribs. "No . . . I'm okay. More than okay. Because of you."

The machines in the background beeped, but the heartbeats were steadier now. The oxygen canula hissed, and Matías asked Claire to loop it off his head.

Tears spilled down her face. "You're back," she said. "You're here. You're—"

"Alive," he said.

"Alive," she echoed.

Matías tried to smile, but the jaw wiring made it only a wisp of a smile. Still, it was enough.

"Come here, churri."

She leaned against the plastic railing of the bed and held his hand. "I thought I was going to lose you."

"Never," Matías said softly, his voice still gravelly from disuse. "You were there for me even when I was lost and didn't know who you were. And because of that, I had something to hold on to—Every word. Every look. Every time we almost touched.

"You slowly let me remember who I was, and you helped me return. And . . . even though everything hurts now, it will get better. I know that as surely as I love you."

Her tears fell onto his bare chest, then rolled off, soaking into his gown.

"Matías, before you left New York—"

"It doesn't matter."

"It does. I found the ring, and I knew you were going to propose if I came with you. I was so relieved that I already had an excuse to cancel. I just . . . I thought we were too different."

"Yes, but—"

"Please, let me finish."

"I'm sorry." Matías stroked her hand.

Claire took a deep breath. "But after everything that's happened since, I get it now. We're perfect together *because* we're different. You push me to think outside of the ordinary and to try things I wouldn't otherwise contemplate. And I get to be the eye of your cyclone, where there is predictability and order, so that you can whirl around as long as you need to, but still have a place to come home to."

"You are the other half of my orange," Matías said.

"What?" Claire laughed, through her tears.

"It's a saying in Spanish—*mi media naranja*. In English, you just say that someone is your better half. But in Spanish—"

"We're halves of the same orange." Claire smiled.

The door flung open, and Claire threw herself over Matías to protect him.

But it was Abuela Gloria creeping through with her walker, followed by Soledad and Armando, then Luis and Aracely, who was shooing away the night nurse who was trying to tell them that visiting hours were over. Claire wondered briefly if they had also snuck in through the laundry delivery entrance, but then she remembered that Soledad could talk her way through any rules when her suffering son was involved.

"¡Mati!" Soledad sobbed. Claire stepped back as his mother rushed in to hug him.

"¡Ay, Matías! ¡Has despertado!" *You woke up!* Aracely covered her mouth as she started crying.

Armando and Luis also approached, unable to speak, eyes red.

"Os dije que ella lo iba a lograr," Abuela Gloria said. She was the first of the family who seemed to notice Claire was there. Not that there was a problem with that. Matías had just woken from a coma. Of course they should pay attention to him.

But whatever Abuela Gloria had said to them, they all looked over at Claire at the same time.

Soledad scrubbed away the tears from her face, even though more fell to replace them. "Claire, lo siento, we are very sorry. We treated you badly. We lost our faith. We prayed for a miracle, and when it arrived, we did not believe it. Thank for saving my son." She burst into sobs, and Claire started crying, too.

Aracely walked around the bed and wrapped her arms around Claire, pulling her into one of her long, soft embraces. "I am sorry, Claire. I hope you can eventually forgive me."

"There is nothing to forgive," Claire said into Aracely's shoulder. "You were protecting Matías because you love him. He is lucky to have a family full of such love."

"Sometimes our love is also smothering," Aracely said wryly. She held on to Claire for a moment longer before she let go. "But you learn to live with it. Right, Matías?"

"They never gave me a choice," he said, and that broke the last of the sadness in the room, because everybody laughed— one part relief, one part happiness, and one part semi-delirious exhaustion.

But there was still something left for Claire to do.

On the bedside table, there was a spool of blue medical tape the nurses had been using to attach Matías's IV tubes to his skin. Claire reached over and picked it up.

She tore off a piece a few inches long and folded it length-wise over itself several times, so it was a long, thin strip. Then she looped it into a circle and used another small piece of tape to stick the ends together.

"I am glad you're here to be part of this," Claire said to his family, who instinctively ceded the space next to Matías's bed to her.

"What are you doing?" he asked.

"Algo muy importante."

Something very important.

"Matías," Claire said, getting down on the linoleum on one knee. She held up the ring of blue tape. "I have lived most of my life without you, but I wasn't *really* living until we met. You are the chaos to my order, the color to my black and white.

"These past eight days have been the worst time I've ever been through, but they were also some of the best because I see you—and us—clearly now. I am better when I'm with you, and I like to think that maybe you're better with me, too."

He nodded, his eyes glistening.

"So, I know you were going to ask me," she said, "but I'm going to do it first, because let's face it, I like being in control."

He laughed.

"Matías de León—mi media naranja—will you marry me?"

A tear rolled down his cheek.

"Yes," Matías said. "Without a doubt, yes. From my body to my soul, all of me belongs to you, Claire."

She took his left hand in hers and slid the blue ring onto his fourth finger. Then she turned his palm up and kissed it, slowly.

"If we're ever parted again, Matías, just press your lips here and imagine your kiss meeting mine . . . And I'll be right there with you."

Epilogue

〜

From: clairewalker@windsorblackllp.com
To: mitch.tahir@intelligentsia.tech
RE: Personal Update

Dear Mitch,

Thank you for your kind email while my boyfriend was in a coma. I should have told you as soon as I knew I had to be in Madrid, rather than waiting until things spun out of control on the merger. But it's something I'm working on now, knowing that no one expects me to wear my armor all the time. We're all just humans, doing the best we can.

I am sorry to hear that you had to suffer through a similar experience with your wife. I appreciate your sharing that with me and hope you're both doing well now.

Matías surprised his doctors by getting back on his feet rather quickly, but that's because they don't know him. He is a man with too many interests to sit still, so he is highly motivated to make a full recovery. We are back in New York now.

I hear the Intelligentsia-Einstein merger closed successfully.

Congratulations on the acquisition! I wish your companies all the best.

—Claire

TWO MINUTES LATER

From: mitch.tahir@intelligentsia.tech
To: clairewalker@windsorblackllp.com
RE: Personal Update

Hi Claire,

What would you say about leaving Windsor & Black? You deserve more than a firm that would toss you by the wayside for having an outside life.

Intelligentsia Tech is looking for a director of international mergers and acquisitions. I think you'd be perfect. And I swear I'm more humane to work for than I usually let on. Besides, if you come work for Intelligentsia, you'll get to boss the Windsor & Black attorneys around.

What do you think?

—Mitch

THIRTY SECONDS LATER

From: clairewalker@windsorblackllp.com
To: mitch.tahir@intelligentsia.tech
RE: Personal Update

Can I split my time between the New York and Madrid offices? And does the job come with Spanish lessons?

Because if so, then HELL YES!

Acknowledgments

Gracias a Juan David Piñeros Jiménez y mi editor Leonel Teti, Kai Vega, y su equipo en Umbriel por toda su ayuda sobre la cultura de España y con las correcciones de mi español. Si hay errores en este libro, son mi culpa.

I couldn't have written this book without my editor, Anne Groell, and my agent, Thao Le, who both fell in love with this story and understood its soul from the moment I pitched it. And enormous thanks to everyone else at my publisher, Del Rey, for your amazing dedication to my books. It is rare to feel like you've found family at work, but you are *it*—I'm so proud to be one of your authors.

Matías's art is inspired by the classical realist painter Sally Fama Cochrane. While words can never capture the depth and visceral beauty of Sally's work, I tried my best and then added a Matías spin. Huge thanks to Sally for so generously sharing her process, as well as for the drawing of Juliet's balcony in Matías's journal. If you'd like to check out more of Sally's work, you can find her at sallyfamacochrane.com.

Thank you to Angela Mann for spending an afternoon talking to me about your family's experience caring for your mother when she was in a coma. I am in awe of how openly you spoke about such a tender, terrible time, and I am deeply humbled that you shared your story with me.

I can't put a book out into the world without also acknowledging my readers and all the book lovers out there who ceaselessly spread their love for my work. It is the greatest honor to get to write stories for you, and I hope to keep doing so for a long, long time.

And finally, thank you to my daughter, Reese, and my husband, Tom. You put up with all my Claire-like rules, and I try really hard not to get annoyed when the dishes are in the wrong spots in the dishwasher, because you are the most important people in the world to me, and I would give you the sun and all the other stars in the sky if I could. *Los amo.*

PHOTO: © ERIN ASHFORD

EVELYN SKYE is the *New York Times* bestselling author of *The Hundred Loves of Juliet, One Year Ago in Spain,* and many other books. A graduate of Stanford University and Harvard Law School, Skye lives in the San Francisco Bay Area with her husband and daughter.

Bonus content and newsletter:
evelynskye.substack.com
Instagram: @evelyn_skye
evelynskye.com